GOATS
JUST WANNA
HAVE FUN

GOATS JUST WANNA HAVE FUN

A
ZEN GOAT
MYSTERY

JANNA ROLLINS

LEVEL
BEST BOOKS

First edition

ISBN: 978-1-68512-880-7

Cover art by Level Best Designs

This book was professionally typeset on Reedsy.
Find out more at reedsy.com

To my sisters – and all those magical nights at the county fair.

Praise for Goats Just Wanna Have Fun

"A smart, sassy heroine, a charming New England town, adorably naughty baby goats, and a skillfully-crafted whodunnit make *Goats Just Wanna Have Fun* a clever and engaging read. A delightful addition to the Zen Goat Mystery Series, this story is fresh and fun, filled with humor, romance, and intrigue. It's sure to leave cozy mystery fans wanting more!"—Kara Lacey, author of the Vermont Camera Club Mysteries

"Callie, Bugsy, and the gang are back for more goat yoga – this time at the town's carnival. Everything is corndogs, ice cream, and thrill rides until the owner of the pig races dies suddenly under suspicious circumstances. Callie and her friends have to solve the mystery before the show's over forever."—Heather Weidner, author of the Jules Keene Glamping Mysteries

"Janna Rollins has crafted the perfect idyllic cozy concoction with her Zen Goat mysteries. From darling animal sidekicks like Bugsy the scene-stealing goat, to mouthwatering food descriptions, to a charming small town. With a heroine you'll root for—not to mention just the right dose of romantic potential in a certain handsome vet—this series will keep you turning pages long into the night, while wondering why your hometown yoga studio doesn't have cute baby goats. A true delight, cover to cover."—Gretchen Rue, author of the Witches' Brew Mysteries

Chapter One

Blue raspberry syrup splashed down the front of my shirt as I sprinted across the fairgrounds. I tossed the uneaten snow cone into the nearest garbage can and poured on the speed. Moments before, I'd placed my order at Sweet Pete's snow cone stand, my mouth watering for the cold treat, when a shrill screeching coming from the direction of the stock barns caused everyone in line to jerk around to find out what in the heck was going on. My startled gaze immediately lasered in on my favorite goat, Bugsy, who had somehow managed to escape his stall in the fifteen minutes since I'd left him happily munching hay in the barn. At a full gallop, the snow-white goat's head was lowered, and his horns were aimed right at the Lupine County Fair manager's narrow backside. Jay Rowe's long arms flapped as he yelled to beat the band and ran as fast as his feet could carry him in a panicked attempt to get away from the speedy goat.

By the time I caught up with Jay and Bugsy, a crowd of laughing spectators had gathered around the open green grass where the impromptu goat versus fair manager high-speed chase was taking place. I joined the melee, pumping my arms and legs faster and faster as I made several unsuccessful attempts to grab Bugsy's collar. With a final burst of speed, Bugsy pulled farther away from my outstretched fingers and successfully butted the fleeing man in the back of the knees, sending him toppling to the ground.

Jay sprawled on the grass, his wire-rimmed glasses askew, and a strand of green grass stuck to his cheek. Bugsy bleated and nudged Jay's side with his nose, but I finally managed to grab the goat's collar and pull him away. I narrowed my eyes at the naughty goat. If I didn't know better, I'd have

1

sworn he shrugged his shoulders with a sly grin as he chewed his cud. I wasn't buying Bugsy's innocent act for a second.

Extending a sticky, blue-stained hand, I offered to help the fair manager off the ground, but he ignored the truce and scrambled to his feet without my help.

"Jay, I'm so, so, sorry. Bugsy is never aggressive with people. I don't know what came over him. It won't happen again, I promise. Are you hurt? What can I do to help? Do you want something to drink? A snow cone, maybe?" I babble when I'm nervous, and my goat knocking the fair manager off his feet made me as skittish as a cat during a hurricane.

Jay adjusted his crooked glasses, then brushed grass and dirt from his dark blue jeans. He pulled himself to his full height, towering over me by about a mile and a half, and glared at Bugsy. The fair manager pointed at the goat and sheep barn. "Get that goat locked into his stall, securely this time, Callie, then see me in my office. Be there in fifteen minutes."

He stalked off while I stared after him. The Lupine County Fair Board, based in Bobwhite Hollow, New Hampshire, had contacted me with an invitation to bring my herd to the fair and conduct a daily goat yoga session on the lawn in front of the sheep and goat building. The same lawn where Bugsy preceded to knock the tarnation out of the fair manager. I'd only arrived with my goats less than two hours ago. How could things have gone so wrong so fast? I had a feeling Jay was about to rescind my invitation and send us packing back to the farm. With a sigh, I tugged on Bugsy's collar to get him turned around and headed to the barn. A crowd of looky-loos blocked my path. Sheesh. You'd think nobody'd ever seen a goat chasing a lanky, red-headed farmer before. We should've sold tickets.

"Sorry about the show, everyone. It's all over. Please enjoy the rest of your time at the fair," I said, hoping to smooth over the chaos Bugsy had caused. When nobody moved out of my way, I realized I might as well make the most of the situation. "You can join The Zen Goat right here tomorrow morning at seven sharp for a fun session of goat yoga. It's free with the gate admission to the fair, and we would love to have you."

"Will this goat be part of the yoga session?" A woman with a baby in a front carrier called out.

"No, he's a little big for yoga," I answered. "He's just here at the fair for moral support for the other goats."

"What's his name?" Someone else asked. "Can my daughter pet him?"

I stopped my progression to the barn. "His name is Bugsy, and yes, he loves to be petted." Maybe Bugsy's little antics were going to make him the star of the show. "He's actually a super nice goat, if you can believe it. He won't bite and, with my hand on his collar, I promise he won't chase anyone. Scratch behind his ears, and he'll be your best friend, though he'll probably try to nibble on your clothes. Who else wants to pet him?" I reached out a hand to invite the woman's small daughter to approach Bugsy.

A handful of people wandered off, but the majority of them crowded around, laughing and talking as they reached out to touch Bugsy and take selfies with him. I allowed the naughty goat to soak up all the attention he could for a couple of minutes before I apologized and excused ourselves. The look the fair manager gave me before he stomped off in a huff was a good indication I'd better not be late for our impromptu meeting if I had any hope of sticking around for the duration of the fair.

Inside the barn, I paused for a moment to allow my eyes to adjust from the bright sunny day to the relative dimness of the cavernous building. The gate on Bugsy's stall was still closed and latched securely. I shook my head, confused. The goat's escape artist talents could put Harry Houdini to shame. Back at the farm, Bugsy broke out of his pen every chance he got, and it always mystified me trying to figure out how he'd escaped. As I reached to unlatch the gate, an enormous sneeze exploded from my nose, catching me off guard. My eyes watered, Bugsy snorted, and a rooster in the poultry barn crowed. I tucked the goat into his new home for the next few days, made sure the gate was locked tight, rubbed my itchy eyes, and headed out to my mandatory meeting.

Jay's office was in a small, barn-red cottage tucked behind the open-class food and textile exhibit hall. I stepped up onto the creaky wooden porch and hesitated before reaching for the doorknob. Raised voices came from inside the cottage. The last thing I wanted was to get involved in someone else's argument. The door opened, and a man I recognized as the owner of Hasty Hogs Pig Racing came barreling out. Brandon Ebersole was about forty, tall with a muscular physique and dark hair.

"I mean it, Brandon. This is the last time. If it happens again, you'll never race at the Lupine County Fair again. I'll see to it," Jay's voice boomed from inside the fair office.

Brandon half turned and bellowed back at Jay. "My pig races are the only reason people come to your sorry excuse of a fair, and you know it. You need me!" His face was purple with rage as he yelled. "Just try to get rid of me. We both know how that'll turn out for you, don't we?"

Brandon flicked his eyes my way and scowled as he brushed past me, tucking a wad of cash into the front pocket of his jeans. He stormed off, disappearing around the corner of the exhibit building.

What was that all about? Nothing too serious, I hoped. Brandon, his wife, and their crew were staying at my great-aunt and uncle's place, Haybeck Farm, in the quaint stone cottage I'd fixed up to accommodate guests who booked goat yoga retreats. With my contract at the fair this week, I didn't need the cottage for yoga guests, so we'd rented it out to the Hasty Hogs crew instead.

Before entering the fair office, I waited a beat to let Jay compose himself. I was already in enough trouble of my own. I didn't need to ride the shirttails of whatever problem the pig race owner was causing. I cautiously pushed open the door. Jay sat behind a cluttered wooden desk, writing something on a yellow legal pad. I cleared my throat to let him know I had arrived for our meeting on time.

"Miss Haybeck. Thank you for coming. Have a seat." He waved a long, freckled hand at a row of chairs lined up against the far wall.

"Jay, please let me stay. Give me and the goats another chance. I'll triple-lock Bugsy's stall and make darn sure he doesn't get out again." I perched on the edge of the chair like a bird about to fly away. "We just got here—"

"I'm not canceling your contract," Jay interrupted. "At least not yet. You probably won't believe it, but right now, you and your devil of a goat are the least of my worries." He grunted and ran a hand through his short red hair, causing it to stand up at odd angles all over his head.

"We're not?" I sat back in surprise.

"No, unfortunately." He leaned back and wrestled a red apple out of his vest pocket, rubbed it on the leg of his knife-creased and brand-spanking-new-looking blue jeans to shine it up, and took a big, crunchy bite. "But if your goat gets out and chases one more person, the whole bunch of you are out of here. Thank goodness it was me he went after and not someone who could sue the fair board."

The crisp snap and sweet scent of the apple filled the small room as the fair manager took another bite. He swiped at the juice dribbling down his chin, then wiped sticky fingers off on his jeans.

"Did you happen to have that apple in your pocket when Bugsy was chasing you?" I asked.

Jay frowned and stared at the juicy apple in his hand. "Uh, yeah. Why?"

I laughed. "Apples are his favorite thing in the world. Bugsy wasn't trying to hurt you. He just wanted a snack."

Chapter Two

Once Jay and I reached an understanding, I hustled back to the goat barn and checked to make sure my little herd was content. Having lived my entire life in Seattle until recently, the Lupine County Fair was my first true rural country fair, and I was excited to experience everything it had to offer. Even though many of the events wouldn't start until the next day, there was still plenty to keep me busy on opening night, including watching the pig races and then eating my weight in corn dogs from the food trucks dotting the carnival grounds. I glanced down at my blue-raspberry-stained shirt. Unless I wanted to walk around looking like I'd wrestled with a Smurf, it looked like I'd better run back to the farm and change. Pulling up my favorites list on my cell phone, I clicked on my cousin's name.

"Hey, girl." Tristan Beck's cheerful voice came over the line. "I'm twenty minutes out."

"Excellent. How about meeting me at the farm? We can ride together."

"Sure, but weren't you supposed to have the goats to the fairgrounds hours ago?"

"Yeah, and I did. The goats are all settled in, but I had a teeny tiny accident with a snow cone and need to run home to change."

Tristan laughed. "Of course you did. Okay, see you in a few."

Tristan, a hairstylist in a Boston salon, was forever giving me grief about my lack of style and tendency to wear my lunch on my shirt. We'd met last winter after I'd spit into a test tube and sent my DNA away to be analyzed. When the results came back, I found out I was a good mix of English, German, and

Irish, which didn't surprise me one bit, and a touch of Spanish that did. The program matched me up with Tristan Beck, my first cousin once removed who had legally changed his last name to drop the 'hay.' He said his Beck moniker made him feel a little less like a country bumpkin. Tristan was twenty-eight, just a year older than me. We'd started chatting online and hit it off straight away, both of us feeling like we'd known each other forever.

A mere three months later, I was as astounded as anybody to find myself in Bobwhite Hollow, living and working with Tristan's grandparents—my great-uncle and great-aunt—Will and Ellen Haybeck.

Uncle Will was my dad's uncle, though they'd never met. My dad's father, Uncle Will's brother, left my grandmother when Dad was too little to remember him, but the hurt he felt due to his father abandoning him never went away. Dad didn't want a thing to do with this side of his biological family. When I told him about finding the Haybecks through the DNA kit, he gave me his blessing to get to know them as long as I left him completely out of it. I'd packed my bags and flown to New Hampshire in late spring, fell in love with my new-found family and the area, and never looked back. Uncle Will agreed to let me open my goat yoga studio, The Zen Goat, on his farm. So here I was, a goat yoga instructor who, as it turned out, was allergic to goats.

Old Rusty, Uncle Will's ancient but trusty pickup truck, sat in the parking lot behind the animal barns. Earlier in the summer, my uncle helped me build livestock racks for the back of the pickup out of pallets we picked up from the local grocery store. The free pallets were a perfect fit for my non-existent budget. In the process, I'd learned to use a drill and an electric handsaw without cutting off any fingers. I was proud of my work and newly acquired skills. None of my friends back home would ever guess I was turning into a farm girl so fast. I patted the livestock rack as I rounded the back of Old Rusty, then climbed into the cab and headed for the farm.

When I wheeled into the driveway bordered by an old stone wall, I laughed out loud at the Pepto-Bismol pink truck parked in front of Haybeck Farm's guest cottage. The cartoon face of a laughing pig and two black-and-white checkered racing flags were painted on each side of the truck with the words

"Hasty Hogs Pig Racing" in black lettering arched over the logo. "Eat My Dust!" was painted on the tailgate beside the round rump and curled tail of a racing pig, along with another checkered flag. Two rubber floppy pink ears protruded from the hood of the truck, and a big round pig nose was attached to the grill. Somebody'd taken it a step too far, but if they were trying to grab people's attention, they'd done a great job of it.

Tristan pulled in behind me in his hunter-green Mini Cooper. His honey-blond curls gleamed in the sun as he wrestled a brown leather duffel bag out of the back seat of his little car. I waited for him on the stone walkway leading up to the two-story, white clapboard farmhouse.

"Are you going to take a lesson from them and turn Old Rusty into a Zen Goatmobile?" Tristan leaned in for a quick hug, careful not to get near my blue-stained shirt.

"Yeah. No." I shook my head and laughed. "I'm happy with Old Rusty just the way he is, thank you very much."

Tristan and I burst through the front door, laughing and talking a mile a minute.

"Keep it down, will ya?" came a gruff but teasing voice from the living room.

I popped my head around the doorframe. Uncle Will was lying on the floral couch, his overall-clad legs crossed at the ankles and his blue eyes merry and sparkling. The ceiling fan overhead rotated at top speed, and a standing fan pulled close to the couch ruffled Uncle Will's thick, white hair.

"Oh, sorry. Forgot it's your nap time." During the heat of the summer, eighty-four-year-old Uncle Will allowed himself an hour of resting time every afternoon.

"Hey, Pop-Pop," Tristan greeted his grandfather.

"Hello, grandson." Uncle Will sat up with a groan, running his hands over his face and down his fluffy mustache. He stretched and blinked the sleep out of his eyes. "No worries, young people. Time for this old goat to get up and around, anyway. You two headed back to the fair this evening?"

Tristan dropped his duffel bag on the floor and gave his grandfather a hug. "We are. Callie made a mess of herself again, as you can see. Since she had to come home and change anyway, we decided to ride back in together. What are you and Grandma doing tonight? Where is she? I didn't see her car out front."

"I'm expecting her back any minute. She took her quilt and a truckload of her baked goods over to get entered into the fair. What time are the pig races starting tonight?"

"Seven."

"Your grandmother and I might join you youngsters, if you don't mind."

Tristan and I both assured Uncle Will we would love to have him and Aunt Ellen join us. I left the two men to chat and went upstairs to change into something a little less sticky.

Earlier in the summer, I'd purchased a great pair of faded denim overall shorts at Whimsical Willow, my favorite boutique in Bobwhite Hollow. They were distressed, fringed cut-offs, and super cute. I pulled them out of my closet, pairing the overalls with a white tank top and a pair of navy blue fringed cowboy boots. Wait a second. White...corndogs...mustard. With visions of yellow mustard stains dripping down the front of my clothing, I swapped the white tank top for a marigold sleeveless T-shirt.

Satisfied with my clothing choice, I took the time to French-braid my hair into a single plait down the back of my head, leaving the dipped sapphire-blue ends unbraided. I washed my face and reapplied a hint of eyeshadow and mascara, then stood back and inspected myself in the mirror. My arms and legs were tanned and muscular from a summer spent lifting bales of hay and working in the garden, and my outfit was on point if I did say so myself. I swung around, scrutinizing myself from all angles. Not bad, but something was still missing. Ah! A swipe of cotton candy pink lip gloss later and even Tristan shouldn't be able to find anything to pick at. I grinned and headed back downstairs.

"Whoa! Girl, look at you. Little miss hot-to-trot Elly May Clampett." Tristan whistled, grabbed my hand, and twirled me around. "See? I told you there was hope for you yet. Now, where's that smoking hot veterinarian who's always sniffing around here?"

I jerked my hand away and smacked my cousin on the shoulder. "What are you even talking about? There's nothing going on between me and Levi and you know it. I am not interested in him even one tiny bit. The only reason he pops by so often is because he's our vet and has to come to the farm on a regular basis," I protested, even though the thought of running into Levi McClure at the fair this evening had crossed my mind. A time or three hundred.

Tristan slid his sunglasses on his face and eyed me over the top of the gold frames. "Mmhmm, so you say. Ready to go?"

"Let's do it." I pulled open the screen door at the same time Brandon Ebersole came striding up onto the porch.

"Is Will here?" Brandon asked without looking me in the eye.

I nodded and hollered into the house for Uncle Will. Half a minute later, my great-uncle joined us on the farmhouse porch.

"Good evening, Brandon." Uncle Will shook the man's hand. "What can I do ya for?"

"We're headed back to the fair, but I wanted to drop off the check for the week's rent on the cottage first, like I promised." Brandon held out a paper check. "I appreciate you being flexible and taking our payment this way. Can't imagine where I left my wallet, but it's going to be a bear to get all my cards shut down and reissued."

Uncle Will accepted the check with a smile. "No worries. A check works just fine, in my opinion."

"You have my word it's good."

"A man's word and a handshake are good enough for me." Uncle Will winked. "We'll all be in the grandstands tonight, cheering on those pigs and expecting a good show. Don't let me down." He patted Brandon on the shoulder.

"I won't, sir. The pigs are ready to race."

Brandon turned and jumped into the driver's seat of his pig-pink truck, where the other Hasty Hogs crew members waited. I waved to his wife, Michelle, who I'd met earlier in the day when they'd checked in.

Tristan took the check from his grandfather and studied it skeptically. "Are you sure about this, Pop-Pop? Not many people do business with paper checks these days."

"I'm sure, grandson. The man lost his wallet. Misfortune happens to all of us at one time or another. The Ebersoles have been bringing those pigs to the Lupine County Fair for half a dozen years or so. The man's good for it."

Except I'd overheard the fair manager threatening to pull the Hasty Hogs Racing Pigs contract. I didn't feel the need to mention the argument since I was sure it had been an idle threat on Jay's part.

Chapter Three

When we got back to the fairgrounds, the parking lot was filling up fast with families arriving to enjoy the first night of county fair fun. The air thrummed with competing squeals of joy and shrieks of fear from the carnival. I eyeballed the giant Ferris wheel. The thing was so high it looked like it scraped the sky. Sun glinted off the several dozen gondola cars painted in vibrant shades of metallic blue, yellow, red, and green. The red-and-white candy cane-striped supports resembled peppermint sticks. I couldn't wait to sit on top of the world in one of those gondolas.

"I better check on the goats before the pig races start," I told Tristan. "If Bugsy's out again, I don't know what I'm going to do with him." On the way back to the fairgrounds, I'd filled Tristan in on the naughty goat's antics earlier in the day. Since Jay hadn't been hurt, my cousin and I had gotten a good laugh about the whole thing.

"You don't need Bugsy here. He can always go back to the farm and keep the mama goats' company if he's going to cause problems," Tristan replied.

The little yoga goats were weaned and old enough to not need their mamas around anymore, so I'd only brought the eight kids and Bugsy to the fair. I agreed with Tristan. If the goat didn't behave, he'd find himself right back in his pasture. Much to his delight, I'm sure.

The goat and sheep barn smelled of fresh straw and musky critters. Sheep baa'd and goats maa'd for attention as Tristan and I walked down the aisle between the wooden stalls. 4-H and FFA kids lounged on bales of hay near their animals, laughing and enjoying the camaraderie being together at the fair brought. My cowboy boots clomped satisfyingly on the hard dirt floor as the fringe on them swayed. I'd never felt more like I belonged somewhere than I did in that exact moment.

Jay had assigned two stalls for my animals near the beginning of the goat section. All eight of the little goats fit in one double-sized pen, with Bugsy in a smaller enclosure. I'd hung a sign from a beam above the stalls proclaiming the name of my business. Aunt Ellen had helped me paint "The Zen Goat" in a soothing teal. Below the words, we'd added a painting of a goat sitting in the lotus position, his eyes closed and his front hooves in the meditation gesture. The drawing of the goat closely resembled Bugsy, who happened to be standing smack dab under the sign, eyes closed and chewing his cud contentedly. This was exactly why I didn't want to have to take him back to the farm. Bugsy was the image of The Zen Goat and a complete sweetie, most of the time. Everyone loved him. Except maybe Jay Rowe. Bugsy was my entire marketing plan, all wrapped up in one white, fuzzy, horned goat.

It took about ten minutes to fluff up the hay in the mangers and freshen up their water with Tristan helping out. The goats all clamored for a snack, so I pulled a bag of carrots out of the cooler I'd stashed beside their stalls. Two young girls in matching yellow sundresses and bouncy brown pigtails approached the baby goat's pen and stuck their hands through the slats to scratch behind the animal's ears.

"Would you like to feed them a carrot?" I asked, glancing at their mom for permission.

When she nodded her approval, I broke a carrot in half and gave each little girl a portion.

"Open your hand and hold the carrot in it, like this." I showed the girls how to lay the vegetable in the palm of their hand, keeping their fingers flat and out of the way. "And hold it out to the goat. She'll take it right out of your hand with her lips. But be warned, it might tickle a little. Are you ready?"

"Yeah," they both said in unison, bouncing with excitement.

While the little girls giggled at the two goats munching on their carrots, Tristan and I quickly gave the rest of the little critters their treats.

"Did you see the posters about our goat yoga sessions we're having each morning of the fair?" I asked the girls' mom. "These are the goats who'll be joining us."

Before she had time to answer, both girls jumped up and down, pulling on their mom's arms. "Can we come? Please, please, please! Can we, Mom? It would be so much fun!"

"Girls. Stop pulling on me. Maybe. We'll see." She wrapped an arm around each of her daughters in an attempt to settle them down, then smiled at me. "What time?"

"Seven."

"In the morning?"

At my nod, the woman grimaced. "Yikes. I'm not sure I can manage to be up and functioning so early."

The adorable girls started up again. Their patient mom laughed and pulled them away from the stalls, promising bags of cotton candy at the carnival.

I called after their retreating backs, "Hope to see you at one of the yoga sessions. We'll be here all week."

Tristan checked his cell phone. "We better get a move on. The pig races start in fifteen minutes, and I want to get a snack first. Let's go."

With nachos and sodas in hand, Tristan and I made our way into the bleachers surrounding the small track set up for the Hasty Hogs to race their little porky hearts out. At the railing, we stopped and peered into the bleachers. A tiny woman with pink lemonade hair glinting in the sun stood up and waved an arm at us. I pointed her out to Tristan.

"There's Aunt Ellen and Uncle Will."

Aunt Ellen moved her purse and light jacket from the metal bench where she'd been saving spots for us. We settled in for an enjoyable hour of pig racing fun.

On the far side of the sawdust-filled track, a podium, in the same nauseating pink as their truck, sat on a platform with the Hasty Hogs Pig Racing logo facing the crowd. A black-and-white checkered tent provided shade for the podium. Michelle, Brandon's wife, stood on the platform, her long dark hair pulled into a ponytail and tucked under a pink ball cap with pig ears and a snout. She wore a white T-shirt with the Hasty Hogs logo splashed across the front. A booth was set up to the side where another woman was selling the T-shirts and ballcaps. I sucked in my lower lip. I could do without the cap, but it might be fun to have one of those cute T-shirts.

"Does anyone want anything from the Hasty Hogs booth?" I pointed the table out to my family in case they'd missed it.

Aunt Ellen chuckled and shook her head. Tristan bugged his eyes out and looked appalled.

Uncle Will said, "No, but I'll take the rest of those nachos off your hands if you're done with them."

I handed the cheesy cardboard tray over and stood to go get my T-shirt.

Tristan grabbed a hold of my small backpack and wouldn't let go. "No, Callie. Friends don't let friends buy pig shirts. I'm saving you from yourself." He tugged harder on my bag.

"Let go." I yanked, but my cousin had a tight grip.

When I threatened to open up my can of pepper spray on him, Tristan scowled at me but finally loosened his hold.

"You're a hopeless case," he teased as, victorious, I sauntered away.

"You're a snob," I retorted, head held high. I wasn't about to let him shame me over my burning desire for a Hasty Hogs T-shirt.

While I waited in the short line, I stared at the pig merchandise, envisioning T-shirts with a goat sitting in the lotus pose and The Zen Goat in a loopy cursive half-circle above the goat's horns. And socks. Everybody would need a pair of Zen Goat socks. My daydreaming had me at the front of the line before I knew it.

"I'll take an extra-large T-shirt, please," I told the doe-eyed woman sitting at the table. The roomy shirt would be perfect to sleep in. My decision to use it as a PJ top had nothing to do with Tristan's low opinion of my clothing choices, of course.

She pulled one out of the stack, and I handed over my debit card.

"I'm Callie Haybeck," I told the woman. "I think you're staying at my family's farm with the Hasty Hogs bunch, aren't you?"

A wide smile split her face, and she held out a hand to shake. "It's so nice to meet you, Callie. I'm Jes Nowak. My husband, Sam, and I are staying in your guest cottage with Brandon and Michelle. It's super charming and cute. The farm feels so peaceful. I wanted to stay there and sink into the comfy couch, but you know, the job calls." Her shrug was accompanied by a high, tinkly giggle. Every sentence out of the woman's mouth sounded excited and like it ended with an exclamation mark. I liked Jes immediately. Her giggle was contagious, and I found myself laughing right along with her.

Jes swiped my debit card through a card reader attached to her cell phone. "Half price for you and any other merchandise you or your family want." Jes giggled again.

I grinned. "Totally not necessary, but I appreciate it." I folded the T-shirt as small as I could get it and crammed it into my small backpack.

"You teach goat yoga, right?" Before I could answer, Jes continued, clapping her hands with excitement as she spoke. "It looks like so much fun. I'm going to make Sam drive me in every morning so I can attend, if that's okay?"

"It's more than okay. I'd love to have you. Have you ever been to a goat yoga session before?"

Jes shook her head no, her big blue eyes sparkling. "Not yet, but I'm planning on fixing that bright and early tomorrow."

"You're going to love it. I promise. See you in the morning." I waved goodbye and headed back to my seat, eager for the races to start.

Brandon and a man I assumed was Sam, Jes's husband, loaded five squealing pigs into metal chutes at the start of the racetrack. Michelle grabbed a microphone and began pumping up the crowd, shouting out the names of each of the racing pigs and asking the crowd to whistle and clap for their favorites. Each pig wore a different colored vest with their racing number stitched on the haunch. I picked a spotted black and pink pig named Petunia Porkchop as my favorite while Tristan rooted for Barbie Q., Uncle Will hooted and hollered for Herbie Hambone, and Aunt Ellen, in true Ellen fashion, cheered for each and every pig Michelle introduced.

Michelle's voice boomed through the loudspeakers. "Ladies and Gentlemen, without further ado, Hasty Hogs Pig Racing brings you the first of tonight's races. Ready, set..."

The traditional trumpet call to start a race flowed out of the loudspeakers. The crowd was quiet while the black metal gates on the chutes lifted, then exploded in cheers, whistles, and stomping feet as we all urged our favorite pigs on to victory. Directly past the finish line sat a row of black rubber dishes, each holding a scoop of pig feed. The pigs had been trained to know those dishes were their prize. They ran full tilt to get at the grain before the other piggies arrived. The racetrack was short, and Hasty Hogs had ten racing pigs, and they rotated them out so each porker could rest between races.

As the pigs rounded the last corner coming into the finish line for the first race, I jumped to my feet, yelling for Petunia Porkchop to pour on the speed. At the last second, Frank N. Swine pushed ahead, winning the race by a snout. Aunt Ellen cheered as loud as ever.

The pigs gobbled up their winnings, then Brandon and Sam scooted them back into the pig pen, shuffling the remaining five pigs out for the next race.

While we waited for the next race to start, a commotion on the other end of the track caught my attention. A sturdy woman tossed a picket sign over the fence, then gripped the top of the five-foot-tall chain link fence surrounding the bleachers and racetrack and began to climb. The fence rattled and clinked under her weight. She jammed her feet into the diamond-shaped pattern one at a time as she climbed, then swung a leg over the top, perched unsteadily for a moment, before dropping to the ground. The woman fell to her knees but grabbed her sign and popped back up faster than exploding popcorn. I glanced around, but nobody else seemed to be paying any attention to her. Apparently, she didn't want to pay the two-dollar admission fee. She dusted off her knees, then started marching between the bleachers and the racetrack, a sign held high as she glared at the crowd of spectators enjoying ourselves. Her sign was made from white construction paper. "Pigs are People Too" was written in big red block letters with "Stop the Pig Races!" printed in black on the bottom half of the sign.

"Looks like old Nancy's at it again," said Uncle Will with a chuckle.

I leaned over Aunt Ellen and asked, "Is she a local? What's her story?"

Uncle Will nodded. "Yep, she's a local. Nancy Achilles is the name. She and her husband divorced, I don't know, a handful of years ago. Never had any kids. She's been protesting the pig races ever since Hasty Hogs has been bringing them to the fair. If you ask me, the woman is bored, and kicking up a ruckus about the pigs is how she fills up her time. Apparently, her house full of cats isn't enough to keep her busy. She's a nuisance, in my humble opinion. Trying to spoil some good, old-fashioned fun."

Aunt Ellen poked her sharp elbow into his ribs. "Now, Will, hold your tongue. It's got to be hard, not having a family to take care of. Nancy's not hurting anyone by marching around with her little signs. Leave the woman alone. All in all, Nancy's a good egg."

Michelle announced the second race, so I forgot all about the protestor and focused my attention back on the hustling hogs. By the time the initial races were over, my favorite pig, Petunia Porkchop, and Tristan's favorite, Barbie Q., had both won a heat, so they would be competing against the other three winners in the big finale.

"If Petunia beats Barbie, you have to go on the big Ferris wheel with me." I nudged Tristan with my elbow.

He narrowed his eyes at me. "Okay, but if Barbie beats Petunia, you have to go on the Mega Drop with me."

I pictured the neon-lit tower stretching into the sky and the sound of terrified screams as the seats dropped back to the ground. My life flashed before my eyes, and those nachos rumbled around in my belly. "Deal."

We shook on it. Petunia Porkchop darn well better win this race, or at least beat out Barbie Q. Otherwise, I had a strong suspicion I'd have to change my clothes again before the night was over.

Michelle amped up the crowd, laying it on thick for the final race. She sounded like an old-fashioned barker selling snake oil as she yelled out each pig's name and their corresponding racing stats. The pigs were lined up in the chutes and ready to go, the bowls at the finish line filled to the brim with pig feed. Brandon stepped up beside the chutes, this time holding a starter gun in the air for the final race. Sam stood behind the racing chutes, ready to flip the lever and release the pigs.

"Ready, set…," Michelle barked through the loudspeaker.

Brandon pulled the trigger while we all collectively held our breath. Clink. Nothing happened. Still holding the starter gun in the air, Brandon frowned and pulled the trigger a second time. BANG. I clapped my hands to my ears as the starter gun exploded in an enormous cloud of white smoke punctuated with red flames. The chutes flew open while pieces of shrapnel shot every which way. When the smoke cleared, Brandon Ebersole lay behind the chutes, a pool of red forming around his still body. Sam squatted beside Brandon, his arms thrown protectively over his head while racing pigs hurtled around the track, and Michelle screamed into the microphone.

Chapter Four

L ike half the county, Chief Dale Barnhart had been in the stands enjoying the pig races with his wife when the gun exploded. In a matter of seconds, he'd hurtled his linebacker-sized frame over the fence, dodging the racing pigs as he ran, until he was kneeling beside Brandon's still form. A team of paramedics who had been on duty at the event screamed onto the scene in the Chief's wake. In minutes, wailing sirens from the Bobwhite Hollow police and fire stations directly across the street from the fairgrounds split the air.

"Is he dead? He looks dead. He's not even twitching." Gasps, tears, and shocked whispers filled the grandstands as we all stood and craned our necks to see what was happening. When the paramedics covered Brandon with a white sheet, our biggest question was morbidly answered. A hush descended over the crowd. The man was dead.

I looked at my family as we all sat back down on the bleachers, each of us too shaky to get up and leave quite yet. "What in the world just happened?"

With eyes as round as Frisbees, Tristan replied, "I think the starter gun exploded, but is that even in the realm of possibility? Can that happen?"

Uncle Will shook his head, dumbfounded. "I've never heard of one exploding before, but I agree with you. It does appear to be what happened. Right before our eyes." He rubbed his white mustache with a thumb and index finger.

"Spectators, please calmly exit the grandstands," an officer instructed through a bullhorn. "You are all free to leave. In an orderly manner, please." He hesitated before adding, "At this time, the Lupine County Fair will remain open, excluding this arena. If anything changes, another announcement will be made."

As we followed the crowd out of the stands, Jay, the fair manager, passed by, fighting the crowd as he made his way in the opposite direction of the surge. His hair stood on end as if he'd stuck his finger in an electrical socket, and his official fair vest flapped open. He frantically attempted to squeeze past us. I narrowed my shoulders to try to provide him with more room.

"Oh, boy. Jay's going to have a terrible number of things to deal with in the coming days with a death at the fair," Aunt Ellen commented. "I don't envy him one bit, poor fellow."

My eyes widened. "Plus, I imagine he'll probably feel horrible and guilty about the spat he had with Brandon this afternoon. Their last interaction was a doozy."

"Spat? What're you talking about?" Tristan asked.

We'd made our way to the goat stalls, so I regaled my family with the tale of Bugsy chasing Jay around the fairgrounds this afternoon and my subsequent visit to the fair manager's office. The chuckle we all got over the story of the naughty goat and Jay's apple felt out of place after the tragedy of Brandon's incredibly public death.

Aunt Ellen pushed herself up from the hay bale she'd been sitting on and turned to Uncle Will. "Are you ready to go, old man? I want to get home to bake a casserole and a fresh pie to have waiting for the Hasty Hogs crew when they arrive. It's going to be a rough night for Brandon's wife and his friends. They could use a little comfort food."

"I'll feed the goats and freshen their water, then Tristan and I will be right behind you to help." I reached for a water bucket.

Aunt Ellen patted my arm. "No, no. There's nothing you can do." She glanced between Tristan and me. "You young people stay here and enjoy the fair, like you'd planned. I'm betting it'll be several hours before those folks get back to the farm, anyway."

Uncle Will pulled Aunt Ellen's hand into the crook of his arm and gave it a squeeze. "My lovely bride has a dozen or more casseroles in the freezer for occasions such as this. The only help she requires is a hot oven. And

I happen to know there's already a couple fresh blueberry pies cooling on the counter. Don't worry. You two concentrate on having a good time." He winked at Tristan and me before they turned and ambled away.

I secured Bugsy's stall gate with the latch, then tightly wrapped two extra bungee cords around it for good measure. Just let the naughty goat try to escape this time. Tristan helped me freshen the goat's water buckets before we were pulled toward the alluring lights and music of the carnival.

The first thing on my mind after witnessing a horrifying death on the pig tracks most definitely shouldn't have been food, but the tantalizing scent of corn dogs frying set my mouth watering as soon as Tristan and I emerged from the goat barn.

My cousin bumped me with his shoulder. "What do you want to do first? The Mega Drop?"

I snorted. "Not on your life. The final race didn't take place. You can't make me get on that death trap with you."

"I beg to differ. The pigs were still released from the gates for the grand finale. While you were rubbernecking the accident, my attention was focused on the pigs. I'm happy to report my girl Barbie Q. came in first place."

Stopping dead in my tracks, I shot Tristan the stink eye. "Bull honky. Did you take a video to prove your pig won?"

"No." He grinned and flung an arm over my shoulders, steering me toward the Mega Drop. "I guess you'll just have to trust me."

I wrapped an arm around his waist and attempted to abort my cousin's mission and navigate the two of us toward the corn dog stand instead. Tristan put all his strength into steering us to the carnival rides. I doubled down with my efforts to fill my belly until we tripped over each other's feet and collapsed in a heap of laughter.

Tristan jumped to his feet and held out a hand to help me up. "Come on, Callie. I guarantee you don't want a corn dog before the ride. I promise to get you one after."

"Dang right, you will." I playfully growled at him before I gave in to my fate.

Dusk was starting to settle over the fairgrounds as we approached a ticket kiosk. We both splurged on unlimited ride wristbands good for the duration of the fair. Reluctantly, I followed Tristan as we took our place at the end of the long line of people waiting to ride the Mega Drop. With darkness descending, the bright carnival lights lit up the night. Despite my fear of the Mega Drop, excitement rose in my chest. Craning my neck, I stared up at the tall yellow tower of the ride and gave myself a pep talk. *Don't be a chicken, Callie. It's two minutes. You're not going to die. Probably.* The height of the thing didn't bother me, it was the freefall after you reached the top that had me shaking in my boots. With the long line moving at a snail's pace, it gave me plenty of time to worry about it and imagine my painful death while we waited for our turn. Teenagers laughed and hooted as they were raised up to skyscraper height and dropped back down. With every ride in front of us, at least one person screamed their lungs out during the drop. No way was the screamer going to be me.

Finally, it was our turn. Tristan and I stepped up and took the last two spots on the end of the bench seat. The carnival worker helped us pull the heavy shoulder pads into place and made sure we were buckled in securely. He stepped back, pushed a button, and the ride began to rise into the night sky.

"Why did I agree to this? Fudge, fudge, fudge, fudge, fudge!" We reached the summit, and as the carriages went into freefall, I tried to clamp my mouth shut, but the scream slipped out anyway. As my hair rose above my head, I no longer cared about being the screamer on our turn. *Don't let me die, don't let me die.* I repeated over and over to myself as my screaming rent the air.

Beside me, my treacherous cousin laughed with glee. The ride jerked to an abrupt halt as the carriage sank into place two feet off the ground. My stomach fell out of my throat and landed back where it belonged with a big thump. I was uber thankful Tristan had steered me away from indulging in a pre-Mega Drop corndog. I stumbled out of my seat and followed Tristan through the short metal gate on wobbly legs.

As soon as we were away from the group getting off the ride, I leaned forward and placed my hands on my knees in an attempt to catch my breath.

"Thank goodness it's over."

"What? Come on. Let's go one more time." Tristan grinned at me and bounced on the balls of his feet. "It was super fun."

I straightened, held up a palm, and walked away.

He caught up with me in a couple of trotting steps. "Callie. Come on. Did you really not have fun? What a rush!"

I jerked my head around. "Are you serious right now? No. It was terrifying."

Tristan studied my no-that-was-not-fun face. "I guess you do look a little green around the gills."

I kept walking. "You owe me a corndog."

I chose the biggest, most expensive corndog I could find, then ordered a basket of curly fries while I was at it. Maybe some greasy food would settle my stomach. Tristan grimaced but ordered his own fried, battered hot dog, then whipped out his debit card to pay for our snacks.

He shrugged while he smothered his corndog in yellow mustard. "When in Rome."

We squeezed into two empty spots at a table in the food court and discussed what we wanted to do next while we ate. As it turned out, Tristan and I weren't the most compatible pair of carnival goers. While I would be content to ride the giant Ferris wheel all night long, Tristan wanted to get back in line for the Mega Drop, followed by the Slingshot, the Zipper, and some contraption called the Hammer. His idea of a good time at the carnival sounded like downright torture to me.

"What's wrong with taking in the sights, throwing some darts at balloons, and going home with a new stuffed animal or a goldfish?" I asked.

"I'm here for the adrenaline rush, not a goldfish that's going to be belly up tomorrow morning," Tristan answered. He turned the full force of his hazel puppy dog eyes on me. "Come on. Go on the rides with me. The whole reason I came down was so we could experience the fair together. You'll love it once you get on them."

His sad puppy eyes almost worked until my stomach rolled at the thought of those scary rides. "No. This is absolutely not my idea of a good time.

None of those rides you mentioned are ones I even want to watch, let alone ride."

Tristan bawk-bawk-bawked at me like the chicken I was.

I brandished my foot-long empty corndog stick his way. "Doesn't matter yet anyway because you promised to go on the giant Ferris wheel with me next."

"Boring." Tristan rolled his eyes. "And no, I didn't. I only agreed to ride the Ferris wheel with you if your pig won the race, but Barbie Q. was the clear winner. Petunia Porkchop came in a mere third." He made an L-shaped loser sign with his fingers, making me giggle despite myself.

"Says you, with zero proof." I gestured at his half-eaten corndog. "Finish up your dog, buddy. You're coming with me, like it or not."

Ten minutes later, we stood in line while classic rock boomed from speakers placed around the carnival. Lights sparkled and flashed from the rides. The man who was working the giant Ferris wheel reminded me of a ringmaster from a circus. He was decked out in black slacks with a red satin stripe down both sides, a red-and-gold paisley jacket with long tails worn over a white ruffled tuxedo shirt, and a black bow tied neatly around his neck. A black satin top hat finished the outfit with a flourish.

A handful of teenage boys in front of us in line were using the bravery afforded them from being in their herd of peers to needle the guy. "Look at this carny," they snickered. "He thinks he's the King of England or something." The boys laughed. "Come on, dude. You're just a greasy old carny. Probably can't even read."

The well-dressed, forty-ish carnival worker simply ignored them. From the way their jeers elicited no reaction, he must've been used to the boys' particular brand of cruelty.

We were next in line when the final gondola filled, so I took the opportunity to say hello and chat with the carnival worker, hoping to make up for the teenager's bad behavior. I wanted him to know there were plenty of nice people in Bobwhite Hollow, too. His hands were fully tattooed, and the edge of more ink peeked from underneath his shirt collar. He was clean and freshly shaven, not at all the dirty traveler the teenagers had accused him of being.

"I love your outfit. That jacket is to die for." I caught his eye and smiled.

His blue eyes crinkled at the corners as he smiled back at me. "Thank you, miss. I appreciate your kindness." His voice, deep and refined, held a strong British accent. "It's one of my own creations."

My eyes must've bugged out of my face. "You made your jacket? That's amazing!"

"I did indeed. I run the Ferris wheel here at the midway in the evenings, but in my free time during the day, I help with costume designs and repairing uniforms."

"It's gorgeous. So elegant," I gushed. "What is a midway, if you don't mind my asking?"

The man winked. "Simply an old-fashioned, more elegant way to say carnival. I prefer the term myself. It harkens back to a gentler era."

"Aha. Makes perfect sense to me. I'm Callie Haybeck, by the way, and this is my cousin, Tristan Beck."

"Keith George. Pleased to make your acquaintance." He shook both of our hands, then directed his gaze back to the Ferris wheel. "Haybeck and Beck? And you're cousins? There has to be a story there."

"Not an interesting one," Tristan replied. "I had my last name legally shortened to Beck a few years ago."

"Much to your family's chagrin, I imagine," Keith said.

"He thinks Beck is more dignified than Haybeck, but deep inside, he'll always be a simple country boy," I teased.

Tristan stuck his tongue out at me.

"I rest my case," I said.

"Are you both local to the area?" Keith asked.

I answered for us. "Tristan lives in Boston. I'm local, though. I teach goat yoga and will have a session here at the fair every morning at seven. You're welcome to join us."

Keith laughed. "I'll barely have gone to bed by seven. No, you won't be seeing me there, but thanks so much for the invitation. It was an honor to meet you both." He brought the Ferris wheel to a stop, and Tristan and I were directed into the first empty gondola.

As soon as we were seated, Tristan gave me the side-eye. "Sometimes I can't believe you were raised in a city."

"Why?" I lifted my cowboy-booted foot and grinned. "Do my cool boots have you confused?"

He laughed but shook his head. "No, it's your complete and utter trust in everyone you meet."

"Are you talking about Keith?" I gestured to the carnival worker.

"Keith? See? You're already on a first-name basis, and you don't know anything about the guy except that he works for the carnival."

"He was perfectly charming. And he sews!"

"Sure, okay. Knowing how to sew means he must totally be the nicest guy in the world. Maybe you can meet up for tea later." Tristan shook his head as if I was a lost cause.

If not judging people by their jobs meant I was a lost cause, so be it.

As the Ferris wheel began to move, I settled back against the seat and gazed out at the view. I loved all the bright lights of the carnival against the dark sky. Once we made it to the top, Tristan scooted to the edge of his seat, causing our gondola to rock. I squealed and grabbed on tight to the pole in the center. Tristan laughed and pointed out how we could see the entire downtown area of Bobwhite Hollow from our vantage point. During the day, the view from the top would've been spectacular.

After the Ferris wheel, I kept Tristan company while he stood in line to ride the Zipper. When he squeezed into the closed carriage with a young couple he didn't know, I stepped back and tried to watch, but the movement made me feel dizzy. While he got his adrenaline rush, I wandered over to the nearest food cart and indulged in a stick of fluffy, pink cotton candy.

By the time Tristan emerged from the fast-moving zipper, I was hyped up on sugar and amped up with the party music pumping through the carnival grounds. The next thing I knew, I'd agreed to ride the Hammer with my adrenaline-junky cousin. Getting into a spinning, rotating wire cage with a belly full of corndog, fries, and cotton candy turned out to be one giant terrible decision. The ride whipped us up into the air, the cage spun, my stomach revolted, and in under two minutes, our fun night at the carnival came to a sour end.

Chapter Five

When my alarm clock rudely jangled me awake at the ungodly hour of five in the morning, my stomach still wobbled from the combination of fried food, pure sugar, and a monster of a carnival ride. I lay with my eyes closed for a minute, calculating last night's damage. While a bit of unsteadiness remained, the nausea had passed. I could live with that. "Nothing a shower and some protein won't fix."

But first, barn chores were calling. I swapped my pajamas for a pair of denim shorts and a T-shirt before trudging outside.

By the time Tristan and I'd made it back to the farm the night before, the pink Hasty Hogs truck was parked in front of the guest cottage and all the lights were out. In the buttery-soft early morning light, Michelle, Brandon's brand-new widow, sat in a rocking chair on the porch of the stone cottage wrapped in a blanket. Her gaze was fixed on the sunrise beginning to lighten up the peak of Mt. Washington. I thought about approaching to give her my condolences, but since I hadn't known either one of them well, anything I could think of saying felt like an empty platitude. Besides, I imagined Michelle was so wrapped up in her grief she didn't even realize I was there or see the small wave I directed her way. I decided to leave her to her thoughts. There'd be time to formulate and express my sympathy later in the day.

I headed for the west pasture where the sheep and mama goats were turned out together. Daisy, Uncle Will's Great Pyrenees farm dog, led the way, her fluffy white tail held high and swishing back and forth like a flag. Daisy earned her keep on the one-hundred-acre Haybeck Farm. With her job as a livestock guardian, she spent her nights with the flock of sheep, keeping watch for any predators. Each morning, Daisy pranced around, tail high, proud to report her charges were all present and accounted for. Nobody was worse for the wear after her shift ended.

During the summer, the flock lived in a pasture with a creek flowing through it, and this summer, my goats had joined them there. The grass was lush, and the water clean and plentiful, so I didn't need to feed hay or even fill water troughs. Even so, I liked to check on them first thing in the morning to make sure none of them had found a weak spot in the fence and broken out. The last thing I wanted was for my goats to escape and destroy Aunt Ellen's garden or one of Uncle Will's crops.

After assuring myself everything was fine, I scratched a couple of goats behind their floppy ears and gave them a quick lecture about behaving themselves. They eyed me and went right back to grazing. Fortunately, with Bugsy, my problem goat, at the fair, I didn't have too much to worry about.

"Fine. I guess this meeting is over."

Frankie bleated at me as if to say, "We didn't need to have a meeting. You could've just sent an email."

On my way back to the farmhouse, I detoured to the hen house to let Aunt Ellen's chickens out of their coop for the day. I scattered some chicken feed around, then hightailed it out of there before the rooster decided it'd be fun to chase me.

By the time I finished my shower, Aunt Ellen was up and had the kitchen smelling like a cozy diner. She handed me a plate filled with a toasted English muffin, a fried egg, and two slices of bacon. I assembled it all into a handy breakfast sandwich, then plopped a kiss onto my great-aunt's cheek.

"Have fun in the parade today," I told her. "I'll be waving at you from the sidelines." I headed off to teach the first-ever Lupine County Fair goat yoga session.

Chapter Six

"What in the heck is going on here?" My mouth gaped open at the sight of the eight news vans in the fairgrounds parking lot. It wasn't even six in the morning, for crimany sakes. What in the world were they doing here so early?

I recognized the logos of three stations out of Boston, one station from Concord, one from Burlington, Vermont, and one out of Augusta, Maine. Given the horrible accident at the track last night, it shouldn't have come as a surprise to find so many journalists covering Brandon's bizarre death. I parked Old Rusty as far away from the commotion as I could and attempted to slink through the gate without being noticed. Luck was not on my side.

A woman carrying a microphone sprinted across the gravel parking lot, shouting to get my attention. "Miss, miss. Would you have a moment to speak with us?"

I froze, then slowly swiveled around to face the reporter, blowing hair out of my eyes and attempting to school my face into some form of pleasant expression. "I'm sorry, I really don't have time. I'm in a hurry to attend to my animals."

A second woman jogged behind the reporter with a whirring camera balanced on her shoulder. Before I could blink, a microphone was shoved under my nose. "Just one quick comment, and I'll let you go."

I fought the urge to make a break for it and reluctantly agreed. "Okay, but I only have time for one question."

"Were you in attendance at the pig races last evening?" She shoved the microphone back in my face, but when I only nodded, she pulled it back.

31

"Can you tell our viewers what happened? What you witnessed?"

The microphone was back in my face. "Um, there was an explosion, lots of smoke, some flames." Never having been on TV before, my brain and my mouth weren't working in tandem.

"And when the smoke cleared?" the reporter asked.

"As you well know, Brandon Ebersole was dead," I responded and turned to leave.

"Wait," the reporter called after me. "Were you acquainted with the deceased?"

"I gave you your one comment." I kept walking, eager to get out of the spotlight. My thirty seconds of fame had been more like thirty seconds of shame. Instead of being articulate, I'd reacted like a deer in the headlights. Fingers crossed they'd choose not to air it.

As Jay had promised, a sturdy round pen had been set up for me on the lawn where Bugsy had given the fair manager the run-around the day before. I lugged a tub of yoga mats inside the pen, then headed to the barn to feed the goats and clean the stalls before the session started. When I spotted Bugsy safe and sound in his stall where he belonged, I let out a relieved breath.

Once my barn chores were finished, there was half an hour before the session was due to start. Barely enough time to wrangle the young goats out to the yoga pen before people started to show up. I shouldn't have stopped to talk to the dang reporter.

Clipping lead ropes to two of the goats' collars, I opened the gate barely wide enough to wedge my leg and hip into the opening, then let the two goats wiggle out one at a time while managing to keep the other six from escaping. Getting the little buggers where I needed them to go was always an adventure, especially since they'd learned their escape tactics from Bugsy. I latched the gate behind myself before jogging out to the yoga pen and depositing the first two goats inside with ease. As I unclipped the leads from their collars and turned to head back to the barn to get their friends, they stuck their adorable little heads through the railings and bleated at the top of their lungs.

"You're okay, babies. The rest of your buddies will be here before you know it." In an attempt to keep the yelling to a minimum, I sprinted to the barn for the next two.

The goats left in the barn were already working themselves into a tizzy from hearing the two out in the pen putting up such a racket. I clipped my leads to Bonnie and Clyde, but Bonnie bucked and kicked her heels up while her twin brother, Clyde, dug his hooves into the ground and refused to move. By the time I managed to get them to the pen, I was sweating bullets, and my shoulders ached. "Four more little devils to go," I muttered to myself. Why hadn't I trained them to lead better? The next two behaved as badly as Bonnie and Clyde had.

As I caught my breath and attempted to wrangle the last two young goats out of the barn, an earsplitting bleat tore through the air. I turned around in time to watch Bugsy rise up on his back legs and frantically beat at the boards of his stall with his front hooves.

"Bugsy, no. Stay," I yelled as the two goats on my lead ropes towed me behind them on the way to join their friends in the yoga pen. Bugsy didn't pay a single bit of attention to my stern instructions. Instead, he launched himself in the air and cleared the stall by a foot, shrieking at the top of his lungs the entire time. In seconds, he'd freed himself from the pen and galloped to catch up with the rest of us. At least he'd saved me another trip back to the barn to get him. We made it to the pen with no more incidents, Bugsy tagging along behind—no lead rope needed. I tucked the two goats inside the enclosure, then grabbed Bugsy's collar and pulled him in behind me. I clipped a lead rope onto the ring on his collar and looped the rope around one of the sturdier corner posts. He could graze and, with him in the pen with us, he was content, so I shouldn't need to worry about the naughty guy escaping while I taught the yoga session.

"Aha. So now we know how he's always escaping. That goat could win a high jump contest."

I looked up from the knot I was securing to find Levi McClure, hands on his hips and an amused glint in his emerald green eyes, standing outside the yoga pen. I couldn't help but notice how the morning sun brought out a hint

33

of red in his brown wavy hair. Laugh lines crinkled the corner of his eyes.

It shouldn't have surprised me one bit to find out Levi had witnessed my morning chaos. I sighed. "What are you even doing here?"

Levi's bright grin slipped into a frown. "Well, considering how I *am* the official veterinarian for the fair, and this place seems to be full of animals, it really doesn't seem too far-fetched for me to be here, does it?" He indicated the entire fairgrounds with an irritated sweep of his arms, then planted his fists on his hips.

Well, hello there, muscles. I couldn't help but notice how Levi's biceps flexed against the burgundy cotton T-shirt he wore. Embarrassed for a number of reasons, I patted Bugsy's furry back and shook my head. "That's not what I meant."

Anytime Levi showed up, he either caught me doing something completely ridiculous or with my foot planted six inches inside my mouth. When I was a teenager, I had a poster on my bedroom wall I'd gotten at a school book fair. The poster read, 'The stupidity of your actions is directly proportional to the number of people watching.' For me, the stupidity of my actions wasn't based on the number of people watching, just one person in particular. Levi McClure.

The vet dipped his chin and stared straight into my eyes. "Then what exactly did you mean, Callie?"

"Only that I'm surprised to see you here this early. Not many people are out and about yet. Did you come to do yoga with us?" I eyed his jeans and steel-toed work boots. "You're going to need to change."

He chuckled. "No, I'm not here to do yoga, but nice try."

My face flamed red at the exchange. At least I was blaming it on the exchange instead of on my attraction to the infuriating vet.

"Aw, Callie. Don't feel sheepish. I didn't mean to get your goat." He tilted his head toward the goat and sheep barn to make sure I noticed how clever he was.

"Believe me, you didn't. You're being udderly ridiculous. Now butt out. I haven't goat all day." Two could play the game.

Levi chuckled while I began to greet the handful of people who were starting to arrive for the first Lupine County Fair goat yoga session. At the same time, I kept one eye focused on Levi's backside as he strolled toward the cattle barn. I could multi-task with the best of them.

Once Levi disappeared into the barn, I invited everyone who was there for the session to come inside the pen and take a mat from the tub if they hadn't brought their own. I was glad to see Jes from the Hasty Hogs crew among the participants.

"Jes, I'm so sorry about Brandon. The whole thing has everyone in shock." I twisted my hands, not sure what else to say to express my condolences. "I'm surprised but super glad to see you this morning, and happy you were able to make it." Spending time cuddling goats would do the woman a world of good.

Her big eyes filled with tears, but she leaned in to give me a hug as if we were old friends. "Oh, thank you. It's all so awful. Poor Michelle. I feel horrible for her." Jes ended the hug and fluttered her hands in a nervous gesture. "None of us could sleep, so I thought why not? Sam was nice enough to drive me in." She pointed at her husband, who sat on top of one of the picnic tables, staring at the phone in his hand. "But enough about all that for now. I'm here for some goat yoga."

"Okay then. Let's get going." I clapped my hands together and turned to unroll my own yoga mat. When I finished, I stretched into the Warrior One pose and asked, "Who here has attended a goat yoga session before?"

Only one of the dozen or so people observing me from their mats raised their hands, so I launched into a short explanation about what they should expect.

"Goat yoga is all about having a good time and relaxing. Sure, we'll be stretching our muscles with simple poses, but I also encourage you to interact with the goats. They'll wander around, maybe wind between your legs, and jump on you from time to time. Goats like to play king of the mountain on the highest thing, and this morning, you're going to be the mountain! Don't worry about your form today; just enjoy yourself and scratch the goats behind the ears when you get the chance. Cuddling goats works as well as meditation for calming anxiety and relieving stress."

I answered a few questions about the goats—Do they bite? No. Will their hooves hurt when they jump on me? Think of it like a bonus massage. Can I pick one up? Absolutely. For a gentle warm-up, I directed the group to their hands and knees for the cat-cow combination. It was my favorite stretch for lengthening the spine and neck. We started on all fours with a straight, tabletop back, then moved into the cow pose by dropping the belly and spine downward for a long breath before arching our backs up like a stretching cat. Knowing their jobs well, the goats took advantage of the situation by scooting under people's bellies, bouncing up onto their curved backs, and jumping from one person to another as if they were playing a game of hot lava. It wasn't long before my entire group of yoga students' form fell completely apart as they hooted and hollered over the silly goats' antics.

A giant sneeze was working its way behind my eyes and nose, so I scrambled to grab a tissue before my face exploded. "Achoo."

A chorus of "Bless yous" arose from my students.

Not long after I'd sunk my entire savings into my little herd of goats, I'd discovered I was allergic to them. So far, I'd tried every allergy medicine on the shelf at White Mountain Pharmacy with little success. Aunt Ellen kept after me to either make a doctor's appointment or go talk to an herbalist friend of hers, but so far, I hadn't made the effort to do either. My watering eyes and runny nose announced it was past time. I made a mental note to get the name of Aunt Ellen's friend again.

When I turned back around from trying to blow my nose with a tiny bit of decorum and privacy, the lady who'd been picketing the pig races the previous evening stood outside the round pen. This time, instead of a sign about pig cruelty, she carried a yellow piece of poster board stapled to a wooden stake. In messy black marker, the sign read, "Free the Goats." My first thought was how Bugsy does an excellent job of freeing himself on a regular basis. And where did she think they were going to go, anyway? Just wander aimlessly around the village eating random people's trees and gardens? Before approaching the woman, I directed the class into the cobra pose, then left them to it while I went to try to diffuse the situation.

"Nancy, is it?" I propped my arms on the top rail of the pen as I addressed her.

Wordlessly, Nancy glared at me.

I tried again. "My name's Callie Haybeck. I think you know my great-uncle and aunt, Will and Ellen?"

This time, she sent a quick nod of acknowledgment my way. I took it as encouragement and plunged ahead. "Can I ask why you think the goats should be freed?" My question was punctuated with a sneeze.

Nancy huffed and brushed thin strands of fading ash-brown hair out of her face. "It makes me incredibly sad to think you have to ask why these sweet creatures should be free. Isn't it obvious? Animals aren't meant to be caged, and what's worse, you're making those poor babies work for their livelihood."

I couldn't help but snort. Unbelievable. I glanced behind me at the goats frolicking over, under, and on top of the morning's yoga participants. Several people sat on their mats with little goats in their laps while they scratched behind the animal's floppy ears.

"Can you honestly look at those goats and tell me they're not enjoying every second of their workday?" I made air quotes around "workday."

Nancy frowned. "I'll admit, they seem to be having a good time. But what happens when yoga is over for the day? They get stuffed in small pens where they can barely move around. Then the poor little things are bored and miserable, sitting in their own filth."

I shook my head. "Nope. You have it all wrong." I nodded toward the sheep and goat barn. "For the few days we're here at the fair, yes, they'll be in their roomy and clean stalls." I placed extra emphasis on the words roomy and clean. "The goats love the attention they get from the fairgoers. Back at the farm, they're out in a green field grazing with their mothers all day, except during yoga sessions. They get mangers full of fresh hay and occasional treats. It's a good life. Trust me."

Nancy blew a raspberry. "I don't see any reason why I should trust you. I don't even know you, for heaven's sake."

"Well, I'm inviting you to get to know me and the goats. Why don't you

37

put down the sign and come on in here. You can see for yourself how well they're cared for." I raised an eyebrow, waiting to see if she'd accept my invitation. "Look here. Little Capone is waiting for you to cuddle him." I motioned to a chocolate-brown kid who'd wandered over and stuck his nose out of the pen to sniff at Nancy's pant leg.

Nancy eyed Capone. She licked her dry lips, sucked in her round cheeks, and stared up at the passing clouds for a moment. Apparently, having come to a decision, she placed her sign face down on the ground and marched over to the gate leading into the round pen. I smiled and held it open for her, but my upper lip involuntarily curled as she walked past. The air around the woman swirled with the sharp, pungent aroma of a thousand cats. I quickly tried to pull my face back under control and quell the sour taste filling my mouth.

Closing the gate behind her, I took a giant step back, gulping in a lungful of fresh air. "Feel free to wander around and meet the goats. Grab a mat and join in the rest of the yoga session with us, if you feel so inclined." Getting Nancy to participate hadn't been even remotely the battle I'd expected it to be, though I'd have to remember to keep my distance, or my sneezing would amp up into a full-blown attack.

While Nancy acclimated herself with the goats, I stepped back to my mat and apologized for the delay.

Jes giggled and waved a dismissive hand at me. "No worries. We're all just snuggling goats anyway." She gave the little brown-and-black goat on her lap a kiss on top of his head. Baby Face Nelson chewed his cud with his eyes closed, a contented smile on his narrow little face.

Since most of my morning students were already sitting on their mats, I restarted the session in the lotus pose with some deep breathing exercises before launching into a couple of sitting stretches. From there, we moved into the tabletop position. With everyone on their hands and knees, the goats bounced onto flat backs and scurried under the students as if they were bridges. I coached the class into the sunbird pose—tabletop with the left arm extended in front of them and the right leg extended behind. Sunbird was one of my favorite poses to bring the levity of goat yoga into play. Unless someone had been practicing yoga for a while, their balance wasn't usually good enough to maintain the pose when goats jumped on them. As expected, within the first couple of repetitions of the pose, most of my students had fallen onto their sides thanks to the playful goats. The air around us echoed with laughter.

By the time the session was over, Negative Nancy had turned into Namaste Nancy. She sat on a purple mat in the lotus pose with one goat in her lap and another nibbling at her hair. The expression on her face looked to me as if she'd found Nirvana.

As everyone rolled up their mats and said their goodbyes, Nancy approached me with a shy smile. "Would it be okay if I joined you tomorrow morning?"

"If you promise to leave your sign at home," I jerked my head toward her protest sign lying abandoned in the grass, "you're welcome here every morning."

"Cross my heart." Nancy smiled the first genuine smile I'd seen from the woman while making a big X across her chest with a pudgy finger.

In my two short months as a goat yoga instructor, I'd seen more than one person's gloomy outlook change after only one session. Maybe all Nancy was truly looking for was someone to pay a bit of attention to her. Whatever had changed her attitude, I was delighted to have played some small role in her new outlook.

I manned the gate as my yoga students left so none of the rambunctious goats would take the opportunity to escape. Jes lingered until everyone else was gone, then approached me and leaned in for another hug.

"Goat yoga was exactly what I needed this morning," she said. "Plus, it was so good to see you again. Thank you."

We don't even know each other. But I hugged her back anyway. Jes had to be one of the friendliest and most effusive people I'd ever had the pleasure to be around. "You're more than welcome. I'm glad you were able to make it. Those little goats are super talented at soothing the soul."

"They really are!" She nodded enthusiastically. "I wanted to come to yoga every morning of the fair, but with Brandon's death, I'm not sure we'll be here the entire week. For however long we are, though, I'll be coming. Maybe I'll see you back at the farm later?"

Suddenly, the ground shook, accompanied by a loud crash. Jes and I both jerked around to find Sam with hands balled into fists and the picnic table he'd been sitting on moments ago turned upside down like a dead bug with its feet in the air. The air around him nearly vibrated with the curse words spewing from his mouth.

"What the heck?" Jes exclaimed, her face draining of color.

I stood there with my own mouth gaping open while Sam aimed a kick at a garbage can, then bellowed his wife's name. "Jes! Come on. We've got to go. The bank called. Our flipping paychecks have bounced again." Sam stormed off toward the parking lot, his face a red mask of fury.

Chapter Seven

I stared after them as Sam practically ran to the pig truck and Jes trotted behind him. Wow, was Sam ever angry. The bounced paychecks must've put them in a terrible financial position for him to show so much anger publicly. From the sounds of it, this wasn't the first time. How often had it happened? To be fair, once was one time too many. I'd be livid, too, if my paycheck bounced, but it'd been a long time since I'd witnessed a temper tantrum like the one Sam had thrown. Tires squealed and gravel flew as the pink Hasty Hogs truck left the fairgrounds parking lot.

The picnic table was bulky and heavy, but after some grunting and groaning, I managed to roll it onto its side and then push it upright. The table wasn't in the exact location it had been, but it was going to have to do for now. Putting the rubber garbage can back in place was an easier task, and thankfully, the fair maintenance crew had already been by to collect the trash from the night before, so there wasn't garbage scattered all over the ground. I dusted my hands off. There. One good deed accomplished for the day.

With the mess of Hurricane Sam taken care of, I left all the goats in the round pen while I downed another dose of allergy medicine, then cleaned out their stalls in the barn and refreshed them with thick beds of sweet, fragrant yellow straw. I made sure the stalls had salt and mineral blocks in easy reach of all the goats, filled their feed bags full of sweet grass hay, then grabbed the water buckets and headed to the outside spigot. I'd turned off the faucet after filling the two blue flat-back buckets when a loud bleat echoed around the fairgrounds. Bugsy had realized I wasn't in the pen with

41

him anymore and was raising an ear-splitting ruckus. Normally, his loud bleating made me roll with laughter, but Nancy threatening to protest my yoga session earlier had my nerves on edge. How many other people thought I might be mistreating my goats?

I glanced around, but the only people paying attention to the screaming goat seemed to be amused by his antics. His outrageous bleating had worked, garnering him the attention he'd been after. A man leaned over the top rail of the yoga pen, scratching the silly critter behind his ears while Bugsy tilted his head into the man's hand with pleasure, his eyes closed, and his mouth turned up in a contented smile. Relieved to have Bugsy preoccupied, I hurried to get the water buckets in the barn and secured them to the stall walls. Once the stalls were cleaned and restocked, I started bringing the goats back in, two at a time.

By the time all nine goats were safe and sound back inside the barn, I was tired and more than ready to indulge in an icy snow cone. Even though it wasn't yet nine in the morning, I had it on good authority the snow cone stand was opening early to provide cool treats for parade watchers. If I hurried, there would be enough time to get a cone and make it to the parade route, where I was meeting up with Uncle Will and Tristan. This time, with any luck, I'd get the delicious ice in my mouth instead of only wearing it.

Sweet Pete Kennison was outside, propping open the awning and sliding open the windows on his ice cream and snow cone trailer as I approached. The eye-catching trailer was painted white with a black-and-white striped awning trimmed with a red triangle-patterned banner adorned with felt ice cream and snow cones. The whole ensemble was lit up with white fairy lights and resembled an old-fashioned ice cream parlor, making it hard to resist.

Pete was dressed in one of his iconic colorful Hawaiian shirts—a dark green fabric covered in bunches of bright yellow bananas. The sight of it made me laugh out loud as the lyrics of "The Banana Boat Song" played in my head.

"What? You don't like my attire?" Pete's eyes sparkled as he spun around from where he'd been busy washing off the outside counter and arranging a selection of plastic spoons and napkins.

"Exactly the other way around. I love it. It's just so…Pete."

"The day's young, but you already look a little frazzled, Callie." He slapped a hand twice against the counter. "What can little Miss Mazzy get started for you?" Pete grinned at the teenage girl who stood on the other side of the counter, waiting to take my order.

I studied the menu. "Can I get a tiger's blood today, please?"

The girl grinned. "Good choice. Tiger's blood is my favorite, too. Well, next to the blue raspberry, anyway." Her light-brown hair was styled in an adorable short pixie cut with the top dyed a deep purple.

"Usually, I order the blue raspberry, but I had a disaster with it yesterday and decided not to press my luck." I chuckled. "I love your hair, by the way." I fondled the blue-dipped ends of my own braids. "I might have to try a royal purple next time."

Mazzy blushed. "You should. It would look good." She thanked me for the compliment before getting to work on my snow cone.

Sweet Pete leaned against the food trailer and crossed his arms over his chest. "So, did you hear about the murder?"

I jerked around from where I'd been watching Mazzy scooping clear ice into a red plastic cone. "Murder?"

Pete pressed his lips together and nodded. "Yep. Brandon, the pig racing guy. Somebody killed him last night."

I shook my head in confusion. "No, you must've heard wrong. I was in the bleachers with my family when it happened. There was a terrible accident with the starter gun. It exploded and killed him, but it wasn't murder."

Pete shook his head in disagreement. "Not exactly. You're right about the gun exploding and killing him, but only because the thing had been tampered with. Somebody rigged the gun to blow. Brandon was murdered."

I gasped. "How do you know? Did Chief Barnhart tell you that's what happened?"

Pete shrugged noncommittally. "I hear things."

I had no doubt. Since moving to Bobwhite Hollow in the spring, I'd become a regular at Sweet Pete's Ice Cream Shoppe. The adorable pink cottage housing the ice cream shop sat in the perfect location next to the riverwalk overlooking the Connecticut River and drew me in right away, but I'd quickly come to adore both Pete and his wife, Claire. The middle-aged couple were always warm and welcoming and seemed to know every single person in the village and half of the people who were only passing through. The Kennisons radiated all the best things about my new town. Pete had a great sense of humor, and we enjoyed joking around with each other whenever I stopped by the ice cream shop, but this time, he wasn't pulling my leg. Murder was no laughing matter.

Mazzy handed my blood-red snow cone out through the window. I thanked her, tucked an extra dollar in the tip jar, and shoveled a spoonful of the sweet and fruity ice into my mouth while trying to wrap my mind around what Pete was saying.

"Yeah, it seems the starter gun was filled with some sort of explosive, and the barrel had been plugged tight so it would explode when fired."

"I don't have a single bit of experience with guns. Do starter guns use actual bullets?"

Pete shook his head. "Not normally, no. Usually, they fire blanks filled with gunpowder. That's what creates the bang and all the smoke. They're completely for show with no bite."

"Were you and Claire at the pig races last night? Did you see it happen?"

Pete flicked his eyes upward as if he were studying a cloud formation. "Uh, no. It'd been a long, hot day, so the truck was busier than I'd anticipated. Claire was holding down the fort at the shop in town, and I was here at the fair scooping ice cream and making shaved ice." He pulled at the neck of his shirt and shook his head. "We missed all the excitement."

"The reason I asked was because when Brandon tried to start the final pig race, the starter gun didn't go off initially. He recocked it and pulled the trigger a second time, and that's when the gun exploded. If the gun was rigged and the barrel plugged, why wouldn't it have blown up the first time?" My snow cone was melting fast, so I shoveled more scoops into my mouth while I waited for Pete's reply.

Pete wobbled his head while he thought about what I'd said. "Kind of makes sense, I guess. With something wrong inside the chamber, the gun didn't discharge the first time, but the movement must've dislodged the explosive enough so when he fired the second time, it caused the hammer to hit in the exact right spot and made the gun explode." He rubbed his bald head. "You would think Brandon would've noticed the gun was plugged when it failed to discharge the first time."

I remembered Brandon frowning, but he had kept his hand high in the air with the gun in it. "He didn't even look at the gun again before he fired the second time."

"Too bad. If he had, it probably would've saved his life." Pete huffed and rubbed a hand over his face. "Well, it's a shame, anyway. A sad way to start the fair. I'd better get in there and help Miss Mazzy out." He hooked a thumb over his shoulder.

A line had formed in front of the food truck while we'd been talking. Mazzy was at the window taking orders and sending frantic glances Pete's way. "Oh gosh. I guess so." And I was going to be late to the parade if I didn't get a move on.

"It was great visiting with you, Callie. Enjoy the parade." Pete winked as he disappeared around the corner of the ice cream truck.

I stared after him. If Pete was right and Brandon really had been murdered, it changed everything.

Chapter Eight

The first image that snapped into my head when Pete claimed Brandon's death was murder was Sam's temper tantrum after the goat yoga session. Bounced paychecks and a hair-trigger temper were the perfect ingredients for murder. But I didn't have time to unpack it all at the moment. Uncle Will and Tristan were expecting me.

Even though the pig races took place the previous night, albeit with a horrifying end, and it had been the carnival's opening night, this morning's parade officially kicked off the Lupine County Fair. Spooning flavored ice into my mouth with every other step, I hurried to the street in front of the fairgrounds where I was supposed to meet up with my family. The parade route started in the parking lot at Bobwhite Hollow High School and wound its way down Main Street before taking a lefthand turn onto Washington Avenue, where the parade would culminate at the fairgrounds. Even though my conversation with Pete had me running a few minutes behind schedule, I was confident I wouldn't miss anything since we were watching from near the end of the route.

The first strains of a marching band announced the beginning of the parade was coming down the street as I wedged my way through the crowded sidewalk. I finally spotted Tristan's mop of golden curls next to Uncle Will's faded straw hat. They were sitting in folding lawn chairs on the edge of the sidewalk. I slid into the empty chair I assumed was for me. "How long have you been here?" I asked my great-uncle.

"Oh, a good couple of hours," he replied with a wink. "Wanted to make sure we were in a prime location to watch your Aunt Ellen go by in all her

46

glory." Uncle Will pointed to a small blue ice cooler tucked under Tristan's chair. "Brought you one of those sweet teas you like. Are you ready for it?"

I shook my head and held up the remnants of the snow cone. "Not quite yet, but thank you. I appreciate it." My last words were drowned out as a police car, blue and red lights flashing, led the first entry, Northern New Hampshire Junior Fife and Drum Corp, down the street. The haunting sounds from the band's instruments drew my complete attention.

The drum Corp was followed by an eclectic mishmash of entries—horse clubs, classic cars, vintage tractors, a fire engine, and firefighters who sprayed the crowd from water-filled fire extinguishers, causing screams of delight. A good portion of the entrants who passed by threw out handfuls of candy. Kids skittered into the street with grocery bags and pillowcases to gather up as much candy as they could. A little girl no more than four years old squatted in the street, trying to get every piece in her chubby little hands, but she'd pick up a lollipop only to drop a tootsie roll. Her dad scooped her up and carried her back to safety over his shoulder, the little girl kicking and screaming the entire way.

Uncle Will pointed down the parade route, then lurched to his feet. "There's my Ellen! Here she comes!"

A pair of beautiful Palomino draft horses pulled a shiny, green wagon with bright white wooden wheels. A colorful geometric-shaped painted barn quilt in vibrant greens, blues, and yellows stood proudly in the middle of the wagon facing us. The wooden quilt was mounted on a large sandwich board with what I imagined was an equally as beautiful quilt facing the crowd on the opposite sidewalk. A banner hanging on the side of the wagon read, "Bobwhite Hollow Barnstormers." Aunt Ellen, along with a group of eight other people, stood on both sides of the heavy wooden quilts. They waved and tossed out candy as they passed by.

Tristan roused himself and used his deepest voice to chant, "Grandma, Grandma," a handful of times. He then stuck his fingers in his mouth and sent out a loud cat-call whistle.

Uncle Will grinned and waved wildly at his wife while I pulled out my phone and snapped a few pictures of the Barnstormers.

A few weeks after I'd first come to the farm, Aunt Ellen asked me if I wanted to tag along with her to her quilting group. Never much for sewing, I passed in favor of an afternoon at home reading. It wasn't until a few weeks later, when Tristan was visiting, and we were driving to town with his then-boyfriend, that I saw my tiny little great-aunt dangling from a harness attached to the roof of a barn. It took me a minute, but I realized Aunt Ellen's little quilting group wasn't anything like I'd imagined it to be. Her group, the Bobwhite Hollow Barnstormers, not only painted huge and intricate barn quilts, but they also installed them on the barns they were painted for. Any profits they made after expenses went right back into our community. The woman made me proud to be her great-niece each and every day.

Coming up behind the Barnstormers float, a vintage red tractor pulled a flatbed trailer loaded down with so many red, white, and blue balloons it looked as if it might lift off the ground at any minute. A banner on tall poles rose above the balloons, proclaiming, "Honoring Our Veterans" and "VFW— Bobwhite Hollow, NH Post." A dozen men and women wearing starched white shirts, dark slacks, and military hats waved miniature American flags from atop the float. As the float passed by, another sign attached to the back of the flatbed caught my eye. "Dedicated to Post Service Officer Orville C. Haybeck."

I poked Uncle Will on the arm to get his attention and pointed. "Look. They dedicated the float to Grandpa Orville." My voice caught on my grandfather's name as a lump filled my throat.

Uncle Will stared after the float and blinked hard. "I sure do miss my brother." He cleared his throat. "It's a well-deserved and long overdue dedication. Orville was a huge advocate for veteran's rights. I only wish I was half the kind and generous man he was."

"What do you mean? You're the kindest person I've ever met."

"But unfortunately, you never had the chance to know your grandfather. He was kind and caring. Generous with his time, to a fault at times." Uncle Will shook his head. "No, there was no one like Orville."

Seeing the dedication and hearing Uncle Will's words about my late grandfather reminded me I needed to call my sister. Almost as soon as

I'd arrived in Bobwhite Hollow, local people started telling me stories about my grandfather. It became clear right away that Orville had been a loved and respected member of the community, which didn't add up with the lurking shadow of a man who would abandon his family. Becoming a little suspicious the miserly dribbles of information Grandma Shirley had unwillingly told us about her ex-husband might not be completely accurate, I'd gone in search of their divorce records.

At the Lupine County Courthouse over in Stonehaven, a clerk spent a crazy amount of time with me, looking for my grandparent's divorce records. After an extensive search, it was clear a divorce between Orville and Shirley Haybeck had never been filed in Lupine County. Which made no sense, because Grandpa lived in Lupine County, and if he had filed for divorce, as Grandma claimed, it would be recorded in this county's books.

I shot off a text to my sister.

Hey, give me a call when you have a minute {{smiley face emoticon}}

Chapter Nine

As soon as the last parade entry rolled by, I ran back to the fairgrounds to check on my goats. This was our first event off the farm, and with Bugsy's escapes, I was a little nervous about leaving them alone for too long. Uncle Will and Tristan went in search of Aunt Ellen. Once they found her, they planned to head back to the farm for a late lunch.

All was well in the goat barn, so I decided to indulge in a fresh-squeezed lemonade from one of the food carts. It wasn't my fault if the cart I chose just happened to sell corndogs, too. And it was lunchtime, so what choice did I have? I had to order one. As soon as I had my treats in hand, I took a big refreshing gulp of lemonade, then found a seat on a shady bench under a tree to relax, do a bit of people-watching, and savor my snacks.

Yoga instructors probably are supposed to eat a little healthier than corndogs. I swiveled my head to see if anyone was judging me. Nope. Not a soul cared. I kicked the guilty feelings to the curb and ripped open a packet of mustard to smear on the crispy cornmeal breading.

The tree-lined fairgrounds were gorgeous, and I found myself daydreaming about adding Zen Goat merchandise for next year while I munched. Unfortunately, my one season of teaching goat yoga here in New Hampshire was quickly coming to a close. When I'd first come to New England, I'd promised myself I'd only stay until fall time, and then jet off to teach yoga on a tropical beach somewhere by the time snow covered the ground here. As soon as the thought slid into my head, I pushed it away. There was still a good two months to enjoy before the snow flew. I hoped. The idea of leaving Bobwhite Hollow and my great-uncle and great-aunt behind wasn't something I was ready to contemplate yet.

I'd shoved the last bite of corndog in my mouth when my cell phone rang.

"Hey, Bree. I didn't expect to hear from you until school got out. Are you on a break?"

My older sister taught fourth grade at an elementary school in Seattle. Even though summer wasn't ready to drift away quite yet, they'd already been back in school for two weeks.

"The little rascals are out at recess, so I had a minute and thought I'd call. What's up?"

"I'm hoping you can do a little research for me. You know how Grandma said Grandpa Orville deserted her and dad before she left for Seattle?"

"Yeah. And?" Bree's voice was hesitant.

"And, as the story goes, Grandpa filed for divorce. But here's the thing: I've gone to the courthouse and searched for the records. Their divorce wasn't recorded here, which it would have been if he filed."

Bree sucked in a sharp breath. "Are you saying they never got divorced? But Grandma was married to Grandpa Ray for years. Was she a polygamist?"

Yikes. The thought hadn't crossed my mind. "Before we jump to crazy conclusions, I thought maybe you could check the King County courthouse. Maybe the divorce was filed there for some strange reason."

I could feel Bree release tension, even over the phone. "Which makes more sense. Yep. I'm on it. In fact, my friend Jennifer works at the courthouse. I'll give her a call this afternoon to see if she can help me out. Text me the details. Their full names and an approximate date range."

"Got it. Thanks, sis. Talk soon."

My fingers flew as I sent Bree the information she'd need. I'd barely hit send when my cell phone pinged with a notification. It was Tristan waiting for me to take my turn on the word game the two of us had been playing all summer long. I grinned and opened the app. When we'd started playing, Tristan had made jokes about wiping the floor with me, but I'd smiled and let him think what he wanted. I was an avid reader and no slouch in the vocabulary department. Two months in and he was no longer joking but instead trying every trick in the book to beat me. So far, he'd met with only limited success, and I planned to keep it that way. I studied the board, then played a word using all but one of my tiles. Yes! With the extra points from the bonus tiles I was able to utilize, it was a fifty-eight-pointer. Put that in your pipe and smoke it, Tristan!

With my cousin thoroughly schooled in the art of word games, I leaned back against the bench and stared up at the blue sky. The day was spectacular, but with what Pete had told me this morning about Brandon's death, the cheery atmosphere of the fair seemed a little more subdued. Murder? At the Lupine County Fair? A layer of gloom clouded the earlier excitement of my first county fair experience.

Why would someone murder the Hasty Hogs pig races owner? Of course, there was the whole thing with Sam and Jes this morning. Sam said their paychecks had bounced. Again. Not getting paid when you expected to be was never a good thing, even once, but it sounded like it wasn't the first time. The couple both worked for Hasty Hogs, so, unless they had a decent-sized savings account, it could be more than rough to have their paychecks bounce. I wondered how often it had happened. Did Sam honestly just find out, or could he have known the day before and killed Brandon over it? Why were the paychecks bouncing to begin with? Was Hasty Hogs Pig Racing bankrupt? Maybe Jes would be willing to talk about it.

From there, my thoughts drifted back to the argument I'd overheard between Brandon and Jay at the fair office yesterday. Tempers were flying. What had they been arguing about? Jay had clearly threatened to pull Brandon's contract from the fair, but for what reason? The Hasty Hogs crew were staying at my aunt and uncle's farm, and they'd only arrived yesterday morning. None of them lived here in Bobwhite Hollow, so how had Brandon already gotten himself into Jay's bad graces? Hmm. How could I find out what they'd been arguing over, short of outright asking Jay?

I shook my head. Why was I even going down that rabbit hole? There was no reason for me to be delving into the reasons behind Brandon's murder. It was a job best left to the police, and Chief Barnhart was excellent at his job. *None of this is any of your beeswax, Calissa Jane,* I scolded myself. *Stay out of it.*

My phone pinged with a notification Tristan had already taken his turn in the word game. I opened the app and focused my concentration away from murder and on winning the game against my cousin.

I sat there contemplating what words I could add to the board with the tiles I had when Pete rushed over to the bench where I sat. The bright afternoon sun glinted off his shiny bald head. He thrust a canister into my face. It was black and sported a bright red label with a cartoon-style drawing of a coyote.

"Look at this, Callie." Pete's voice was high and excited as he shook the canister under my nose.

"What is it?" I squinted into the sun and read out loud, "Wiley Explosives." I frowned. "Is it a gag joke from Looney Tunes?"

"No. This is actual explosives. Don't you get it? The powder from this canister is what was used to kill Brandon. It's evidence, and I'm on my way to turn it over to Chief Barnhart." Pete trotted away at a fast clip, the shirttails of his Hawaiian banana shirt streaming in his wake.

I was still staring after Pete when someone slid onto the bench next to me. "Hello, pet."

With mouth still gaping open over Pete's declaration the contents of the empty canister he found had been used to kill Brandon, I turned to the person who'd addressed me. I found myself sitting next to the British carnival worker who'd been running the giant Ferris wheel last night. Trying to refocus, I scoured my mind for his name. *Come on. He has a first name as a last name, but what is it?* A light bulb went off as his name slid into my head. Keith George.

"Are you alright, mate?" the man asked. His British accent was soothing to my ears.

I blinked and nodded. "Yeah. Yeah, I'm fine. How're you doing today, Keith?"

The man's top hat and fancy showman attire of the night before had been replaced by a simple, dark gray, tweed flat cap. He wore a heather-gray T-shirt over a pair of navy-blue cotton trousers and a pair of black leather sneakers. All visible skin on his arms, from his biceps down to his fingers, was covered in tattoos. A leather-bound copy of George Eliot's *Middlemarch* rested on his lap. Even without his fancy duds, the man managed to look like he belonged strolling the streets of London as opposed to working a carnival ride at a small-time county fair.

When I called him by name, he jerked his head back and looked at me in amazement. "I'm impressed. You remembered my name. Callie, isn't it?"

I nodded. "Names are important. When I meet someone, I try to remember their name. It's the only superpower I've got." I laughed.

"Brilliant. I happen to agree wholeheartedly with you. Names are extremely important for how the world views you. More than one person in history has been known to hide behind a moniker different than the one they were assigned at birth." Keith held up the copy of *Middlemarch*. "Take George Eliot, for example. The author's name was everything. Given the era the book was published, it most likely wouldn't have found the success it did if the public was aware it was written by…" He paused.

"A woman." We both said at once.

Keith dipped his head and winked. I felt as if I'd received a nod of approval from my favorite college professor.

"Yes. Mary Anne Evans had the cheek to trick the public by using a man's name. If she hadn't, this book would've had a much harder path to its inclusion on the lists of best literary classics. If it had seen the light of day at all. You are correct when you say names are important. They can change everything."

I smiled, pleased with the compliment but not wanting to admit I'd never read *Middlemarch*. The library probably had a copy I could check out. "Take my cousin, Tristan, for example. Remember last night how we told you he'd legally changed his last name?"

"Yes, exactly. Tristan dropped the 'Hay' in order to sound more," Keith swirled his hand in the air, "posh."

Our conversation soon segued from the importance of names into a chat about my morning yoga session, the disrespectful boys at the carnival last night, and Keith's history with the carnival. Excuse me, the midway.

"I've been traveling with the midway for several years now," he said, elusive as to exactly how many years he'd been on the road with them.

"It doesn't get monotonous?" I asked. "Where do you call home when you're not on the road?"

"The midway is my home and the other showmen, show people, my family." Keith spread his arms wide, taking in the entire fairgrounds with his gesture. "I love the travel, the experiences, the people I work with, and the kind and interesting people, like you, I meet along the way. The stories I could tell you!"

"I bet you have some great stories." I loved how he referred to the simple carnival as a midway and his fellow carnies as showmen—show people, actually. It added a touch of romance to an experience I was sure was full of hard work and long hours.

"Indeed, I do. In fact, I'm writing a book I've tentatively titled *Stories of the Midway*. My agent already has a few large publishers on the line, waiting to bid on my manuscript."

"Ooh. It sounds intriguing. I'll be purchasing a copy the minute it comes out. When will your book be available?"

Keith flapped a hand as if he couldn't be bothered with the details. "Oh, blimey. I have no idea. They're forever pushing me for the final manuscript, but you can't rush creativity. These things take time."

"Well, let me know when it does come out. In fact, tonight I'll bring you one of my business cards so you can email and keep me updated about the release." I stood up, wanting to check on the goats one more time before I left for the farm. "Will you be at the giant Ferris wheel again this evening?"

Keith nodded. "Most definitely. That wheel is my baby. My pride and joy. I don't let anyone else run her."

My eyebrows raised of their own violation. *A Ferris wheel as your pride and joy?* To each their own, but it came across as a bit sad to me. "Okay. See you later, then. It was nice chatting with you, Keith."

"You as well, Callie. See you around." He opened his book and began to read.

Chapter Ten

The goats were calm and content. Even Bugsy was lounging in his stall, happily chewing his cud, so I freshened up their water and headed for home to see what help I could offer at the farm. My great-aunt and uncle weren't getting any younger, and I wanted to make sure my living and teaching goat yoga at their farm didn't create any additional burdens for them.

When I pulled Old Rusty into the driveway, Aunt Ellen was sitting in a rocking chair on the front porch with a colander of fresh green beans on her lap. With one fluid, practiced motion, she snapped the end off each bean, pulled the string down the middle, then snapped off the other end before tossing the discarded pieces into a can at her feet to feed to the chickens later. The bean was then snapped in half and dropped into a ceramic bowl. From helping Aunt Ellen in the garden all summer, I'd learned the next step would be to blanch the beans for five minutes before packing them into mason jars and processing them in her pressure canner.

"Would you like help with the beans, or is there something else you'd rather have me tackle?"

With it being late August, we'd been in full harvesting mode for a couple of weeks. Aunt Ellen had grown a massive garden for more years than I'd been alive and had expressed how much she'd appreciated the help I'd given her this growing season. Even so, she was contemplating cutting back the size of the garden by half for next spring.

She gestured to the other rocking chair on the porch. "Pull that chair over and help me out here, if you will. This is the last of the beans that were ready, though if the weather holds out, we could get a whole other bumper crop before first frost."

This far north, fall could come early, or so I'd been told. I had yet to experience it for myself, although the daytime temperatures were already hovering around the mid-seventies. Perfect for this Pacific Northwest native.

"Where's Tristan? I thought he'd be helping you out today. Don't tell me my lazy cousin is napping."

"No, he's off gallivanting somewhere. Helped me pick the beans, then took off to meet someone in town. He said he'd see us back at the fairgrounds this evening."

"Huh." I frowned. "Do you know who he was meeting up with?"

Aunt Ellen shook her head. "I'm not sure. I didn't ask, and Tristan didn't say."

Tristan hadn't grown up in Bobwhite Hollow. He'd spent summers on his grandparent's farm, though those carefree days came to a halt when he was a teenager and having too much fun with his friends in Boston to spend as much time with his grandparents as he did when he was younger. So, it was a conundrum to me as to who in the world he was still acquainted with well enough in our little village to meet up with. And why the heck hadn't he texted me to go along? But fine. Whatever. I'd try not to pout too long.

"Go on in and get a bowl," Aunt Ellen directed. "And you'd better take another dose of allergy medicine while you're at it. Your eyes look like cherry bombs."

"Yeah, they're super itchy. Nothing I've tried is working with any level of success." I groused.

She raised her eyebrows. "Have you made an appointment with Althea like I keep harping on you to do?"

"Althea. That's the herbalist's name." I snapped my fingers. "Not yet. I've been meaning to get that done, but I couldn't remember her name."

Aunt Ellen shrugged with a wry smile. "Well, nobody's going to do it for you, ladybug."

"Soon. I promise."

I ran into the house to drop off my folksy canvas backpack, grab a bowl, and take Aunt Ellen's advice about the allergy meds. On my way back outside, I brought glasses of dark, lemon-flavored iced tea for us to sip on as we worked. It'd taken me a bit to get used to how strong my great-aunt made the tea, but once I'd acclimated to it, it'd become my favorite way to quench my thirst on a warm day.

With a bowl full of green beans on my lap, I got to work. All was quiet over at the quaint stone guest cottage across the yard, and the Pepto-Bismol pink Hasty Hogs Pig Racing truck was nowhere in sight.

I nodded my head in the direction of the guest cottage. "Have you seen Michelle today?" I asked Aunt Ellen.

"Not a glimpse, but the other two, Sam and Jessica, have been in and out a couple times. They left about fifteen minutes ago again. Chief Barnhart was here talking to them shortly after you left for your yoga session this morning."

I told Aunt Ellen how Jes had shown up for this morning's session and filled her in on what Sam had said about their paychecks as the couple was leaving.

A deep frown creased Aunt Ellen's forehead. "Those poor people. They have young children to provide for, and now all this trouble. What a shame."

"Young children?"

"Mmhmm. Jessica told me their two little ones stay with her parents when they're on the road working the pig races. A boy and a girl, I believe she said."

"To make matters worse, Pete seems convinced Brandon's death wasn't an accident at all."

Aunt Ellen's mouth dropped open, and she stared at me wide-eyed. "What do you mean?"

"He said the gun was tampered with, and it'd been packed with some sort of explosive that caused it to explode like it did. Last I saw him, Pete had somehow found the container the explosives were in and was taking it to Chief Barnhart." I tossed another snapped green bean into the bowl. "I'm not sure where he got his information from, but he seemed to be pretty darn certain Brandon was murdered."

"Pete Kennison isn't a gossip, but he certainly does have his finger on the pulse of Bobwhite Hollow. I wouldn't discount anything the man says. Not by a long shot." My aunt slowly shook her head. "Another murder in our small burg. What is this world coming to?"

We snapped beans in silence for a few minutes. I'd reached for the last handful when Uncle Will pulled into the driveway, gravel cracking under his tires. He cut the engine, slid out of his truck, and slammed the door with a powerful thrust of his arm.

Aunt Ellen's head jerked up. "Well, what's gotten under your hat?"

Uncle Will marched up the porch steps, steadying himself on the handrail as he climbed. Once he stood in front of the chairs where we sat, he wrestled a piece of paper out of the front pocket of his faded bib overalls and waved it through the air. "You know I don't like to speak ill of the dead," he said, "but if Brandon was standing in front of me, I'd give him a scathing piece of my mind."

"What seems to be the problem?" Aunt Ellen asked.

Uncle Will tapped the paper with an angry finger. "The check for their stay in Haybeck Farm's guest cottage isn't worth the paper it was written on, that's the problem."

"Well, my lands." Aunt Ellen snapped her beans with more gusto.

"You've got to be kidding me," I said and jumped up to take a look at the check squeezed between Uncle Will's fingers.

"Let's not get all up in arms. With the tragedy of Brandon's death, I was going to mention we should reimburse Michelle for their stay anyway. It would help with the unexpected expenses she's facing." Aunt Ellen attempted to calm Will's anger.

"I agree, my dear, but it isn't the point. Giving us a worthless check took the decision away from us, and that's what has my dander up."

He wasn't wrong.

Uncle Will rubbed his temple with his free hand. "I've got a nagging headache. I'm going to go lie down for a bit."

As the screen door of the farmhouse slammed behind my great-uncle, Aunt Ellen and I looked at each other with concern. The fact the Hasty

Hogs check wasn't any good was not surprising, considering the status of the crew's paychecks. The most concerning thing to me at the moment was how Uncle Will had a headache bad enough to make him lie down. Had finding out the check was bogus caused Uncle Will's headache? Steam came out of my ears. If Brandon hadn't already been dead, I would have gladly killed him myself for causing undue stress to my elderly uncle.

Chapter Eleven

While Aunt Ellen and I banged around in the kitchen getting the green beans preserved in quart-sized Mason jars, Uncle Will tossed, turned, and grumbled on the couch in the front room. From the sounds of it, his nap wasn't going well, and his headache hadn't abated. Aunt Ellen frowned in her husband's direction, then flitted through the kitchen door into the backyard. In two shakes, she was back with a handful of lavender stems topped with the delicate purple flowers. With a pair of kitchen shears, she chopped off the flowers and dropped them into a tall water glass, then mashed the aromatic buds up with a long teaspoon. She filled the glass with cold water from the tap and took the concoction, along with a cold washcloth, to Uncle Will.

"Good grief, woman. You're going to be the death of me with your crazy remedies."

"Don't you give me any trouble, old man."

I chuckled to myself as I listened to the two of them fussing and fuming at each other from the other room.

"The old coot finally drank it," Aunt Ellen informed me when she bustled back into the kitchen with the empty glass in hand. "He should rest well now for a bit."

"You think the lavender will take away the headache?" I asked.

"It hasn't failed me yet," she replied.

The next time I peeked my head around the corner, Uncle Will was sleeping like a lamb.

After a dozen jars of green beans were canned and cooling on the kitchen counter, Aunt Ellen and I curled up in armchairs with our books. She flipped the pages of a true account of a Canadian homesteader while I got lost in *Caught on Camera*, Kara Lacey's Vermont-based cozy mystery I'd picked up at the bookshop in town the other day. The two of us spent the rest of the afternoon reading while Uncle Will slept off both his mad and his headache.

The Lupine County Fair Demolition Derby was on the agenda for this evening. Tristan had warned me the derby would be loud and stinky, but I'd been looking forward to it anyway. He'd sighed and shook his head, apparently resigned to his fate. With me for a cousin and best friend, Tristan was going to have to partake in way more countryfied activities than he ever imagined.

I drove Old Rusty to the fairgrounds while my great-aunt and uncle followed behind in Uncle Will's pickup. I checked on the goats, stuffing their mangers with hay and filling their water buckets with fresh, cool water. Finishing quickly, I sprinted over to Sweet Pete's snow cone stand, beyond curious to hear what Chief Barnhart told Pete about the empty explosives canister he'd found. I only had a few minutes before I was supposed to meet back up with the family, so I hoped the stand wasn't too busy.

I was in luck. Only three people stood in line waiting for their cones. I joined the queue and craned my neck, looking for Pete, but Mazzy and a teenage boy with dark floppy hair were the only two people working at the stand. When it was my turn at the window, the boy stepped up and asked to take my order. I glanced at his name tag.

"Hi, Noah. I'm looking for Pete. Is he around?"

The freckle-faced boy shook his head. "Nope. Are you going to order a snow cone?"

Before I could answer, Mazzy popped her head through the window and grinned at me. "Hi, Callie. Do you want another Tiger's Blood?"

I shook my head. "Hey, Mazzy. No, not tonight. I was hoping to talk to Pete. Is he here?"

"Nah, the boss isn't here. He left this morning and hasn't been back yet."

"Really? Didn't he leave around ten this morning? He's been gone this whole time?"

She nodded, her purple hair bouncing with the movement. "Yep. He found something in the trash and took off. Said he'd be back, but he's never shown up. Good thing Noah was scheduled to work today."

Noah grinned and placed both fists on his hips like a superhero who had come to save the day.

Pete had never returned from the police station?

"No kidding," I answered. "Are you two doing okay? Do you need anything?"

"We're good. Claire called and will be here after she closes the shop in town to relieve me. It's not the first time Pete's been gone for hours."

"Not the first time? What do you mean? It's only the second day of the fair."

Neither Mazzy nor Noah had worked at Sweet Pete's main shop this summer. He'd told me earlier he'd hired them just for the fair cart. I was shocked he'd already been leaving them alone to handle the business.

"True, but he must trust me already." A pleased smile spread across her face. "Pete left early yesterday afternoon, too, and I was alone here until closing time. It was my first day!" Mazzy bugged her eyes comically.

"It seems odd he'd abandon you without any help when you're so new."

She shrugged and grinned, clearly proud of herself for stepping up to the challenge. "I guess, but I handled it just fine."

"I'm sure you did." She seemed like a capable young woman.

The whole scenario felt off to me. And hadn't Pete told me he wasn't at the pig races last night because the snow cone cart had been so busy? Why would he lie? More importantly, where had he been instead? I hated to even think it, but with Pete supposedly finding the Wiley Explosives container and his long absences from the snow cone stand, the lie about his whereabouts seemed like the cherry on top, pointing to his participation in Brandon's murder. If it indeed was murder, as Pete claimed. But if Pete killed Brandon, why would he be the one spreading the rumor of murder around?

"Okay, well, thanks for answering my questions." I started to walk away but thought better of it. I dug in my backpack and pulled out one of my business cards, handing it to Mazzy. "If you need anything before Pete or

Claire gets here, give me a call."

"Thanks, but I'm sure we'll be fine." Mazzy tucked my card into the back pocket of her jeans.

Chapter Twelve

By the time I got back to the goat pens, Uncle Will and Aunt Ellen had finished their tour of the sheep and goat barn and were waiting for me. Tristan was still nowhere in sight. We headed over to the building housing all the home economic type exhibits—garden produce, canned goods, baked goods, and arts and crafts. Judging had taken place this morning behind closed doors, so Aunt Ellen was curious to find out if her entries had been decorated in winning ribbons this year.

Right away, we found her plate of homemade maple bars. The purple "Best of Show" ribbon was no surprise since Aunt Ellen's maple bars were famous around the area. Rumor had it a couple of women had practically come to blows over the last half dozen at the Christmas charity bake sale back in December. Aunt Ellen's eyes twinkled every time she told the story.

A jar of her canned carrots had earned a red second place ribbon and her green beans a blue first place, but it was the dozen fresh eggs that caused Aunt Ellen's back to stiffen. No ribbon adorned the carton. I took a quick peek at the other eggs entered in the category. Aunt Ellen's eggs were not as uniform in color and size as the cartons displaying winning ribbons.

She studied the eggs with a stern twist of her lips. "Well, those hens of mine are going to get a piece of my mind when I get home. No ribbon." She harrumphed. "Whoever heard of such nonsense. They better be careful, or they'll wind up in the stew pot." With a last glance at the eggs, my disgruntled great-aunt wandered toward the quilts.

Dang. Those hens had better watch their necks. Though we all knew Aunt Ellen's threat of the stew pot was all bluster.

Uncle Will winked at me and leaned over conspiratorially. "As you may have noticed, Callie-Kat, my bride isn't used to coming out on the bottom of the pack." He hooked a thumb in his overall suspenders and whistled quietly as we trailed Aunt Ellen to the next exhibit.

When we caught up, Ellen spun around and beamed at us, pointing to an enormous quilt held high on the wall by a galvanized metal bar and fishing line. "Now, this is more like it. Best in Show!" Her magnificent radiating star quilt done in bright yellows, deep reds, and sea greens had the coveted purple ribbon hanging from it.

"Are you happy, dear? All your hard work has paid off. You deserve it. I'm proud of you." Uncle Will wrapped an arm around her shoulders and planted a loud kiss on her cheek. "Are we ready for a sausage on a stick?"

"Not quite yet. There's someone I want Callie to meet first." Aunt Ellen winked and linked her arm through mine. "Come along."

Uncle Will spied an empty spot on a bench. He pointed. "I'll be right there when you're finished."

My elderly aunt fairly dragged me along as we made our way to the large metal barn housing commercial vendors. The salesman barked at us in the same fashion as the carnival workers did, trying to drag our attention to their hot tubs, television satellite systems, candles, cooking demonstrations, and a million other things we didn't need.

The alluring scent of frying peppers and Italian sausage made me stop short and follow my nose to a booth where a barker was making the crowd laugh with his hilarious reasons why we all needed to purchase his set of nonstick pots and pans for the low, low price of two hundred and ninety-nine buckaroos.

"Ow." I spun around at the pinch on the back of my arm.

Aunt Ellen scowled at me. "What's the holdup? Come on." She whirled and hurried away.

Fine. I hadn't even had time to whip out my credit card. It's not like I cooked much. Or even had my own kitchen. But the demonstration made me want to get my hands on those pans. I shot one last covetous glance his way, then turned to follow my great-aunt. In doing so, I slammed into the shoulder of a slight, dark-haired man no taller than I was, knocking him hard enough to make him take a step backward.

"Oh, gosh. I'm so sorry. Are you okay?"

With a smile that didn't reach his brown eyes, he replied, "Don't worry about it. It's super crowded in here. Hard not to bump into people."

A woman with long, dark, curly hair reached out and grabbed his forearm. "Evan. I've been looking all over for you. I have your money."

Michelle, Brandon Ebersole's brand-new widow, flicked her eyes to me and was instantly startled when she recognized me. Purple, bruise-like shadows lay under her eyes. "Oh, Callie, right?" Her face tightened as her gaze jerked between me and the man. "Do you two know each other?"

"Not at all. I was just apologizing for slamming into him," I said.

A small hand reached through the crowd and pulled me away from Michelle and the stranger. Aunt Ellen had realized I wasn't following her and had come back for me.

"Sorry again," I called as the crowd closed in and blocked them from view.

But not before I saw Michelle slip the man a folded stack of green bills, a one-hundred-dollar bill perched on top.

This time, Aunt Ellen wasn't about to let go of my arm. She pulled me along in her rush to get…well, wherever we were going. I was almost out of breath by the time she stopped in front of a booth with a display reminiscent of a high-end apothecary. A wooden cabinet displayed shelves laden with jars filled with liquids of varying hues alongside clear jars full of dried herbs. Two menu boards flanked the shelves, one listing tonics and tinctures, the other a list of various herbs. A large wooden sign over the display proclaimed "Isis Herbal Apothecary." A high counter ran the length of the booth, keeping the public's hands away from the bottles.

A thin, deeply tanned woman dressed in a flowing marigold summer dress had her hair held back with a headscarf the color of Fanta Orange Soda. A chunky necklace of green jade adorned her neck while beaded bracelets jangled on her arm. The woman tipped her head and smiled at us in greeting. "Ellen. I'll be right with you." A man ahead of us stood at the counter, his credit card held out. The herbalist swiped the man's payment card and handed him a dark blue bottle of liquid in return. "Now, don't forget. Three drops under the tongue twice a day will keep the rash away."

The man tucked the bottle into the front pocket of his shirt before he scurried away. Aunt Ellen and I stepped up to the counter. She and the proprietor greeted each other with a warm clasp of hands.

"Althea, I'd like to introduce you to my great-niece, Callie."

Althea held her hand out to me. "So nice to finally meet you, Callie. Your aunt has told me great things about you."

I couldn't help but smile under the woman's warm gaze, even though I was a bit irritated at Aunt Ellen for bulldozing me to get me here. What was this, anyway? A sneezing intervention? I sent a mock side-eye to my aunt.

Unfazed, she carried on. "Callie here has been having some trouble with allergies. I thought maybe you could help her out."

"Of course." Althea drummed her fingers on the counter and focused her gaze on my face. "Tell me, Callie. What type of allergies are you experiencing?"

"Type? The usual, I guess. Sneezing, itchy eyes and ears, runny nose."

"Hay fever allergies, perhaps? As opposed to food allergies?"

I nodded. "I think so. I teach goat yoga, and it seems the biggest things I'm allergic to are the goats and hay." I smiled wryly and shrugged. "Go figure."

Althea clucked her tongue. "Such a shame, but we can fix you right up."

"We can?" With my track record so far, I wasn't nearly as confident as she sounded.

"Sure." She spun around, causing her dress to twirl around her sandal-clad feet. Althea pulled a drawer below her display shelves open.

From my vantage point, I could see rows of small bottles inside the drawer with round labels on top of the lids. Althea ran a fingertip over the tops of the bottles, picking out three and setting them on the shelf. Coming back to the counter where Aunt Ellen and I stood, Althea placed the bottles in front of me, along with a dropper and a small bag of clear, empty capsules. She unscrewed the lids, took out an empty capsule, and used the dropper to precisely place three drops from each bottle into the capsule. Once finished, Althea poured a small cup of water from an icy glass dispenser on the end of her counter. Handing me the water and the capsule, she smiled. "Give this a try."

I pushed the capsule into my mouth and slugged it back with the water. For the next fifteen minutes, the herbalist explained in great detail what each bottle contained, why, and how these essential oils could work to curtail my allergies. She spouted off not only the science backing up her claims, but also several anecdotal stories about other allergy sufferers who swore by her remedy.

While Althea rambled on in her enthusiasm for her product, my mind wandered back to the encounter with Michelle. Who was the guy I'd nearly taken out, and why did Michelle give him money? The way her face had tensed when she recognized me made me think she was doing something she didn't want to get caught at. What could it be?

I gasped. *Did I just witness the grieving widow paying the hitman she hired to kill her husband?* My left hand flew up to clutch my chest over my heart.

"What is it, Ladybug?" Aunt Ellen asked, panic in her voice. "Is it the tincture? Are you having problems breathing?"

"No, no. It's nothing like that. I'm fine," I assured both her and Althea, who was also staring at me wide-eyed. "I had a thought about something else. Nothing to do with the oils at all. I'm sorry. Carry on."

Maybe it was a poor choice of words because Althea carried on about all things homeopathic for what felt like a lifetime. By the time she finally rang up my purchase, my eyes were glazed over, and I didn't remember a single thing she'd said.

"Don't worry," Althea gripped my wrist as I reached for the brown paper bag holding my items. "Place three drops from each bottle in an empty capsule in the morning and take it with a glass of water, exactly like I showed you. Easy peasy."

Aunt Ellen and I headed back to find Uncle Will. "What do you think?" my aunt asked.

"I'm willing to give it a try," I answered. "Althea seems really nice and knowledgeable, but wow, is she ever passionate about her tinctures!"

"She certainly is," Aunt Ellen chuckled. "She has a tendency to wear a person thin, that one, but she's a good egg."

Chapter Thirteen

U ncle Will was exactly where we'd left him, lounging on the bench while watching people go by. As soon as he spotted us making our way to where he sat, he pulled himself to his feet.

"Did you happen to see Michelle while you were people-watching?" I inquired.

Uncle Will pushed his lips out as he searched his memory. "Can't say I did. Why do you ask?"

"No reason. I was just curious." There was no sense getting anyone else riled up until I verified my theory about Michelle paying off a hitman.

"Ready for your sausage on a stick, old man?" Aunt Ellen smiled and hooked her arm through Uncle Will's elbow as we headed off to the food carts. We split up. Each of us aimed toward different booths for our snacks.

By the time we met back up, our arms were loaded down with treats. I'd bypassed the corndog stand this time and went for the tantalizing smell of pulled pork instead. I had a powdered sugar and honey-coated elephant ear balanced on top of my sandwich as we joined the end of the line moving slowly into the grandstands for the demolition derby. Aunt Ellen held a bowl of clam chowder in one hand and a chocolate whoopie pie in the other. Uncle Will's fist was gripped around the biggest smoked turkey drumstick I'd ever seen, and he had a red-and-white checkered container of curly fries resting in the crook of his elbow.

"I thought you were jonesing for a sausage on a stick?" I teased Uncle Will.

He shrugged. "Eh, the line was too long. I'm sure I'll need another snack later."

Aunt Ellen sighed and eyeballed his gigantic turkey drumstick over the top of her glasses. "Not likely, old man."

He grinned. "Watch me."

She smiled indulgently and shook her head.

"Hey, you've got your whoopie pie there," he pointed at Aunt Ellen's treat, "and I'm going to need dessert, too. What better dessert than a sausage on a stick? Yes, siree!"

I changed the subject. "Anybody heard from Tristan yet?"

The words had barely slipped out of my mouth when I spied my cousin approaching. A wide grin lit up Tristan's face. His golden curls bounced as he walked, and the sun glinted off the gold-rimmed frames of his tinted sunglasses. He was hand in hand with a tall and delicious, if I did say so myself, dark-skinned man. The guy was a good six inches taller than Tristan. His black curly hair was cut close to his head, and a trim beard framed his handsome face. He wore a red button-up cotton shirt over a pair of slim-fitting chinos in a buttery khaki. An infinity symbol tattoo adorned one slender forearm while a trio of stone bracelets encircled his wrist. *Who in the world is this hottie, and where did Tristan find him?*

The question must've shown out of my eyes, because Tristan answered it before any of us said a word. "Glad we caught up to you all. Spencer, this is my family." Tristan swung out an arm, indicating me and his grandparents, then introduced us each by name. "Family, meet Spencer Lempriere."

Spencer dipped the top half of his body toward us in greeting. "Callie, it's a pleasure to meet you. Will and Ellen, it's good to see you both again."

Aunt Ellen studied the man. "Spencer Lempriere. It's good to see you. How long's it been since you've graced Bobwhite Hollow with your presence?"

A crooked smile lifted the corners of Spencer's lips. "It has been a hot minute, ma'am."

"How're your folks?"

"They're doing well. Thank you for asking. My father's recovering from hip surgery, but he's healing rapidly. The doctor is pleased with his progress. Not much keeps that stubborn man down for long."

"Well, give them my best," Aunt Ellen said.

The line had surged forward and was building up behind us, so we got caught up in the flow. I had a million questions. How did Tristan and Spencer meet? Aunt Ellen and Uncle Will obviously knew who he was and were acquainted with his parents. Which must mean he was a local. Were Spencer and Tristan friends when they were kids? I couldn't wait to find our seats so I could get my questions answered.

Uncle Will led us through the packed grandstands until he came to a section right up front where only a handful of spectators sat. From our vantage point, we not only had a great view of the arena, but I could see a good section of the carnival and the gates at the back entrance of the fairgrounds. Looking around at the amount of people pressed into the bleachers, I was confused by how easily we were able to find such great empty seats. Why were they still available?

"Are we not supposed to sit here, maybe? Is this section reserved?" Something felt off.

"Nope, just lucky, I guess." Uncle Will's eyes twinkled as he slid down the silver bench, making room for the rest of us to sit. "You're going to love being this close to experience your first demolition derby, Callie-Kat."

If Uncle Will said everything was fine, who was I to argue? Though the glint in his eye and the way Aunt Ellen rolled hers made me think he was up to no good. I shot one more suspicious glance around the grandstands before shrugging and sliding onto the bench seat beside Aunt Ellen.

We'd barely gotten seated before Tristan stood. "I know where you're sitting now, so Spencer and I are going to run and get ourselves some chow. Be back…soonish."

And they were off. I placed my elephant ear on the empty bench in front of me and balanced my sandwich on my knees. I took a big bite, causing barbecue sauce and coleslaw to squish out of the bun and plop onto my bare legs.

Uncle Will handed me a stack of paper napkins. "Here. You'll need these. I've seen you eat." He chuckled.

It was my turn to roll my eyes, except he had a point. After I'd wiped up my mess, I turned to Aunt Ellen.

"Who is Spencer, and how do you know him and his parents?"

"Spencer grew up here. His father is the principal at the high school, and his mother teaches first grade. The Lemprieres are a nice family. Spencer was the valedictorian of his class, and he's done well for himself, from all accounts. Last time I ran into his mother, she mentioned he'd been made a partner at the architect firm he's with in Washington D.C." She frowned.

My eyebrows pulled together. "He's handsome and successful. So why the long face?"

"I'm not sure he's right for our Tristan, is all. Spencer was always one to put on airs when he was growing up in Bobwhite Hollow. He thought he was too good for this town and couldn't wait to see it in his rearview mirror. I'm glad he lowered his standards to come home and check on his dad, at least."

I didn't mention the fact Tristan made it clear he felt the same way about Bobwhite Hollow. Maybe they were a bit more perfect for each other than Aunt Ellen cared to admit. My worries were of another nature. My cousin had a tendency to fall in love whenever he could, which wasn't necessarily a bad trait, but his last, short-lived relationship had gone terribly wrong before it even got started. Maybe Spencer was the change of luck Tristan needed, but I planned to keep a close eye on him to make sure he didn't break my cousin's heart.

Uncle Will gestured for me to pay attention. The first cars were being driven into the dirt arena, which had been soaked in water to create thick mud. "You've got to pick which car you're rooting for this round."

All the windows in the cars had been removed, and each vehicle had been painted with what looked like cans of dripping spray paint. After careful consideration, I picked a VW bug painted to look like Dory from *Finding Nemo*. Eight cars formed a large circle facing each other and revving their engines. I waved a hand in front of my nose to waft away the smell of exhaust coming from the cars closest to where we sat.

As soon as the first round started, it was easy to determine why only a handful of brave—foolhardy—spectators sat in the section where we were. With the eight cars spinning their tires in the mud and smashing into each other as soon as they found traction, exhaust fumes and bits of thrown mud funneled their way directly into our section. We were straight in the line of fire. I glanced at Uncle Will, who sat rocking back and forth in glee. With arms crossed against his chest and hands tucked into his armpits, he winked at me.

"Up close and personal, eh, Callie-Kat?"

Aunt Ellen shook her head. "You old fool." She patted his leg and smiled indulgently.

"Hello, Haybecks." Chief Barnhart and his wife slid onto the bench directly below where we sat. The chief was dressed in jeans and a light blue, untucked, short-sleeved cotton shirt.

"Almost didn't recognize you out of uniform, Dale," Uncle Will teased. "Nice to see you, Jackie," he addressed the chief's wife.

When it was a little quieter between rounds, I leaned forward. "Chief Barnhart?"

He half-turned. "Yeah?"

"Pete Kennison showed me an explosives canister he found and said he was taking it to you. He thought it had something to do with Brandon's death."

"Yeah," the chief grunted again as if to tell me to get on with it.

"Well, that was hours and hours ago, and Pete has never come back to the snow cone stand. I was wondering if everything is okay. Is he still at the police station?"

"No, of course not. Sure, I questioned him a little bit, but he couldn't have been at the station more than half an hour." Chief Barnhart swiveled back around, then pointed to the back gate of the fairgrounds. "In fact, there's Pete now. You can't miss that ridiculous shirt of his."

Sure enough, a bald man wearing a dark green shirt covered in bright yellow bananas was rushing through the back gate. Pete carried what looked to be a large cardboard box with a...I squinted to see...*Is that a telescope sticking out of the box?* He veered off the main path and disappeared inside a small shed on the other side of the derby arena. Thirty seconds later, he emerged from the shed sans the box and scurried away toward the snow cone stand. Or at least I hoped he was on his way to relieve those poor kids who'd been working all day.

If Pete hadn't been at the police station all day, where had he been? Certainly not working at his snow cone stand. And Mazzy mentioned she'd called Claire, so Pete hadn't been working at Sweet Pete's Ice Cream on the riverwalk either. I checked off his infractions on my fingers. One—he seemed to know Brandon's death wasn't an accident. Two—he'd lied about being at the pig races when Brandon was killed. Three—he'd somehow found an empty canister for explosives he claimed was used in the murder. Four—he'd been missing in action all afternoon and a good part of the evening. If his speculation that Brandon had been murdered was correct, things wouldn't look good for Sweet Pete's innocent act.

Forty-five minutes later, Tristan and Spencer still hadn't returned. Three rounds of cars had smashed the smithereens out of each other. The air stank of exhaust, radiator fluid, and all other manner of automotive fluids. My face was gritty from the mud and dirt thrown our way, we'd narrowly missed being hit by pieces of a flying metal bumper, we had to yell at the top of our lungs to communicate with each other, and a headache was forming between my eyes. I was officially over demolition derby day.

Aunt Ellen screamed into my ear, "Are you ready to get out of here?"

"I thought you'd never ask!" I bellowed back.

She nudged Uncle Will with an elbow, indicating we were ready to leave. Breaking his concentration away from the crashing cars, he frowned and remained seated, then swiftly pointed between himself and the arena a couple of times. Aunt Ellen shrugged and followed me out of the grandstands.

Chapter Fourteen

A pair of public restrooms were situated under the grandstands, so Aunt Ellen and I exited through a set of stairs leading below the bleachers. We found Tristan and Spencer sitting close together on a bench directly across from the Grandstand Bar. The small bar served beer and wine in clear plastic cups that could only be consumed inside the confines of the grandstands. My cousin and his date each had a cup of red wine in hand.

"There you are!" I cried when I saw them. "What are you doing? You were supposed to come back and watch the derby with us."

Tristan shook his head. "No way. Not where Grandpa had you sitting. Look at you. You're covered in mud." He wrinkled his nose. "And you stink."

I smacked him on the shoulder. "Why didn't you warn me?"

"Grandpa pulled the same thing on me when I was about eight." Tristan's eyes sparkled as he laughed at me, then he pointed his chin at the stairs. "He still up there?"

"Yeah. Aunt Ellen and I decided we'd had enough. I'm going to try to clean up a little bit in the restroom. Don't go away." I shook my finger at my cousin, but smiled at his date to show Spencer I wasn't always a bossy cow. Okay. Maybe I was, but he didn't need to know it yet.

The restrooms at the fairgrounds weren't exactly the best place to clean up, but after Aunt Ellen and I stood in line for five minutes, I found a dirty sink and a piece of abrasive paper towel. Using the scratched and foggy mirror, I proceeded to wash my face, hands, and arms the best I could.

"You missed a spot right there." Aunt Ellen poked my left cheekbone.

I wet the paper towel and gave the spot she'd indicated another quick rub. Tossing the paper into the overflowing trash can, I followed my great-aunt out of the restroom.

Aunt Ellen left us "young'uns" to it and wandered off in search of a piece of peach pie and another look through the arts and crafts exhibits. When the demolition derby was over, she and Uncle Will would head back to the farm. Tristan, Spencer, and I gravitated toward the alluring lights of the carnival. Darkness had fallen, and with it, the entire atmosphere of the fair had changed. The neon lights radiating from the rides were brighter, the joyful sounds of people laughing mingled with the pings, whooshes, and comical sounds emitting from rows of carnival games. Party vibe excitement filled the air.

"So, where did you two meet?" I asked the guys as we strolled through the carnival. It was time to get some answers.

They grinned at each other, then answered in unison. "At the swimming pool."

"Swimming pool? When did you go swimming?"

"Let's see." Tristan tapped his chin with a finger. "Pretty sure I was twelve, so what…sixteen years ago?"

Spencer nodded. "Sounds about right. Which would've made me fourteen. It was a fun summer."

"For sure," Tristan agreed. "Swimming, riding bikes, and generally running wild." He nudged Spencer with his shoulder. "By the next summer, you were too cool to hang with us younger boys, if I remember right."

Spencer raised his eyebrows. "Too dignified," he clarified. "While the rest of you barbarians were wrestling in the dirt, I was looking ahead to the future and planning for my ticket out of Bobwhite Hollow."

"Why were you so eager to leave at such a young age?" I asked.

He lifted an elegant shoulder. "I'd started to figure out who I was and already felt like small-town life was suffocating me."

"Were you bullied for being gay?"

"No, I had four brawny older brothers who weren't about to let that happen." Spencer shook his head. "No, it was nothing drastic, just a sense of better things waiting for me somewhere other than Bobwhite Hollow."

"Sure, I get that." I circled a finger between the two of them. "So, you guys have stayed in touch all these years?"

Tristan shook his head. "Nope. Neither one of us had a second rider for the Zipper last night, so we got thrown together. Literally."

"Yeah, when Tristan screamed like a little girl, I remembered him. The boy screams exactly like he did when he was twelve and I picked him up by his shorts and threw him into the deep end of the pool." Spencer chuckled.

"Enough." Tristan laughed at his own expense but tugged Spencer's hand. "Come on, let's get our money's worth out of these bracelets." He held up his wrist to show off the blue carnival bracelet.

"We can all three go together on the giant Ferris wheel," I offered.

Tristan rolled his eyes and Spencer sighed.

"We're not going to only ride the dang Ferris wheel all night, Callie." Tristan glared at me.

I glared right back.

"Fine. Let's get it over with, but then you're going to have to either buck up and go on some more exciting rides, or you'll be on your own."

Unbelievable. My cousin came from Boston to enjoy the fair with me, but one handsome man later, and he was ready to ditch me. Not what I'd imagined when we'd made our plans, but I guess I couldn't blame him. Spencer was easy on the eyes. The three of us got in line for my favorite ride, and I did my best to get over my irritation.

Keith was manning the controls of the Ferris wheel, just like he'd told me he would be. I dug one of my business cards out of my backpack and handed it to him while we waited for our turn.

"My phone number and email address are right there," I pointed out my information, "so you can let me know as soon as your book is available for purchase. I'm excited to read it."

"Will do, m'lady, thank you." Keith tucked my card into an inside pocket of the black satin showman's jacket he wore, then tipped his top hat at me.

Once we were seated in the carriage, Tristan went for my jugular. "What do you think you're doing, Callie? Why in the world did you give that carnie your business card? What were you thinking?"

"For one thing, he's a showman, not a carnie."

Tristan snorted. "His words, nobody else's."

"For another, Keith is writing a book full of stories of the midway. It sounds fascinating, and I want to read it. I gave him my email address so he can let me know when the book gets published."

Tristan put on his best British accent and turned his nose into the air. "Oh, the midway now, is it?" He shook his head. "I hate to break it to you, but this is a small-town carnival, and your new best friend is a smarmy carnie." He glanced at Spencer for approval.

What a showoff. "Why are you being so condescending? You don't know a thing about Keith." Tristan wasn't usually so judgmental. I had to believe his attitude had a lot to do with present company.

"And neither do you." Tristan cocked an eyebrow at me, challenging me to argue.

"Anyone who works for a traveling carnival has something to hide," Spencer added to the conversation with a sneer. "You seem like a smart enough girl, so you should be smart enough to steer well clear of that type of person. Though I suppose anyone who teaches—what is it again?—goat yoga?—mingles with all manner of people."

Talk about condescending. Spencer's tone of voice and the way he'd called me a girl made it clear he thought I was anything but smart. I wanted to clap back but held my tongue, feeling a clench in my belly at the fact Tristan hadn't come to my defense. From the time I'd found my long-lost cousin, we'd been tight, both of us feeling like we'd known the other forever. Sure, we poked and prodded at each other, but giving each other grief was our love language. Tonight, Tristan was making me feel like the third wheel, an irritating little sister he wanted to shake off, and I didn't like it one bit. I sighed, ready for the ride to be over. Next time, I would go by myself. At least I could enjoy the spectacular view from the top without someone I barely knew degrading me and my cousin letting him.

As soon as the ride ended, I left the snotty guys to their own devices and went in search of a bag of cotton candy. *Only the lower class indulges in such a pedestrian treat.* The voice in my head sounded suspiciously like Spencer's condescending tone. I shoved him out of my head and continued my quest. At a well-lit food truck, bags of tan cotton candy hung next to the typical pink and blue bags. When it was my turn at the window, I ordered a fresh-squeezed lemonade and pointed to the bags of spun sugar.

"Tell me about the brown cotton candy, please."

"You must not be from around here," the window attendant replied. "It's maple cotton candy. A New England specialty. Would you like a bag?"

I licked my lips, intrigued. "Yes, please!"

For the next half an hour, I wandered the fairgrounds, drinking my lemonade and enjoying my maple cotton candy. I stopped into the goat barn to check on my flock. Bugsy yelled when he saw me coming and jumped up with his front hooves on the top board of his stall. I slipped him a taste of the cotton candy. One little nibble wouldn't hurt, and he'd been such a good boy, only escaping once. So far. Digging in the ice chest, I gave each of the goats a carrot and a scratch behind the ears before I headed back to the lights of the carnival.

With only a cursory look around for Tristan and Spencer, I got back in line for the Ferris wheel. While I waited, with the line slowly inching forward, I snapped a dozen or so pictures. The bright lights of the giant wheel shone against the dark sky, where twinkling stars sparkled overhead. Swiping open the Instagram app, I added the best one of the pictures to my Zen Goat profile and added #lupinecountyfair. My fifty-seven followers would love it.

At the front of the line, Keith greeted me then craned his neck to look behind me. "Where's your partner in crime?"

I blew a raspberry. "Off with his date. I'm on my own this time."

He frowned. "I regret to inform you..." Keith pointed at a sign attached to the metal fence around the giant wheel. It read, "No Single Riders."

"Oh no. Really?" I threw my head back in a dramatic display.

"I'm afraid so." Keith stretched to his full height and looked down the line. "Are there any single riders? Anyone who would like to ride the wheel with this lovely lady."

A hand rose up from the sidelines.

Keith waved the person in. "Come on, then. We don't want to keep her waiting."

My heart did a little pitter-patter when I spotted Levi and his broad shoulders weaving his way through the crowd and to my side.

"I suppose I can sacrifice myself to help a damsel in distress." The veterinarian grinned at me.

I huffed. "I'm far from a damsel in distress." But I climbed into the Ferris wheel carriage anyway.

Levi slid in after me. "Hey there...nice segment on the news tonight."

My mouth gaped open while my face flushed as hot as a furnace. "Are you kidding me? They aired it?"

"They sure did." Levi grinned.

Mortified, I tried not to make eye contact as we jerked forward while Keith finished filling the carriages. Levi attempted to make small talk until our carriage came to a swaying stop at the top of the wheel.

The bright lights below me made me forget all about my embarrassment. I propped my arms on the edge of the carriage and took in the view. What was it about summer nights and the lights of the fair that made everything feel so magical?

As our carriage came down the front side of the wheel, a woman with long, dark, curly hair spilling halfway down her back caught my eye. Michelle again. She was standing by herself, arms crossed defensively over her chest and gazing upward as if looking at the stars. When the same man who I'd nearly knocked over at the cooking demonstration approached and handed Michelle a corndog, her posture relaxed and she smiled. The two of them walked away arm in arm. Seemed a strange way to behave with the hitman she'd hired to kill her husband. Did I have that part wrong? Was Michelle involved in an affair instead? Maybe both. Maybe she'd paid her lover to murder Brandon.

I glanced over at my companion to ask him if he'd seen Michelle and the stranger, but instead I found Levi with his eyes squeezed shut and white knuckles gripping the post in the middle of our carriage. The handsome and masculine veterinarian's face was the same shade of green mine had been after the Mega Drop last night.

I forgot all about Michelle and tentatively touched Levi's arm. "Are you okay?"

Without opening his eyes, Levi nodded. "Did I mention I hate heights?"

"You did not. I guess when you said you'd sacrifice yourself to ride with me, you meant it."

Levi nodded. "Sure did. I'm an idiot."

I wanted to tease him mercilessly, but at the same time, it was fantastic to know someone who was worse on carnival rides than I was. Choosing compassion over teasing, I patted his arm as our carriage jerked forward and we headed back down. After three more rounds of the wheel, all with Levi's fists clenched firmly around the post and his eyes squeezed shut, the ride was over.

With a hand on my lower back, Levi guided me through the other riders departing from the wheel.

"Well, that was embarrassing." His cheeks flamed red, and he dipped his head so I couldn't see his eyes. "It's the first ride I've been on in years, and I just got a good reminder why."

"There's nothing to be embarrassed about. Just so you know, the Ferris wheel is the only one I can ride without losing my cookies." I glanced around. "Tristan can attest to me being a scaredy cat. In fact, it's the reason he ditched me. Well, and wanting to hang around with his new boy toy."

Levi threw his head back and let loose with a deep belly laugh. "I guess we're two peas in a pod, then."

"It would appear so." I scuffled the gravel with my feet. "Why were you in line for the Ferris wheel anyway if heights bother you so badly?"

He glanced away. "I wasn't."

"Sure you were. When Keith asked if there were any other single riders, you raised your hand."

He nodded. "Yeah, but I was only walking by. I heard the guy call out and noticed it was you waiting up front, so I volunteered. Couldn't pass up the chance to get on a ride with the intriguing Callie Haybeck, could I?"

Levi thought I was intriguing? Huh. Never would've guessed that in a million years. I thought I'd cemented my irritating, snarky, and dumb as a post traits solidly in his mind.

"And for what it's worth," Levi continued, "I'm glad you decided not to tuck tail and run when your dad sent you the ticket home."

When the first Zen Goat yoga retreat I'd hosted at Haybeck Farm had resulted in the death of one of my guests, my parents were beside themselves with worry. They'd gone as far as sending me a plane ticket home like I was a teenager misbehaving on spring break. To be honest, I'd thought about going back to Seattle. Moments before the ticket had been delivered by priority mail, Uncle Will and Aunt Ellen's son, Jim, had shown up and yelled at everyone about how I was trying to scam his parents out of the farm. I only thought about escaping back to the safety of home for all of thirty seconds before I grew a backbone and made the decision to stay.

I grinned at Levi. "Really? If I recall correctly, after the first time we met, you called me a city girl and told Uncle Will I'd never make it on the farm."

His green eyes flicked to me, and he held my gaze. "Turns out I was wrong."

A ball of heat sent sparks shooting around inside my belly. "To be honest, I don't miss Seattle. I feel like I can hear myself think here."

Without discussing spending more time together, the two of us wandered side by side through the rows of brightly lit rides and carnival workers hawking their games. We took two empty stools in front of the horse race game and tried our luck at frantically rolling balls up the ramp in an attempt to propel our horses forward. When the final bell rang, my mighty cardboard steed was one step in front of Levi's. A boy who looked to be about eight years old cheered as the man running the booth handed over a stuffed chocolate donut plushie the size of an innertube.

As we rambled through the carnival, I kept half an eye out for Michelle. When I finally spotted her and her companion about to enter the two-story circus-themed fun house, I pulled on Levi's sleeve.

"Come on. Let's go in."

He threw his head back and groaned. "Seriously? I hate clowns."

The entrance to the funhouse was through the gaping mouth of a grinning clown, his diabolical eyes flashing between vibrant hues of reds and oranges.

"I'll keep you safe. I promise. It'll be fun." It was a small-town carnival. How bad could it be?

Levi drug his feet in the dirt, but reluctantly followed me. "It absolutely will not be fun."

I grabbed his hand and tugged him along, trying to not lose sight of Michelle. We held up our wrists for the attendant to see our bracelets and stepped between the clown's sharp teeth.

"Yeee…" I tried to smother my cry of fright when we were immediately greeted by a two-foot-tall Jack-in-the-box clown who sprung out of his box with maniacal laughter. The scary doll's eyes flashed red, and his purple hat bobbed as he swayed with the movement.

Levi jumped a mile in the air and squeezed my hand so tight I thought my fingers might be broken. "You said it was going to be fun."

Instead of replying, I glanced around for Michelle. As soon as I spotted her and the man she was with, the two of them disappeared around the corner of the next room. I sped past the still-bobbing clown to follow.

Levi and I immediately found ourselves in a hall of mirrors. Every way we turned changed our perspectives. Tall, tiny, as big as a house, as thin as a toothpick. The room was a dizzying maze made up of our own images. I stepped to my left but was body checked by a mirror, causing a peal of laughter from Levi.

He gripped my hand tighter. "This way, I think. And don't let go of my hand."

The thought hadn't even crossed my mind.

Whack. We smacked into another mirror. I swiveled my head and had the sense of the entire room twisting and turning around us as our images were reflected back to us a hundred-fold. *Fudge nuggets.* The out-of-body sensation was exactly why I never went into these crazy things in the first place, though I wasn't about to admit it to my companion since I was the one who insisted we give it a whirl.

Up ahead, a woman laughed, reminding me of my mission to snoop on Michelle. The man she was with called out her name.

"Michelle, where are you?"

"Over here," she laughed.

I turned in what I thought was the direction of their voices, only to be met with both Levi and my face reflected back to us in a scary image reminiscent of a horror movie.

"We gotta get out of here." Levi turned and raised his left arm in front of him as we inched our way forward.

Every turn took us to another dead end, but we finally managed to make our way out of the crazy maze. A ramp led us to the second floor and into an area filled with bouncy circus music. The walls and ceiling were covered in red and white striped fabric as if we were inside a circus tent. Several brightly clad clowns with big red noses performed sideshow antics, while a clown with a curly mop of red hair drove a tricycle in circles around and between us. He honked a horn attached to the handlebars, producing the deep aooogah sound of an old-fashioned car.

A grass-green curly slide spilled visitors out of the funhouse. I caught a glimpse of the back of Michelle's head as she whooshed down the slide.

Welp. So much for spying on the widow and her friend. All I'd managed to do was see the back of her head. Not super helpful.

Levi and I stepped up to the exit. I went first, with him right behind me. The slide swirled us around and dumped us out between the funhouse and a row of portable toilets the same color as the slide.

Levi good-naturedly glared at me. "Never again. I'd rather ride the Ferris wheel ten times in a row than ever step foot into one of those pits from hell again."

"Duly noted." I pulled an I'm-so-sorry face. "How about I make it up to you with an elephant ear?"

"You're on."

Later, after sharing the sweet, crispy treat dusted with powdered sugar and drizzled with caramel sauce, Levi stopped at another game booth. This time, he plunked his money down in exchange for a handful of darts. After all three of his darts met their mark, he bought another round, then traded his small prize for the next level up. While he leaned in, focused on his targets, I couldn't help but admire his jean-clad behind. I looked away the second his head started to turn in my direction. No need to get caught ogling the veterinarian. One more round of popped balloons and I found myself grinning with my arms wrapped around a ginormous bright pink unicorn. Levi and I'd had our differences in the past, but I was ready to forgive and forget. Nobody had ever won a prize for me at the carnival before. The way to a man's heart might be through his stomach, but it was possible the path to mine was paved with carnival game stuffed animals.

Chapter Fifteen

When I got out of the shower the next morning, the allergy oils I'd purchased from Althea mocked me from the bathroom counter where I'd deposited them when I'd gotten home. I stared at the bottles for a minute, then shrugged. Heck, why not? Might as well give them a try. I carefully measured out three drops of each oil, putting them one at a time into an empty capsule as the herbalist had instructed, then placed the capsule onto my tongue and chased it down with a glass of water. Done. No way were they going to work, but at least once I could report an unsuccessful try, Aunt Ellen would let up on me about calling Althea.

The evening with Levi took on a movie quality as it scrolled through my mind while I drove to the fairgrounds for the morning goat yoga session. My daydreaming left me unprepared for the police presence I encountered as I pulled into the parking lot. Every one of Bobwhite Hollow's police cars—two cruisers and the chief's Bronco—were parked in the otherwise nearly empty lot. Three uniformed officers were busy setting up a shade tent and table inside the grounds a few feet past the ticket booth.

I hesitated before getting out of the truck. Had something else happened, or were the police amping up their investigation into Brandon's death? Maybe their table was simply part of the county fair. A way to make the police force approachable to the community. I bit my lip. *You're not going to find out by sitting here in the truck.* I slid out of the passenger seat and grabbed my bag. After I showed my fair pass to the attendant and entered the grounds through the metal turnstile, an officer waved me over to their table.

"Please step over here, ma'am."

Alrighty then. Not a friendly get-to-know-your-local-cop booth.

"Good morning. Is there something going on I should be aware of?" I asked.

"Are you aware a death occurred here at the fairgrounds the other night?" The police officer hooked his thumbs into his belt and eyed me from behind dark sunglasses.

I nodded.

"Were you in attendance at the pig races that evening?"

Boy, the guy was awfully formal. I swallowed back a smile. Murder talk with a police officer was no time to grin like the Cheshire cat. "I was."

"I regret to inform you Brandon Ebersole's death was not the tragic accident it seemed."

"It wasn't?" Holy fudge nuggets! Pete was right. "Brandon was murdered?"

"Yes, Ma'am, he was. Did you see anything suspicious either before or after the explosion?"

I shook my head. "No, I'm sorry, I didn't." The questions made me think they didn't have a clue who had murdered Brandon. "Do you have any suspects? Any idea who killed him?"

The officer lowered his head and studied me over the top of his sunglasses. "This is an active investigation. Therefore, I am not at liberty to share details of the case with the public at this time."

The officer took my name and phone number, then told me to contact the Bobwhite Hollow police department if I happened to think of anything useful.

"You have my word." I hurried off to get the goats fed and watered before the yoga session.

You'd think early morning at the fairgrounds would be quiet with fairgoers not out and about yet and the carnival still and silent, but the air buzzed like a hive of busy bees. 4-H and FFA kids hustled around with wheelbarrow loads of bark chips and straw as they shoveled out animal stalls and filled them with fresh bedding, getting ready for the new day. The outside animal washing stations were filled with kids scrubbing their sheep and cattle before the day's competitions got started. A girl was blow-drying a milk cow with a canister-style livestock dryer while a young boy fluffed his sheep's wooly coat with a carding brush and trimmed any out-of-place clumps of wool with a set of wicked-looking hand shears. Country music blared from various cell phones plugged into portable docking stations, and the kids laughed and teased each other as they worked. I loved the jubilant camaraderie the kids shared and made a mental note to watch some of the showmanship competitions they'd be competing in later in the day.

I'd been paying attention to all the activity around me, and hadn't noticed the commotion going on at my own goat stalls until I was ten steps away.

"Chief Barnhart? What're you doing?" I called out.

The big man had one beefy hand gripping Bugsy's green collar while he tried to open the gate on the empty stall with the other. He leveled me with a glare as he shoved my goat into the stall and re-latched the gate.

"Putting your wayward goat back where he belongs. Again."

"I see that, but what do you mean again?" Confused, I looked between the chief and Bugsy, who was content to chew his cud and watch the exchange.

"Just what I said. What part is causing you confusion?"

Well, the whole thing, actually. I held up a hand, trying to keep up. "Okay, you found Bugsy out this morning, and you've put him back. Got it. And I can't thank you enough. But you're telling me it wasn't the first time?"

The chief snorted. "Not by a long shot. In fact, if I get a report he's running loose again and snatching food out of people's hands, I'm going to have to ticket you for goat-at-large." He winked to indicate he was kidding. I hoped.

I crossed my arms and glared at Bugsy. And to think I'd given the naughty goat a bite of my maple cotton candy as a reward for being so good last night. What a trickster.

With all the distractions this morning, time was ticking away. Instead of the hour buffer I'd wanted, there were only forty minutes left until I needed to start the morning's goat yoga session. Once Chief Barnhart left, I took a lesson from the 4-H and FFA kids and got my hustle on filling mangers with hay, refilling mineral feeders, and carrying buckets of fresh, cool water from the outside faucet. The last scoop of dirty bedding was on my shovel when I swung it around to toss it into the wheelbarrow and almost threw it straight into Pete's face instead.

He stepped aside just in time to avoid my shovelful of goat droppings. "Callie! You've got to help me!" The ice cream man appeared anything but cool. Droplets of sweat rolled down his red face, and his usual calm countenance had been replaced with a frantic energy.

"Help with what? Have you been jogging?"

"Me? Jogging? No. Don't be daft." Pete grimaced. "Pay attention. Remember how I told you I found the explosives canister yesterday and was taking it to the police station?"

I nodded.

"Apparently, that was a big mistake."

"It wasn't what caused the starter gun to explode?"

"No, I was right. It was definitely Wiley Explosives used in the gun."

"Okay." I drew the word out. "So why was it a mistake taking the canister to the police?"

"Because I'm apparently their number one suspect. They think I killed Brandon." Pete stared at me, wide-eyed, waiting for my response.

But what if Pete was the murderer? I couldn't imagine the usually happy and friendly Pete killing anybody, but he had bald-faced lied to me about working at the snow cone stand the night Brandon was killed, hadn't he? If he wasn't involved in the murder, why would he lie about where he'd been? Even yesterday, he'd been missing in action for hours. But, then again, what possible reason could Pete have for wanting the Hasty Hogs Pig Racing owner dead?

"Callie. Hello?" Pete snapped his fingers in my face to get my attention.

I shook the terrible thoughts away and focused on Pete. "Why would the police think you killed Brandon?"

A muscle twitched rapidly in his cheek "I guess because they don't have any other suspects, and I'm the one who found the empty explosives container, so my fingerprints are all over it. Yesterday, they questioned me at the police station for hours."

I frowned. His story about his unexplained absence yesterday certainly didn't match up with what Chief Barnhart told me. "Where did you find the container, by the way?"

"In my snow cone stand. I actually found it wedged between the garbage can and the wall when I moved the can to put a new trash bag in it."

Oh. I blinked and sucked in a sharp breath. Another check against him. "That's not good." What if Pete was the person who packed the starter gun full of explosives and had to find a way to explain his fingerprints being all over the empty canister? "Did anybody witness you finding the canister?"

"Mazzy came in right after I picked it up." Pete nodded rapidly. "You're right; it doesn't look good, and that is the reason why you have to help me."

"I still don't quite understand what you need. Help you with what exactly?"

He huffed and rubbed a hand down his face in frustration. "Help me find out who killed Brandon, of course."

I yelped. "Me? Why?"

"You have experience flushing out killers." Pete lifted his hands as if it was obvious. "Plus, I thought we were friends, and you'd want to help me out."

I continued to stare at him.

"Would free ice cream for the rest of the season help?"

Low blow, buddy. Low blow.

Chapter Sixteen

My mind spun as my body raced to get the goats out to the enclosure in order to start the morning's goat yoga session on time. Earlier in the summer, a retreat guest had been killed at the farm. With a tiny bit of snooping, I'd helped the police uncover the murderer, so apparently Pete was under the impression I possessed the skills to nose out Brandon's killer. *He's barking up the wrong tree. It was pure dumb luck last time. I can't help.* But my brain latched on and wouldn't let it go. Who killed Brandon, and why?

Pete claimed to be innocent, but his innocent act could be a front. Though most murders weren't random. If Pete had killed Brandon, what was his motive? Sweet Pete didn't seem like a murderer to me, so I didn't hesitate to agree to help him when he'd asked. But then again, from the true crime documentaries I watched, it wasn't unusual for serial killers to smile at their neighbors as nice as could be and make small talk right after they'd buried the bodies. And Pete's actions in the last few days made it clear he was hiding something.

Beyond finding out what Pete was hiding, I didn't have a clue how to help. Who had it out for the pig racing owner? The image of Brandon brushing past me at the fair office the other morning came to mind. He and Jay were arguing, and Jay had threatened to pull the Hasty Hogs contract. What had the two of them been arguing about? And how could I find out? I didn't know Jay well, only in his capacity as the Lupine County Fair manager, and even then, my acquaintance with him was limited. I'd have to ask Pete what he could tell me before I approached Jay with my questions. But first thing first. Any snooping I was going to do would have to wait until after yoga.

People were already crowding around the round pen as I brought the last two young goats into the enclosure. Bugsy tagged along, not wanting to be left behind. Yesterday, there'd only been eight yoga students at the session, but word must've gotten out, because this morning, twice the number of people filed through the gate as I held it open and welcomed them in. I was pleased to see the woman and her two young daughters, who I'd invited a few days ago, had shown up. The little girls were already enthusiastically hugging goats. A handful of yesterday's students had returned, including Jes from the Hasty Hogs crew and Nancy of the notorious "Free the Goats" signs. I was pleased to note Nancy wore a big smile and had lived up to her promise to leave her picketing signs at home.

As everyone rolled out mats and cuddled goats, I took two minutes to take some deep breaths and calm my mind. A yogi with her thoughts all in a tither wouldn't make for the most peaceful of sessions. Once I got myself together and felt able to present a decent class, I asked everyone to stand on their mats with their feet together and backs straight.

"Now, press the palms of your hands together, fingers splayed, and hold them over your chest." I demonstrated the prayer pose. "Close your eyes and inhale. Hold for a count of three, exhale. Good. This time, calm your mind and imagine the sun's rays filling your body with energy. On the next inhale, keeping your hands together, raise them over your head, lift your face to the sky, and arch your back slightly. Hold for three counts, then bring your hands back to chest position on the exhale. Good." I glanced around at the class. "Let's repeat that for ten rounds."

I'd chosen to start the session with a sun salutation pose, giving myself more time to push Brandon's murder out of my mind and center my breathing. After the sun salutations, I moved the class into the triangle pose to give the goats more opportunity to interact with the students. The energetic goats immediately took advantage of the wide stances, weaving their way in and out between legs and arms, much to the human participants' delight.

During the class, we moved through various other poses, all with goats using their backs and rumps to play King of the Mountain. For part of the session, I walked between the participants, helping people with their poses and answering questions about the goats.

Seeing Jes here again this morning got me thinking about what I'd overheard her husband say to her about their paychecks yesterday. If this wasn't the first time their checks bounced, didn't it give Sam, or even Jes for that matter, a motive to kill Brandon? But how would killing the man solve the problem? Wouldn't Brandon's death make it even harder to get the money owed them? After all, Brandon's check to Uncle Will for the stay in the guest cottage bounced, too. My guess was Hasty Hogs Pig Racing was on the verge of bankruptcy. It was a delicate subject, and I wondered if there was any way to broach it with Jes. The woman was effusive and friendly, so maybe I could invite her to spend some time with me at the farm later and probe her for answers.

I checked the time and was surprised to see it had moved so fast. Our hour was nearly up, so I moved the class into the final, restful child's pose. I lifted my head to glance around, and my gaze landed on Nancy. With the rest of the class face down, I studied the woman. Aunt Ellen had said Nancy was harmless, but what if she had a darker side my aunt wasn't aware of? From all accounts, Nancy had been a vocal opponent of the pig races for several years. Could her passion for freeing the pigs have caused her to get rid of their owner? I planted my head face down on my mat and reprimanded myself. *That makes zero sense, Callie. Someone who is such a big advocate for animal lives wouldn't murder a human being. Would they?* I sighed, came out of the pose, and ended the session.

Before Jes left, I caught up with her. "Hey, how're you doing?"

She smiled but quickly broke eye contact. "Oh, fine. Good, I guess."

Her demeanor was so different from what it had been yesterday, I wondered if she was embarrassed because I'd witnessed Sam's temper tantrum the day before. Or maybe it was because Brandon's death had been reclassified as a murder.

"Glad to hear you're doing alright." Though I wasn't sure I believed her. "Are you going to be at the farm later? I've got some chores to do and wondered if you'd like to keep me company."

"Yes, please!" Her eyes lit up as she answered, and this time her smile was genuine. "I think we'll be at your farm most of the day. The rest of the pig races scheduled for the fair have been canceled, but the police chief asked us to stick around for a while anyway."

"Great. I should be back at the farm by early afternoon. There's a weak spot in the fence I've been needing to fix. I'll come find you when I'm ready to head out to the pasture."

"It sounds perfect. Put me to work. I'm a good hand, and Lord knows I could use something to take my mind off everything else going on right now."

Crap. Here I go making plans to wander the farm alone with a possible murderer. The thought dissipated as quickly as it had formed. I wasn't super worried. I could take care of myself, and I didn't honestly think Jes had anything to do with Brandon's death. Sam, maybe, but Jes, no.

Jes leaned in for a hug. As we separated, she commented, "Look at you, lady! No sneezing today. You must've found a better allergy medicine. That's great news! I'll see you a little later." She threw a wave my way as she left.

I stood there staring after her. Wow. Jes was right. I hadn't even noticed it, but not one tiny sneeze during the whole session. No runny nose. No watery eyes. No itchy ears. A big smile cracked across my face. Those crazy snake oils had worked, after all. I shook my head. Nah. Had to be a coincidence.

All the other students had wandered away, and I was left alone with the goats. I didn't mind one single bit. Sometimes the goats were better company than people, but I wouldn't have said no to a little help getting them back to the barn. I was contemplating which goats to take first when someone cleared their throat right behind me.

I spun around to find Tristan with a cup of coffee extended in front of him like a peace offering.

"What's this?" I asked, arms crossed against my chest. It was all I could do not to grab the coffee, but at the same time, I didn't want to give my cousin the satisfaction of being forgiven too easily.

"It's coffee, Callie. Just take it." He thrust the cup toward me. "Look, I'm sorry I ditched you last night and sorry I acted like a big jerk."

I reached for the cup and took a sip. "You should be." My mouth had a mind of its own. Before I could stop myself, I launched into a tirade. "All summer we've had plans for you to come up from Boston for the week to enjoy the fair with me, but one pretty face comes along, and you abandon me. And treat me like I'm an idiot. Do you have any idea how miserable it is to wander around a carnival all by yourself when everyone around you is having the time of their life?"

Tristan's deadpan stare made me fidget.

"What?" I asked, eyebrows raised, daring him to challenge me.

And challenge me he did. "Girl, I saw you more than once last night. Far from wandering around all by yourself and miserable, as you want me to believe, you appeared to be enamored with the hot veterinarian you were walking arm in arm with."

I gulped. "I didn't see you."

"I'm aware. The two of you were too busy making goo-goo eyes at each other."

Hot coffee streamed down the back of my throat as I swallowed hard. "We were not making goo-goo eyes at each other!"

"You were. Believe me, it was nauseating." Tristan bobbled his head. "And don't think I missed the pink monstrosity of a unicorn lounging on your bed this morning. I suppose Levi won that ugly thing for you?"

"Fine. Whatever." I glared at him. "Why're you giving me so much grief about Levi anyway, when you've been attached at the hip with Spencer since you ran into him the other night?"

"Because I wasn't the one pulling the whole woe is me charade, now was I?"

"Guess not." I shrugged. "But, to set the record straight, there's nothing going on between me and Levi."

"Uh-huh. If you hurry up and finish your coffee, I'll help you get these goats put away."

I wasn't about to argue with his offer to help.

After the goats were tucked away in their stalls and happily chewing their cud, I pulled Tristan into a quiet corner of the barn and told him all about the police's revelation this morning and Pete's request for help finding the killer.

When I finished my story, Tristan shook his head. "No, no, no. Callie, you can't get involved in a murder investigation again. Let the police do their job. It's what they're trained for."

"Pete's my friend, and he asked for my help. I can't sit back and let him be accused of killing Brandon while the actual murderer goes free." I didn't mention my own suspicions about the ice cream man.

Tristan closed his eyes and took a deep breath. "Okay. I guess I know you well enough by now to realize you're not going to leave it alone." He twirled his sunglasses in his hand, then pointed the earpiece at me. "Since you're bound and determined to do this, you know I'll have your back, but you have to let me help."

"I don't have to let you do anything." I mock glared at him. "But yes, two heads are better than one. You can be my trusty sidekick."

"Like Watson?"

"Well, I was thinking more like Scooby-Doo, but sure, Watson works."

Tristan rubbed his palms together. "Alright, so what's our game plan?"

"The first thing we need to do is sit down with Pete and get some questions answered." I woke up my phone to check the time. "We have an hour before the snow cone stand opens, so let's head over. Pete should be there prepping for the day."

Chapter Seventeen

Tristan and I approached the colorful snow cone and ice cream trailer, but there didn't appear to be anyone around. The place was locked up tight. I went around to the back and knocked on the metal door just in case, but the only sound was the humming of the freezers inside the trailer.

"Well, he's not here. What's next?" Tristan asked.

With a huff, I blew my bangs out of my eyes. "Pete's got to get here soon. He was already at the fairgrounds before I started the goat yoga session, so let's wait for a few minutes to see if he shows up."

A handful of colorful metal tables with closed sun umbrellas were placed near the stand so customers had a shady place to sit and enjoy their cold treats. Tristan and I chose the yellow table and opened the umbrella to take advantage of the shade it provided. I was swinging my leg over the bench when Pete arrived, dragging a red wagon behind him filled with syrup flavors and supplies for his business.

"You're here!" Pete exclaimed. "Let me get these things into the stand, and I'll be right with you." He appeared to be much calmer and far less rumpled than he'd been two hours before. Today, he wore a sky-blue Hawaiian shirt with bright pink flamingos scattered all over it.

Five minutes later, Pete joined Tristan and me, three creamy, caramel-colored, ice cream cones in hand. Even though it was only nine in the morning, I didn't hesitate to reach for one.

My eyes flared wide as I took my first taste. "What is this magic?" The ice cream was somehow creamier than any soft-serve I'd ever had before and exploded with flavor. I swiped a finger across the ice cream left on my bottom lip.

Tristan stared at me in shock. "It's a maple creemee, dummy. Do you live under a rock or something?"

"To be fair, maple creemees are usually a Vermont thing, but being so close to the border, Claire and I wanted to serve them," Pete added. "We've actually had a few Vermonters upset when they discover we're serving them in New Hampshire."

"Whoa! This is so good! I can understand why they'd get a bit territorial about them. We don't have anything like this in the Pacific Northwest. Why haven't I had one before?" My ice cream was disappearing at an alarming rate, but I didn't care. It was the most delicious thing I'd ever shoved in my mouth.

Pete shrugged. "Beats me. They've always been on the menu at Sweet Pete's. Guess you've never ordered one."

I wanted to say, "I'll be ordering one every day now," but my mouth was too full. After I finished gobbling down my creemee, I wiped sticky fingers on the napkins Pete had thoughtfully provided along with the ice cream cones. "Okay. That was super delicious, but it's time to get down to business," I announced while my companions finished their cones.

I let Pete know Tristan was going to be helping us with our unofficial investigation. Pete gave his consent, but then it was time to ask the hard questions.

Whipping a small notebook and pen out of my backpack, I opened the notebook on top of the table and tapped the pen against a blank page. My legs jittered as I tried to come up with a non-accusatory way to ask my first question. When nothing came to me, I simply blurted it out. "Pete, I hate to ask this, but it's the first step. Did you kill Brandon Ebersole?" I watched my friend closely for his reaction.

Pete jerked his head back but quickly recovered. "Of course not. No, I did not kill Brandon. The only thing I'm guilty of when it comes to Mr. Ebersole was selling him too many ice cream cones, but that was on him, not me."

Satisfied with his reaction, I pointed my pen at him. "You're guilty of the same thing with me."

He threw his hands up in the air. "You can't blame me. A guy's got to make a living. I'll sell you as many ice cream cones as you can hold." He chuckled. "Next question."

I took a deep breath. "Yesterday morning, when you told me Brandon's death wasn't an accident, I asked you if you'd been at the pig races. Do you remember what you told me?" *Would he lie to me again?*

Pete nodded. "Sure. I was here at the food truck while the races were underway."

Trying to raise just one eyebrow, I kept eye contact and didn't say a word. The technique worked on murder mysteries I'd watched, so it was worth a try. Pete set his jaw and stared back. I flipped my notebook closed and looked at Tristan, who was shifting his gaze between me and Pete.

"Looks like we're done here." I stood to leave.

"Wha…? What do you mean we're done here?" Pete sputtered. "Don't we need to formulate a plan?"

I shook my head. "Nope. There's nothing Tristan and I can do to help if you're not going to be honest with us."

Pete dropped his chin to his chest and sighed heavily before gesturing for me to sit back down. "Alright, alright. You caught me. I wasn't at the food truck during the pig races."

We were finally making progress.

"Where were you? And why are you lying about it?" Tristan asked. "Makes you look guilty."

"Not only that," I broke in, "but you were gone for hours yesterday and told me you were at the police station the entire time. What you don't know, is Chief Barnhart informed me you'd only been there about thirty minutes. Both the chief and I saw you coming into the back gate of the fairgrounds about eight o'clock last night. So there's another big chunk of your time unaccounted for. You've got to come clean with us, or we walk." I scowled at him.

Pete rubbed a hand down his face. "If I tell you, will you promise this information stays between us?"

Tristan and I looked at each other, and I shook my head again. "Nope, this is about a murder. We can't promise to keep your secret if it involves Brandon's death," I said.

"It doesn't. Not at all," Pete answered. "I just have a hobby that might seem strange to most people. Something I like to keep to myself. Well, and the other members of my group. And Claire's aware of what I do, of course."

Yikes. A strange hobby? Did I even want to know?

"Either you tell us, or we don't help," Tristan replied. "The choice is yours." My cousin did have my back.

"Okay, fine. I wasn't working the snow cone stand like I said, or even at the fairgrounds at all. A member of my group called and said there'd been a sighting. When it happens, we have to go immediately, so I left Mazzy and Noah with the stand and took off to see if I could locate it."

I tilted my head and chewed on my bottom lip, trying to make sense of what Pete was saying. "A sighting of what? What were you trying to find?"

"A UFO. I'm a UFO chaser." He stared me down as if daring me to laugh. Tristan snorted. I kicked him under the table.

"A UFO chaser, huh?" Tristan asked. "Have you found anything?"

"Not yet, but we will. They're out there."

Clearing my throat, I got back to business. "So, you got a phone call about the…UFO…then went in search of it. You said you belong to a group. Was someone with you who can verify your story and where you actually were?"

Pete leaned back and stared at me. "Yes, my buddy can verify, if he'll agree. Most of us chasers like to keep the location of the spacecraft under our hats. We don't need every looky-loo out there."

"Right." I tried to keep the disbelief out of my voice. "And yesterday?"

"Same. This time the sighting was down near Henniker, so we were gone quite a while."

"When you came through the back gate, you were carrying a cardboard box with a telescope, I think, poking out of the box. You left the box in a shed near the track. What was that about?"

Pete shook his head. "You don't miss a beat, do you?"

"You'd be amazed at what you can see from the grandstands," I answered.

He sighed. "The box has our UFO hunting gear in it. A telescope, binoculars, night vision equipment, stuff like that. One of our guys was running a car in the demolition derby, so I left the box in the shed for him to pick up when he was done."

I pursed my lips and blinked at Pete.

"What? Do you not believe me, Callie? Do you think I murdered Brandon?"

I shook my head. "No, of course I don't, though it seems to me your name could easily be cleared off the suspect list by telling the police the truth about your whereabouts. Seems like a no-brainer to me."

Pete sighed heavily. "I know. I know, but I gotta talk to my buddy first. There's no way I'm going to blindside him with this. We don't do that to each other."

"What's his name? Maybe Tristan and I can talk to him."

"Nice try, but nope."

I studied Pete with a frown. "It still doesn't make any sense to me why you'd protect your friend and your UFO club when you're worried you're about to be charged with murder. Promise you'll talk to him as soon as possible?"

"Yes, I said I would, and I will."

"Fine. I'm trying to get all our ducks in a row here." I studied my notes. "So, if it wasn't you, who do you think killed Brandon? Any ideas?"

Pete relaxed his shoulders and shook his head. "Don't have a clue. I'm as baffled as you are."

I filled Tristan and Pete in on the argument I'd overheard between Brandon and Jay, about the bouncing paychecks and the bogus check Brandon had written to Haybeck Farm for the guest cottage rental, and about seeing Michelle giving money to the stranger I'd smacked into at the cooking demonstration.

"It sounds to me like we have a handful of suspects to look at already," Pete said.

"Yep. I agree. Why Brandon was arguing with Jay needs to be checked out. Sam Nowak could use a closer look." I jotted down their names in my notebook. "I'm planning on talking to Jes this afternoon."

"Don't forget to add Brandon's wife to the list," Tristan added. "The spouse is always the first suspect the police look at."

I wrote Michelle Ebersole on the list. "True enough. Generally, when a spouse kills, it's about love or money. We've already ascertained there are money issues, yet Michelle gave money to whoever the mystery guy was, and then the two of them were together later at the carnival."

"Love and money for a motive?" Tristan asked.

"Seems feasible," Pete said.

I tapped my pen against the notebook. "And how about Nancy? The lady who was protesting at the pig races? She's been coming to goat yoga the last two mornings, but what do you think about her as a suspect?" I asked.

Pete wrinkled his nose. "Nancy's harmless. Just bored, I think, but sure, write her down. Don't want to overlook someone because we think they aren't capable of murder."

I added Nancy Achilles to the bottom of the list.

"Tell me more about the explosives container you found. You said you found it behind the garbage can in the snow cone trailer?"

"Yeah," Pete nodded. "We were having some issues with the ice maker the other day, so I came in early yesterday morning to make sure it was working. When Mazzy and Noah had closed up, they'd wiped everything down but had forgotten to sweep the floor. I grabbed the broom and got to work, but when I moved the trash can, I found the empty Wiley Explosives container behind it. Mazzy came in and found me standing in the trailer holding the can."

"How do you think the canister got inside your food trailer?"

He shook his head. "Your guess is as good as mine."

I turned and studied the snow cone and ice cream stand. The window where orders were taken and cones handed out stretched over half the length of the trailer. "Bear with me for a minute." I got up and trotted to the window. "If the killer came up to the open window," I leaned my elbows against the counter, "ordered his-"

"Or her," Tristan inserted.

"Right. Or her cone, they could've reached over and dropped the container inside when your employee's backs were turned to make their order."

Pete nodded. "Sure. That's possible. Since I wasn't here that night, Mazzy would've most likely been taking orders while Noah scooped ice cream and made snow cones. They were busy enough they might not have noticed someone slipping it in."

The possibility we had a feasible idea of how the empty container got into Sweet Pete's stand excited me. I flipped to a blank page in my notebook and jotted down a second list of the same names. Ripping the page out, I handed it to Pete. "When Mazzy and Noah get to work today, ask them if they remember seeing any of these people at the stand that night. And ask them to write down the names of anyone else they remember being there."

Pete studied the list, then looked up at me with a frown. "Will do, but I wouldn't count on the teenagers knowing the Hasty Hogs crew, since the pig racers aren't local."

My shoulders sagged. "Fudge nuggets. You're probably right, but ask them anyway. You never know. They should be able to tell us if Jay or Nancy stopped by, at least."

"So, what's next boss?" Tristan asked.

I tapped my pen against my chin. "I'd like to figure out what Jay and Brandon were arguing about. I don't know Jay well at all. Can you tell us anything about him?" I looked at Pete.

"He's a nice enough guy. A local fruit grower, though apples aren't the only thing Jay's raising out there on his farm, if you get my drift." Pete winked and pushed himself up from the table. "Good session, but I gotta get to work." He walked off, leaving Tristan and me sitting at the table with our mouths gaping open.

Chapter Eighteen

"Jay's growing pot on his farm? I wouldn't have guessed that in a million years. He looks like such a strait-laced guy." I stared at Tristan. "Is marijuana legal in New Hampshire?"

Whenever I'd been around someone smoking pot, my nose would immediately get stuffed up, and I'd start sneezing, so I'd never had the slightest desire to indulge myself. Even though it was legal in Washington, I hadn't had any reason to find out if wacky tobaccy was illegal in my new home state.

"Beats me." Tristan shrugged. "I live in Massachusetts, where weed is legal."

I titled my head. "Do you smoke?"

"Nah. I've tried it more than once, but never saw the big appeal. Just makes me hungry." He shrugged. "I guess I'm relaxed enough already."

While we chatted, I pulled up the internet on my phone and entered a few key words. I had my answer in the shake of a lamb's tail. "Get this. Medical marijuana is legal in New Hampshire with a qualifying card from a doctor. Recreational use is *not* legal, but it's not criminalized either. More like a minor violation if someone is caught with it in their possession. However, if someone is caught growing weed, they can get in major trouble."

Tristan stuck out his lower lip. "Hmm. Interesting. If Pete's right about Jay, makes me wonder if Brandon stumbled onto something he shouldn't have."

"Why don't we take a walk over to the fair office and see what we can find out?"

Tristan's eyebrows shot up past the top of his sunglasses. "You think Jay's going to tell us, do you? Just outright admit he's growing weed and killed Brandon over it? I think we need to be a little stealthier in this investigation instead of running off half-cocked. Drug dealers and murderers aren't generally the safest people to confront about their shady dealings."

"You might have a point." I huffed and flung one of my braids over my shoulder. "I guess one of our first tasks is to try to figure out who had access to Brandon's starter gun. Off the top of my head, I would think Michelle, Sam, and Jes, for sure. They were all right there when it happened."

Tristan nodded. "Agreed. They were all in close proximity to the crime scene and most likely had access to the gun. It's got to be one of them, so this should be fairly easy to figure out."

I chewed on my lip for a few seconds, mulling it over. "Not necessarily. From what I understand, the gun had been tampered with. Explosives were shoved down into the barrel and caused the gun to blow up. Do you remember they used a trumpet sound to start all the races until the finale?"

"Yep. Go on. What're you thinking?"

"Well, if the gun was only used for the last race, it could've been tampered with at any time before the pig races started. The killer didn't have to be on the scene when Brandon picked up the gun. They could've been anywhere by then. Not even at the fairgrounds."

We both swiveled around and stared at Sweet Pete's stand. "No," we said in unison.

I put up my hand, palm out, dismissing the idea. "It wasn't Pete. I'm sure of it."

"How can you be so sure?"

I shrugged. "It's a gut feeling. And why would Pete beg me to help find the killer if he did it?"

"To get you tangled up in the whole thing and throw the police off his scent?"

I dropped my ink pen and it fell through the slot of the table. "You think Pete's trying to set me up?"

"It's something to think about." Tristan cut his eyes over to the snow

107

cone stand again and frowned. "You're probably right, though, and Pete's completely innocent." He pushed up from the table. "Anyway, give some thought to what our next move should be. I will, too, then I'll check back with you a little later."

"Where are you going?"

"To meet up with Spencer." He checked the time on his phone. "I should've already left."

"What? I thought you were going to be my trusty sidekick." My voice came out a lot whinier than I'd intended.

"I am, just not right now."

Mmhmm. "Scooby never would've ditched Shaggy," I yelled after Tristan's retreating figure. He ignored me.

I sighed and grabbed my backpack from underneath the table, picking up my rogue pen from the ground in the process. With Tristan off gallivanting with Spencer again, I figured I might as well head out to the farm and get some work done. Physical labor was one of the best ways to get my mind focused and think about what needed to be done next to figure out who the killer was.

Chapter Nineteen

Once I got home, I made a beeline to the barn and loaded an orange, five-gallon bucket with the fencing supplies I'd need. Into the bucket went a long black fence stretcher, a container of silver fencing sleeves, a pair of wire cutters, a heavy-duty staple gun, and two pairs of pliers. I'd dropped a couple pairs of thick leather work gloves into the bucket when Uncle Will strode into the barn, wiping his greasy fingers on a red rag.

He eyed my bucket of supplies. "What're you up to, Callie-Kat?"

"I noticed a weak stretch of fence out in the west pasture," I replied. "Thought I'd head out and fix it before we end up with loose livestock."

Uncle Will nodded his approval. "You want a hand?"

"Nope, I can handle it. My teacher taught me well." I grinned.

Uncle Will put his palms together in front of his chest and bowed slightly from the waist, imitating the instructor in the classic *Kung Fu* television show. "You have learned well, grasshopper." He chortled over his own cleverness.

When I'd arrived in New Hampshire in the late spring, I'd had exactly zero skills for living on a farm, but after overhearing Levi tell Uncle Will he'd bet I'd be hightailing it back to Seattle before the summer was over, I'd dug in my heels, bound and determined to prove him wrong. Only two months had passed, and while I still had years of learning to do, with Uncle Will's help, I'd acquired a few new skills. Fixing a woven wire fence was one of them. An added bonus to my stubbornness and desire to prove the handsome vet wrong was that I was starting to take some of the load of farm chores off the backs of my elderly relatives. It wasn't nearly enough, but it was a start.

Uncle Will pushed back the round brim of his faded straw hat and clamped a weathered hand onto my shoulder. "I'm proud of you, kid."

I ducked my head to hide my watery eyes and picked the bucket up by the handle. "Thanks. I'd better get out there. The fence isn't going to fix itself."

"And I'll get back to work on my cantankerous tractor. We're going to need to get the second cutting of orchard grass done next week, but I'd rather not do it with a spitting and sputtering tractor."

So far, I'd left the tractor repair up to Uncle Will. The cussing and turning red in the face as he tried to fine-tune the hydraulic system gave me pause. Mechanically inclined I was not, and it wasn't a task I wanted to tackle anytime soon. There were plenty of other farm chores to keep me busy without the added bonus of mechanic grease under my fingernails.

"Hey, Uncle Will. Can I ask you a question?"

He'd made it out of the barn, but turned and sauntered back over to me when I called out his name. "Sure. What do you need?"

"Can you tell me where Jay's farm is?"

"Jay Rowe? The fair manager?"

I nodded.

"Sure, he's out there on Wilson Pond Road. East of the village about five miles or so. Why?"

"Just curious. I heard a rumor he might be growing something illegal out there."

Uncle Will pulled his head back in surprise. "Jay? No. I can't imagine."

"Do you know him well? Have you been to his farm?"

"Well, let's see." Uncle Will pulled off his hat and scratched his head. "Jay's dad and I were friendly back in the day, but we lost Wally to a tractor accident years ago. Such a shame. The man made the best cider in New England. I counted him among my closest friends." Uncle Will slowly shook his head. "Probably been twenty years since I've had any reason to go out to the Rowe farm. Still, I'm sure there's no substance to whatever rumor you heard. They're an upstanding family."

"Okay. Well, thanks." Maybe Pete had his gossip all wrong this time.

With the bucket swinging by my side, I stepped out into the blinding

August sunshine and nearly ran smack into Jes. She'd changed out of her yoga clothes and had thrown on a Hasty Hogs T-shirt and a pair of jeans.

"I was about to come over to see if you still felt up to helping me out."

She clapped her hands with excitement. "You won't even believe how ready I am to get out of the house. But maybe you noticed by the way I came running when I saw your truck in the driveway." Her eyes widened, and she touched my forearm. "I didn't mean to sound like there's anything wrong with the guest cottage. It's great! It's just with Michelle grieving Brandon, she's keeping all the curtains pulled tight so it's dark and depressing in there. I tried to get her to get out of bed and come with me, but no luck."

I nodded. "It's only been a couple of days. I'm sure she's still in shock. The poor woman. I can't imagine what she's going through. At least she got out last night for a couple of hours."

Jes cocked her head. "Uh, I don't think so. As far as I know, Michelle hasn't left the cottage."

"Not to throw her under the bus, but yes, she has. I ran into her twice at the fair last night. She must've left without you noticing."

"Sam and I went to the fairgrounds for the demolition derby, so she must've left after we were already gone." Jes reached back and adjusted her ponytail. "But we had the truck. How in the heck did she get to the fairgrounds?" She asked in a bewildered tone of voice.

I shrugged. "The guy she was with must have picked her up."

Jes stared at me. "The guy she was with? What guy? You're sure she was with somebody?"

I told Jes about the encounter with Michelle and the mystery man.

She shook her head and stuttered around. "Seriously, I don't have any idea who the guy could've been. I thought she hadn't left the house at all since Brandon died. So weird."

Jes and I started walking as we talked. Daisy roused herself from where she'd been napping in the shade of a large oak tree and followed us. The big dog's tongue hung out as she ambled along beside me.

"You didn't have to come, silly girl." I dropped my hand to Daisy's soft head and stroked her fur. She wagged her fluffy tail and added a bounce to her step as if to say she wouldn't be left behind for all the dog treats in the world.

I opened the gate and waved Jes into the pasture, then pointed to a fence in the distance. "The fence we're going to repair is in the next field." Sheep and goats dotted the far pasture.

"Lead on," Jes said. Daisy loped ahead, happy to oblige.

As soon as the goats spotted us coming their way, they raced each other to the fence and watched us through big oval eyes. "Shoot. I should've brought some treats for you to feed them," I told Jes. "We'll just have to come out again later."

"That'll work! It'll give me another excuse to get out of the house."

"You're more than welcome to wander all over the farm. It's one of the perks of staying in our guest cottage. Please make sure you close any gates behind you so none of the critters get out."

"Seriously? I can?"

"Of course. I'm sorry we didn't make that clear when you guys checked in," I said.

"Oh, it says we can on the welcome letter and information you guys left on the table, but I still wasn't sure if I should without asking permission first."

"Yes, please. Enjoy the farm while you're here. We want you to!"

We'd entered the sheep and goat field and, while the sheep ignored us entirely, the mama goats tagged along, curious to find out what Jes and I were doing.

"Look at them following us." Jes giggled. "I'm the pied piper!"

I laughed. "You don't even need a flute, just an orange bucket."

The section of fence I wanted to repair didn't have any holes in it, but the wire was loose and sagged between the wooden fenceposts. Wiry goat hair was stuck in the knots of wire at the corners of each square. I set the bucket down and handed Jes a pair of leather work gloves.

She eyed the sagging fence. "Hmm. How did this happen? With the pigs, we always wind up with holes from them trying to burrow under and through the fence, but I've never seen it sag like this."

I pointed to a brown goat with white socks who was leaning against the fence and moving her body down the entire section while pressing hard on the fence. "Heidi heard you ask, so she thought she'd give you a demonstration."

"What in the world is she doing?"

"Rubbing. The goats love to scratch themselves on anything they can find, and they're constantly rubbing themselves down the fence like she's doing. It doesn't take long before the wire loses tension." I laughed at the goat's antics. "They're kind of a menace."

"But a cute menace."

"Agreed." I smiled and gently smacked the goat on the haunches. "Knock it off, Heidi."

Heidi bounced away, kicking up her heels like a kid.

Jes pulled on the work gloves. "What do you need me to do? I've been repairing fences my entire life, so put me to work!"

I grabbed the top of the fence near a fencepost and pulled hard until the metal fence was once again standing at the correct height. "Pull on the other end," I pointed to the next fencepost down the line from where I stood, "and let's see if we can get it tight enough again."

Jes put her weight into her end, and I put mine into mine. While still tugging on the wire, I reached into the bucket and found the staple gun. With the fence in place where I wanted it, I shot staples around the wire and into the fencepost at intervals up and down the wooden post.

While we worked, I used the opportunity to ask a few of the questions burning holes in my mind. Keeping my head down so as not to embarrass her, I started in. "Jes, is it okay if I ask you something kind of personal?"

"Uh, sure. I guess," she replied. "Though I reserve the right not to answer."

"Fair enough."

"Ask away, then."

"I don't mean to pry, and like you said, you don't need to answer me if you don't want to." I paused, but when she didn't say anything, I plunged ahead. "Yesterday morning after yoga, I couldn't help but overhear Sam say your paychecks bounced. From his comment, it sounded like it wasn't the first time. Have they bounced before?"

Jes sighed. "Yeah, I thought you might've heard that. Sam can be loud sometimes, especially when he's mad. I'm sorry you had to witness his temper tantrum. He has a short fuse sometimes."

"Well, I don't blame him for being mad."

"No, me either, but the whole world didn't need to hear about our money problems. And dumping the picnic table over was ridiculous."

I wasn't about to comment on Sam's bad behavior. "So, it wasn't the first time your paychecks have bounced?" I tried again to get her to answer my question.

"Far from it." Jes sucked in a deep breath, then slowly released it. "We haven't been paid for the last two months. The entire summer, basically. Brandon and Sam were working it out and Brandon assured us this time the checks were good."

"What does Michelle say about it?"

Jes shook her head. "Michelle doesn't know anything about it. Brandon took care of all their finances. Sam promised not to mention it to Michelle as long as the checks cleared the bank this time. I haven't had the heart to bring it up with her since he passed. Now doesn't feel like the appropriate time."

"She's bound to find out sooner or later," I said.

"Of course. Just not today and not from me." Jes's voice held a touch of sadness.

Holy cow. Should I tell her about the bounced check for the guest cottage? From what I could tell about Jes, I was sure she'd feel guilty about staying at Haybeck Farm if she knew, and I didn't want to be the person to add any more stress to her life. No, I agreed with her. It didn't feel like the right time for that particular conversation, either. I'd let Uncle Will and Aunt Ellen handle it however they saw fit.

I finished stapling the wire to the fencepost and moved over to staple the post Jes had her end of the fence stretched to.

"It's got to be hard not getting paid for two months. It's none of my business, but how are you getting by?"

"Actually, we're doing okay. Sam and Brandon were partners in the Hasty

Hogs business until recently, but Sam sold his portion to Brandon last spring. We'd agreed to continue to work through the summer, but this was supposed to be our last pig racing event. We've still got the money socked away from the sale. It'll make a nice down payment on a house with a little to spare. Plus, Sam starts his new job on the first of next month. I'm sure the paycheck mess will get straightened out soon."

"So, you don't think Hasty Hogs is on the verge of bankruptcy?"

"Oh gosh, no." Jes flapped a dismissive hand. "I did the books before Sam sold out, and the business wasn't going to make anyone rich soon, but there was always plenty of money to pay the bills and for us all to draw a paycheck during racing season. No, Brandon said it was some kind of a misunderstanding at the bank he was supposedly working to clear up. The problem has something to do with getting all the accounts switched over."

I thought back to Brandon's need to write a check for their stay in the guest cottage using the excuse his debit card was lost. I wasn't as optimistic as Jes that the money problems would be cleared up soon. Poor Michelle. Besides the sudden loss of her husband, I was suspicious she was about to find out she was dead broke on top of it.

"And Sam's been understanding about it?" Jes' husband didn't strike me as the type of person who'd let someone walk all over him without a fight.

Her big eyes widened, and she shook her head. "Oh, no. Sam's been all worked up over it. Ranting and raving. You witnessed some of it yourself. He's gotten in Brandon's face about the bounced checks more than once, but I'm super thankful the two of them worked it out before Brandon died. It would've been awful for him if they'd still been at each other's throats. They've been good friends for a long time, and sometimes friends get in spats. Sam would never have murdered Brandon, if that's what you're thinking."

Uh-huh. She'd seen right through me. "Oh gosh, no. I wasn't thinking that at all. Just curious." I kept my lying eyes focused on the task at hand as I sank the last staple in the fencepost, then stepped back to admire our work. "Well done, Jes. Thank you."

"You bet. I'm glad to be able to help out."

I eyed the fencing tools in my bucket. "I could've used the stretcher to get the wire tight, but I haven't quite got the knack of it down and have broken a few pieces of fence trying to use it. I'm glad you were here to help. It went way smoother and a whole lot faster than I expected."

"It did. We didn't even have to cut any wire or use the fencing sleeves." Jes grinned and looked up and down the fence line, her hands planted on her hips. "What's next? Are there any more sections needing fixed?"

"I don't think so, but let's go ahead and walk the fence to make sure. Do you have time?"

"All the time in the world."

I picked up the bucket full of fencing supplies. "Is there anyone you can think of who had it out for Brandon?" *Besides your angry husband?*

She shook her head. "No. Brandon wasn't always the nicest guy, but I can't think of anyone who hated him enough to kill him."

While Jes and I walked the fence line, I mulled over what she'd told me. What if Michelle wasn't as in the dark about the Hasty Hogs' finances as Jes thought? If Michelle had found out they were destitute, could it have made her furious enough to hire a hitman to off her husband? She had motive and access to the weapon, that was for sure. And like Tristan said, the spouse was always the most likely suspect. But why wouldn't she have found another way to kill him instead of making it such a public spectacle? And a gun exploding? In everything I'd read, a woman's weapon of choice was usually poison. On the other hand, she definitely would have had easy access to the gun, and a hitman wouldn't have any qualms about using it.

Something about the way Michelle let Jes think she'd been holed up in the guest cottage this whole time set my teeth on edge. Her relationships with her husband and whoever the mystery man was warranted a closer look.

Chapter Twenty

An hour later and two more sections of loose wire fence fixed, Jes and I parted ways. She skipped up the path to the guest cottage while I lugged the bucket to the barn to put my fencing supplies back where they belonged. Tidiness was another thing Uncle Will had taught me this summer. "Don't put it down. Put it away." Part of doing a good job was to clean up after myself once the work was finished, he'd lectured, and I'd taken the lesson to heart.

Tristan's Mini Cooper was in the driveway when I finished. I bounced up the porch steps and jerked open the front door but had barely taken a step inside when Uncle Will's voice boomed out of the library.

"Jeez'um crow, Jim. You've got a barrel of explaining to do. Who do you think you are, pulling this kind of garbage on your mother and me?"

A ball of dread ricocheted around in my belly. I glanced back outside. *Is Jim here?* I hadn't seen an extra car in the driveway, but maybe I hadn't paid close enough attention earlier. Tristan's father, Jim, was Uncle Will and Aunt Ellen's only son. He was an attorney who lived in Chicago and had convinced himself I was in Bobwhite Hollow for the sole purpose of scamming his parents out of their farm. I'd had the distinct displeasure of meeting him in person exactly one time and was not eager to repeat the experience. I closed my eyes, sucked in a sharp breath, and slowly released it before poking my head around the doorjamb leading into the farmhouse's front room that Aunt Ellen referred to as the library.

Perched on the edge of armchairs like birds waiting to fly away, Tristan and Aunt Ellen watched as Uncle Will paced around the room. He had the

117

phone receiver pressed to his ear with one hand while the other gripped a white piece of paper. He held the sheet of paper over his head and jabbed it into the air as punctuation while my normally laid-back great-uncle ranted and raved into the telephone. I pressed a hand to my heart and allowed my shoulders to relax, beyond glad to find Jim on the other end of the line as opposed to here in the house with us.

I took a seat on the couch and mouthed to Tristan, "What's going on?"

My cousin clamped his teeth together, pulled his lips back tight, and shook his head. Whatever it was, it couldn't be good. Aunt Ellen's blue eyes were laser-focused on Uncle Will. Her lips moved as if she was yelling along with him, and her pink hair bobbed in agreement with each thrust of the now-crumpled paper into the air. Every so often, we heard Jim's voice sputter through the line, but the second he started to speak, Uncle Will cut him off.

"No, you listen to me. You've completely disrespected your mother and me with this utter nonsense. Why are you doing this? Is this the type of person you've become in your grandiose office and fancy suits? A mean-spirited person who enjoys causing pain to others?"

Sputtering from Jim.

"This is not a negotiation, James. There is no way on God's green earth we're going to give you power over us so you can attempt to use your little bag of tricks on us. You have misread this entire situation so thoroughly it makes me worry about your mindset. Not mine. Not your mother's. Yours. We have done nothing your entire life except support and love you, and this is the way you repay us?"

Uncle Will paused.

"No, don't you dare hang up on me, son. I've called you to try to talk this out and so far, you haven't given me one solid reason why you've done what you've done. The last thing I want to do is to be estranged from my son, but I have to tell you, if you insist on moving forward with your wild accusations, I guaran-dang-tee you, that is exactly what will happen."

I'd never heard a person give someone such a thorough dressing down without using a single curse word. I was impressed. It was a skill that could come in handy and another lesson I was pleased to take from Uncle Will.

Jim Haybeck wasn't the cowering type, but with the tongue-lashing he was receiving from his father, I pictured the pompous attorney shrinking behind his desk until he reached the size of a twelve-year-old.

Note to self: Never get on the bad side of Uncle Will.

The call went on for what seemed like forever, but I still wasn't able to put my finger on what the catalyst was to cause Uncle Will to be so bent out of shape. Finally, Uncle Will slammed the phone back into its receiver. I opened my mouth to ask what was going on, but when he turned around, the glare pouring from his eyes was enough to make me reconsider.

Not so for Aunt Ellen. Worry scored every line of her face. "Well? What did that rotten kid of mine have to say for himself? Is he going to drop this guardianship nonsense, or do I have to fly to Chicago and give him a piece of my mind?"

Tristan and I stared at each other. "Guardianship nonsense?" we mouthed in unison.

Uncle Will dropped onto his desk chair and rubbed his temples. "Some rubbish about protecting us from ourselves, but I didn't let that weasel get a word in edgewise."

"Now, now, dear. Don't call my son a weasel." Aunt Ellen stood and rubbed Uncle Will's back with a slender hand. "Only I can call him names, the little cockroach!" She balled her hand into a fist and pounded it on top of the treacherous paper lying on the desk.

Aunt Ellen finally looked up and remembered Tristan and I were there. "Don't worry, kids. We're going to fight this. The dirty rat won't get away with it."

Tristan spoke up. "Fight what, Grandma? What exactly is Dad trying to pull on you?"

She handed my cousin the sheet of paper that had started all the commotion. I jumped up to read over Tristan's shoulder. It was an official document, signed, sealed, and notarized. In bold print at the top were the words "Petition for Guardianship of Estate." Tristan and I silently read through the document. It claimed Will and Ellen Haybeck were disabled persons and listed Jim Haybeck's full name and signature as the person requesting guardianship over their estate.

"Disabled? What the..." Tristan looked at his grandparents with a frown. "Neither one of you is disabled. I'm incredibly confused right now."

Aunt Ellen whipped the petition out of Tristan's hands. "You and me both, grandson. You and me both."

"Isn't it only considered an estate when you're...," I tapped my lips with a forefinger, not wanting to finish saying what I'd started. "Dead." The last word came out in a whisper.

Uncle Will chimed in. "Not necessarily. What my son is trying to do here is to have your aunt and me declared incompetent. If he succeeds, he'll pull all the strings with our finances and with the farm." Uncle Will ran a weathered hand over his face. "We would no longer be allowed to make those decisions ourselves."

"Why is he doing this? Does he want to sell the farm out from under you?" As soon as the words were out of my mouth, realization hit. "Oh. I get it. This is because of me."

Uncle Will's bushy eyebrows flew up to his hairline, and he pointed a weathered finger at me. "Bingo. Jim is trying to take our rights away so we aren't suckered in by your charm. In his delusional mind, before we can blink, you'll have convinced us to sign the family farm over to you."

My mouth flopped open like a goldfish. Or gold digger, according to Jim. "I would never."

Aunt Ellen pulled me into a hug. "We know you wouldn't, ladybug. This whole thing is far more about Jim and his need to control everything than it is about you."

Tristan had been silent for a few minutes, but now he jumped to his feet and clenched his fists. "Dad's always been a hard-nosed guy, but this is the worst stunt he's ever pulled. It's the last straw. I'm done with him."

Aunt Ellen swapped her hug from me to my cousin. "Don't go off half-cocked and do anything rash, sweetheart. No matter what, he's still your daddy. Misguided yes, but we'll get through this. As a family." She stretched out an arm and included me in the family. My heart warmed.

Tristan pulled out of the hug. "There's no way he'll ever be able to get a judge to sign off on this. You two are still the most competent people I've ever met. We can gather a thousand witnesses who'll say the same thing."

"I hope you're right, grandson." Uncle Will swiveled in his chair and picked the phone receiver back up. He punched in some numbers.

"Who are you calling?" Aunt Ellen inquired.

"Roger Fisk." Uncle Will replied matter-of-factly. "It's a cold day indeed when we have to hire an attorney to defend ourselves against our own flesh and blood."

By the time Uncle Will had hung up the phone after talking with the attorney, we all felt better. Roger Fisk had assured Uncle Will, even though Jim was an attorney himself, his petition didn't have a leg to stand on. "He'll be laughed out of court," were his exact words.

The petition would need to be filed here in Lupine County. The county seat and courthouse were in Stonehaven, only twelve miles down the road from Bobwhite Hollow, and Fisk agreed with Tristan. Getting as many people as possible to attest to Uncle Will and Aunt Ellen's competency would be a major part of his game plan. The attorney stated he had no doubt any evaluation by a professional would sway my aunt and uncle's way. With that weight off our shoulders, the heaviness left in the room came from the idea that Jim would try to have his parents declared incompetent to begin with.

In true Aunt Ellen fashion, she attempted to see the good in her only son. "Jim is just concerned about us. He's a good boy and has our best interests at heart. He needs time to get to know Callie and set his mind at ease." She rapped her knuckles on the table. "I'm going to give Jim a call tonight and get him to come home to spend some time with all of us." Not quite under her breath, she muttered, "The slimy snake."

Oh, please, no. I cringed inside but plastered on a smile, trying not to let my dislike for the man show on my face.

Chapter Twenty-One

"What's the plan for tonight?" Tristan asked after all the excitement surrounding the vile guardianship petition died down.

I fiddled with my braids. "Not much. I need to go back to the fairgrounds to check on the goats and give them their evening feed, but there's nothing else on my agenda."

"You're not planning on hanging around at the fair tonight?"

I yawned. "No. With late nights the last few days and then early morning yoga, I'm feeling a bit wiped out. Think I'll make it an early night."

"Let me know when you're ready. I'll go with you to help tend to the goats."

I glanced at the clock. "There's no time like the present."

Tristan gave me a cursory glance from top to bottom. "You're going to change, aren't you?"

The yoga outfit I wore was the same one I'd tugged on at the crack of dawn. Glancing down, I noticed a dribble of ice cream from the maple creemee stained my sea-green tank, and the black cropped leggings were more than a bit dirty from working on the fence. I frowned. "No, I hadn't planned on it. I'm going to feed the goats and come right back home. I'm exhausted. Why in the world does it matter to you what I'm wearing?"

Tristan raised his eyebrows and cocked out a hip. "Your appearance always matters, girlfriend. Always be prepared. You never know who you'll run into or what might come up." He flopped back into a chair, crossed his legs, and flicked a finger at me. "Stop arguing and go change. We're not in any rush and, believe me, you'll feel better after you clean up."

Ugh. If I didn't change my grubby clothes, Tristan would never let me hear the end of it, so I plodded up the stairs to my room as fast as a slug moving through syrup. Digging around in my closet, I rejected my favorite faded denim shorts and T-shirt, knowing Tristan would give me the side-eye if I went back downstairs wearing them. I slid several hangers across the closet rod until my hand landed on a summer dress. *Perfect.* Cute, casual, and, most important of all, comfortable. Plus, it didn't feel like work to slip it on. The swingy skirt of the light blue sundress hit me midthigh. I twirled to make the skirt flutter around my legs and was surprised by the rise of energy. Okay, so Tristan was right, but I didn't have any intention of telling him so. *The guy's already smug enough.* I pulled the elastics out of my hair, brushed it out, and redid my braids.

By the time I'd made it back downstairs, Tristan was standing at the foot of the stairs waiting for me while Aunt Ellen hovered over Uncle Will, who was stretched out on the couch. He held an ice pack wrapped in a kitchen towel to his forehead and Aunt Ellen was applying drops of lavender essential oil to his temples.

"Does he have a headache again?" I whispered to Tristan.

Before my cousin could answer, Uncle Will piped up. "Now, don't go getting your knickers in a twist. It's just a little headache. I'll be right as rain in a few minutes."

"Hush yourself," Aunt Ellen reprimanded him. She screwed the top back on the bottle of oil and joined Tristan and me in the hall outside the library door. She shook a finger at us. "This headache was caused by my son and his terrible petition. The dirty rat."

"Is there anything I can do to help?" I set my backpack down, ready to tackle any chores needing to be done at the farm so my uncle could rest.

Aunt Ellen shook her head, and Uncle Will protested from the other room. "No, no. All the farm animals are taken care of. Nothing to do around here right now. You go and see to your goats. We'll be fine."

"Okay, but promise you'll call if you need anything." Tristan held up his cell phone. "We can be home in ten minutes flat."

Back at the fairgrounds, my resolve to make it an early night faded with the seductive hubbub of an evening at the fair. Mixed in with the cheerful sounds from the carnival, music rang out from a country band playing on a small stage near the enclosure we used for goat yoga in the mornings. With an extra pep in my step, Tristan and I checked on the goats and had the evening feeding and watering done in record time.

"Are you getting together with Spencer later?"

Tristan shook his head. "Nah. They have a bunch of family visiting, so they're having a barbecue tonight. Lots of cousins and aunts and uncles he hasn't seen in a while."

I cocked my head. "You're not going? Sounds like the perfect opportunity to meet his family."

"No, it's not like that. Spencer and I are...well, it's just a summer fling."

With the condescending way Tristan had acted in Spencer's company the night before, I couldn't say I was sorry to hear their relationship wasn't too serious yet. I smiled and pointed to the stage. "Do you want to go listen to music for a while, then?"

"Sure. The band sounds pretty decent."

About three-quarters of the folding chairs set in rows on the grass in front of the stage were full. Tristan and I scooted onto empty seats halfway to the stage and next to the middle aisle. The band was playing a rousing rendition of Zac Brown's song "Chicken Fried." I couldn't help but move my feet and clap along to the music. Tristan side-eyed me but I noticed he bobbed his knee and swayed in his seat to the rhythm. The band segued into "Watermelon Crawl," and I was about to jump to my feet to show off my less-than-stellar dance moves when something cold and wet touched my elbow. I about jumped out of my skin before swiveling around to find a white furry face smiling at me.

"Bugsy!" I shrieked. "What are you doing here, you naughty goat?" I grabbed his collar before he could take off and got up to escort the escape goat back to his stall.

As soon as I began to move away from my chair, the music stopped abruptly. "Hey, lady. Where're you going? Sit down. The goat can stay, too. Apparently, he appreciates good music when he hears it."

Flames leapt into my cheeks as I spun around. Was the lead singer honestly heckling me? *I suppose that's one way to get the audience to stick around. Shame them into staying.* Nervous to be in the spotlight, I giggled. "The naughty goat needs to go back where he belongs. I'll be right back. I promise." Whirling around, I tripped over my own feet as I tried to hurry away.

"Oh, and where do you think you're going, sir? Joining the lovely lady? Can't say I blame you, she's a looker!"

The audience twittered, and I glanced behind me, expecting to see Tristan following. Instead, Levi was five steps behind me. I instantly bristled. *I can take care of this myself.* Unaware of my irritation, he grinned, held a hand up in greeting, and trotted to catch up with me and my wayward goat. Unlike me, Levi ignored the heckling coming from the stage. As soon as we were past the chairs set up for the audience, the band picked up the chords of "Watermelon Crawl" once again.

My face was still on fire as I picked up my pace and glanced at Levi, who jogged beside me. "You didn't have to leave on my account. I'm perfectly capable of making sure Bugsy gets back in his stall, you know. I don't need some self-proclaimed superhero to come to my rescue."

"I'm well aware of your competency." Levi held up his cell phone. "As it happens, the only one I'm trying to rescue is a rabbit who seems to be experiencing some heat distress I've been called to see if I can help. It's only coincidence it happened at the same time as Bugsy here made his appearance." Levi's emerald-green eyes smirked at me.

The heat on my face progressed from a smoldering fire to an inferno engulfing my body from head to toe. Without another word, I ran for the sheep and goat barn in an attempt to escape my mortification while Levi jogged toward the small animal barn.

"It was nice to see you anyway, Callie. The lead singer was right. You do look amazing tonight," he said as he took off in a sprint to save a struggling bunny.

Fine. So, Levi actually was a superhero, and I was nothing but an enormous jerk. An enormous, humiliated jerk.

Industrial-size fans were blowing inside the sheep and goat barn to keep the animals comfortable. The swirling air cooled my bare skin but did nothing to relieve the fiery waves of mortification rising from the pit of my belly. Why did my mouth insist on separating from my brain whenever Levi was around? Honestly, I wouldn't mind spending a little time with him, but with the way I behaved every time he was near, it was a miracle he even gave me the time of day. Most likely, the only reason he ever approached me was because, as the local veterinarian, Levi needed to keep a good relationship with the farmers, and my Uncle Will was one of them. Me too, if you counted my small herd of goats.

I blew my bangs out of my eyes and marched Bugsy over to his stall. Everything was exactly how Tristan and I'd left it ten minutes before. Except for the rebellious horned goat being on the wrong side of the fence. Good thing Chief Barnhart wasn't anywhere in sight, or he might've gotten a big kick out of presenting me with the ticket for 'Goat at Large' he'd threatened me with.

After tucking Bugsy back into his stall and giving him a firm talking to, I started for the music venue again. *But do I really want to be publicly humiliated again?* The clear answer was a giant "No thank you." Instead, I turned around and wandered the aisles inside the barn, loving the comforting scent of sweet-smelling hay mingling with the pungent mustiness rising from the animals. I wiggled my nose, waiting for the sneezes to start. *Huh.* Nothing. Maybe it wasn't a coincidence. I was beginning to think Althea deserved a huge round of applause for fixing my sniffles.

A white lamb with a black face shoved his nose between the slats and bleated at me as I walked past his stall. Laughing, I squatted down and patted his soft nose. "Hi, little buddy. You're a sweet guy, aren't you? Oh, yes, you are. What a good boy." The sign hanging above the stall indicated the lamb was a local boy's 4-H project and listed the lamb's name—Ichabod Snoozer. I laughed out loud.

Farther down the row, I found a couple of stalls filled with goats belonging to the president of the Bobwhite Hollow Dairy Goat Association. I leaned against the wooden stall and crossed my arms over the top, studying the sturdy, fawn brown Toggenburg does in the pen. Both does sported the distinctive white-striped faces particular to their breed. Two blue ribbons dangled from the bottom of the Alpine Toggs Dairy sign. I'd met the goat's owner, Emily, earlier in the summer when I'd signed up for a workshop the association put on to teach newbie goat owners like me how to trim their goat's hooves. Emily was about my age, and we'd gotten along great. We'd talked about meeting up for drinks, but so far, we hadn't made it happen. It'd be nice to have a female friend in Bobwhite Hollow, but nothing would come of our acquaintance if I didn't pursue the relationship.

"Hi, Callie. How are you? It's fun you have your herd here at the fair. I should join you for yoga one of these mornings." Emily slid up beside me with the last few bites of an elephant ear in her hand.

I grinned at her. "Yes, you should." I pointed at the blue ribbons. "Congratulations on your first-place wins. Your ladies look beautiful."

"Thanks. These are my sweetest does. I left the ornery ladies at home."

I laughed. "Good idea. If I was smart, I would've left Bugsy at the farm. That goat is going to be the death of me. All the young ones have behaved perfectly."

"Speaking of your goats, I've been meaning to ask if you've bred your does yet?"

Wide-eyed, I shook my head. "No. It hasn't even crossed my mind. Remember, I mentioned my plan was to teach goat yoga only this one season. I haven't solidified my plans yet, but most likely, I'll be selling my herd."

"I know that's what your original plan was, but you genuinely should think about breeding them anyway. A goat's gestation period is about five months, so if you breed in September and happen to still be here next spring for whatever reason, those kids would be big enough to be your new yoga babies. And even if you do end up selling the herd, a pregnant doe is always a good selling point."

None of what Emily was saying had been on my radar even the tiniest bit. As a goat farmer, even a temporary one, I sure had a lot left to learn. "Wow. Okay, yeah, I see your point. But I don't have the slightest idea how to go about making it happen." I chuckled at my own ineptness.

With the hand holding her elephant ear, Emily gestured to her goats. "My ladies are already bred. If you want, you can hire the services of my buck. He's done with my herd." When Emily turned back to look at me, one of her well-behaved does snatched the elephant ear out of her hand. "Hey! Miss Permelia, where are your manners?"

The goat chowed down the sweet treat, then belched to show her approval. Emily and I chortled.

I was still chewing on the idea of breeding the goats. "How does it work? Do I bring my does to your farm and we stand back and watch your buck do his thing? I honestly have no idea."

Emily laughed. "You're too funny. No, I would bring Rambo over and turn him out with your does. He'd live on your farm for a month. Plenty of time to service your ladies in his own sweet time. Without an audience."

I nodded, already thinking her suggestion wasn't a half-bad idea. "What's his stud fee?"

Emily quoted a price that sounded perfectly reasonable to me, but what did I know? I hadn't made it my business to stay apprised of the going rates for goat gigolos.

"Okay, let me think about it for a couple of days and talk to Uncle Will. I'll get back with you later in the week to let you know what we decide."

"Sounds good. Maybe I'll see you in the morning for yoga."

The music from the bandstand had stopped, so I decided it was safe to venture back outside. Tristan grabbed my arm as soon as I stepped out of the barn.

"Where've you been? I've been looking all over for you." A bead of sweat dripped off the end of his nose.

"You didn't look very far, then. I was in the barn talking to another goat lady. Why? What's wrong? Did Aunt Ellen call? Do we need to get home?"

"No, everything's fine at home, as far as I know." Tristan swiped an arm across his face. "A few minutes ago, I ran into the fair manager and his wife and kids. They had wristbands and were headed into the carnival."

"Sounds like a fun family night." I looked at Tristan with confusion. "What am I missing?"

"Well, Sherlock, since we know they're all at the carnival, I thought it would be a good time to do a little snooping around at Jay's farm. See if Pete's right about the illegal grow."

A slow grin spread across my face. "What are we waiting for, Watson?"

Chapter Twenty-Two

As Tristan drove, I rehashed the small piece of the argument I'd overheard between Jay and Brandon.

"Okay, so they were yelling at each other...Jay said whatever they were talking about was the last time, or Brandon wouldn't be racing his pigs at the fair, correct?" Tristan asked.

"Yep. Then Brandon come barreling out the door and nearly ran into me." I squeezed my eyes shut to envision the scene better. "He said Jay needed hi—wait! There's one more thing I'd forgotten. When Brandon flew out the door, he had a wad of money in his hand. He stuffed it into the pocket of his jeans. I assumed the money was his fee for racing the pigs at the fair, but that doesn't make sense."

"Why not?"

"Because the fair board paid me with a check. It stands to reason they would have paid Hasty Hogs the same way."

Tristan shrugged and made a face. "Not necessarily. He told Uncle Will he'd lost his wallet and cards, so it stands to reason he asked to be paid in cash since his bank account was compromised."

"True. Or maybe Brandon knew about Jay's marijuana grow and was blackmailing him," I said.

"And Jay got fed up and killed him," Tristan added.

We drove the rest of the way to Wilson Pond Road in silence.

Tristan drove, since his Mini Cooper would be easier to hide than Old Rusty. Slowing down at each mailbox along the paved road, I hung my head out the window to read the names on the boxes. About two miles down the road, we finally found the mailbox with the name Rowe painted on the side, but it turned out we didn't need it to find the farm. A carved wooden sign in the shape of an apple hung from a post, reading *Rowes of Apples Farm*. The driveway veered off to the right, but Tristan braked and backed his hunter-green car into a thick hedge of bushes on the opposite side of the road.

As soon as we got out of the car, I regretted my short sundress and sandals. I glared at Tristan. "If you hadn't of harassed me to change, I would've been dressed a whole lot better for this adventure."

"And Levi would've seen you looking like a hot mess. Again," he hissed back.

Touché.

Using the old stone walls lining the driveway for cover, we slunk up to the Rowe farm. Despite my big toe bleeding from jabbing it into a thorn while wearing open-toed sandals, I felt like we were walking into a postcard. A white, two-story farmhouse sporting gingerbread trim and a bright red tin roof sat at the head of the driveway, surrounded by white rail fencing and a white picket gate. The gate leading to the house and surrounding yard stood wide open. A tall, weathered barn reigned over the farm from halfway up a green grassy hill several hundred yards from the house. The rising luminous moon appeared to be balanced atop the weathervane on the peak of the barn roof. Behind the barn, the apple orchard the farm was named for stretched endlessly up the hill. Dusk was just beginning to fall, leaving pink and purple highlights streaking the sky.

"We should have enough time to look around if we hurry. Hopefully, they're planning to get their money's worth out of those carnival bracelets." I scrambled out of the ditch but stayed in the tree line to avoid any security cameras the Rowes may have had aimed at their driveway.

Tristan and I both froze in place when a large white goose barreled around the corner of the house and out through the open gate. The creature's wings flapped as he ran straight at us. He put up a huge racket, honking and hissing. The goose slowed down as he got close, but by the way he stretched out his neck and pumped his head up and down, an attack was imminent. With only three feet left between me and the oncoming bird, I screamed and ducked behind a tree.

Wrong move. I circled the tree. The goose circled with me, keeping up his aggressive hissing the whole way. The wind his beating wings created sent me moving faster and faster until I could almost grab his tail feathers. There was no time to look around for an escape route. Where in the world was Tristan? Why was the goose chasing me and not him?

"Tristan! Help me," I cried out as the goose's sharp beak and teeth made contact with the back of my bare leg. I screamed again and began to run blindly.

"Callie, stop running." Tristan's voice finally penetrated my frantic brain. "Turn around and face the goose. Stand still."

His advice sounded like pure nonsense to me, but so far, my evasive maneuvers had only gotten me chased and bitten. I stopped and swiveled around to face my attacker. The goose came to a screeching halt, his neck still extended. "What do I do now?" I asked my cousin out of the side of my mouth.

"Copy me." Tristan narrowed his eyes and extended his arm, index finger pointed straight at the goose. "Don't you dare come one step closer." Tristan's voice was firm and in control.

The goose eyed him but pulled his neck back slightly. I extended an arm and copied my cousin. It took about five minutes, but finally the goose had pulled his neck fully in and stood upright, appraising us.

Tristan clapped his hands as loud as he could and stomped his feet, yelling, "Go. Get out of here!"

The goose backed off, turned, and waddled back the way he'd come. As soon as he disappeared around the corner of the house, I slammed the gate closed on the fence surrounding the Rowes' home.

"Are you okay? Did he get you?" Tristan asked.

"Oh, yeah." I twisted my leg to look at the bite. A thin trail of blood ran down my leg where the goose's sharp teeth had penetrated the skin. A raspberry-red blood blister the size of a half-dollar had welled up on the side of the open wound, with blue bruising already covering an area the size of my fist. "He got me pretty darn good."

Tristan bent to take a closer look, then clicked his tongue. "The good news is, you're going to live. Aren't you glad I saved your life?"

"How did you know what to do? You're just as much a city kid as I am."

"Except you're forgetting I spent summers on Grandma and Grandpa's farm."

"Did they have a mean goose when you were a kid?"

"No, but Uncle Orville did."

"My grandfather? He did?"

"Yep, and he taught me what to do in case one went after me. He always said having a goose was better than having a watchdog."

I rubbed the bite on my leg. "I think he was right." Strange to think that even though I'd never met my grandfather, the advice he'd given to my cousin all those years ago saved my skin tonight. Well, most of it, anyway. I liked the idea of his wisdom reaching through time to help me. It was a thought I'd have to chew on later when I had more time. Right now, we had some serious snooping to do.

I glanced around the Rowe farm. "Where do we start? If Jay's growing cannabis, it's going to be hidden. Not out in the open where anyone who comes to pick apples would be able to see it."

"Yeah, I suppose it could even be an indoor grow." Tristan nodded. "That would make the most sense, actually, since the growing season this far north is fairly short."

I studied the house. "Maybe it's in the basement."

"I am not breaking into anyone's house." Tristan thrust out his chin and shook his head.

Since breaking and entering wasn't on my list of to-dos either, and a killer goose lived in the yard, I gave up the notion without a fight. Seeing how Rowes of Apples Farm was open to the public, we weren't necessarily trespassing by walking around the farm. Sure, the apple barn was closed as tight as a drum, and the owners were nowhere around. Semantics. "Let's walk the property and see what we find."

After a cursory exploration of the apple barn, which didn't reveal any unlocked doors, Tristan and I snooped around every outbuilding we could find. The doors on all the other buildings opened easily. No illegal pot was growing in the tool shed, the chicken coop, the well house, or the sugar shack. And thankfully, no more crazed and territorial geese interrupted our snooping. Before giving up entirely, we headed up to the orchard. Although beautiful, with ripe red apples ready to be picked, there was nothing unusual. No skunky scent of pot, no spiky-leafed plants growing under the trees. With acres and acres of apple trees, it would take us forever to explore the whole farm.

I leaned against a tree and pulled another sticker out of my toe. "There's no pot in the orchard. It would be ridiculous to think there would be. Like you said, his grow wouldn't be out in the open, anyway." I huffed. "I've got a feeling Pete's got this one all wrong. There's nothing underhanded going on here. It's getting dark, and my leg and toe hurts. Let's get out of here before we end up getting caught." When Tristan didn't answer right away, I pushed off the tree to look for him. "Tristan?"

"Over here," he called. Tristan stood at the far edge of the orchard, gazing down the backside of the hill into a grass-filled valley. "Look." He pointed.

I squinted in the direction he indicated, barely able to make out the shape of a long, squat building in the gathering darkness. "If you weren't looking for it, you'd never know that building was there."

Tristan and I glanced at each other then took off, running down the hill. I stubbed my toe on something hard and tumbled head over heels until I landed with a thud against the building, causing weird chitters and grunts to come from inside. Tristan grabbed my arm and pulled me to my feet. We stood silent, listening to the noises from inside the building.

"Something is in there," I hissed in Tristan's ear. "Something alive."

He threw his hands up. "Girl, this isn't fun anymore. I'm getting out of here."

I grabbed his arm and pulled him back as he attempted to twirl away. "We've gotten this far. We have to find out what it is."

Tristan huffed but agreed. Our movements had caused more eerie sounds to come from the building. I listened carefully, trying to determine what was making the sounds, but couldn't pinpoint anything. Once the noises died down, we tiptoed around the side of the building and found a door facing away from the orchard. Tristan glanced at me and nodded. I held up my phone and jerked the door open, shining my light into the long room.

"AAAAAH!" A scream boiled out of my mouth and my heart thumped like a drum as my flashlight beam picked up a gleaming black eye staring back at me. My phone landed with a thump at my feet as I stumbled backward, smashing into Tristan in my hurry to get out of there.

"Cock-a-doodle-doo!" A symphony of crows shattered the silence, and the stench of chicken poop filled my nose.

Tristan jumped a mile high and dashed behind a tree.

"Don't be a scaredy cat. It's only a shed full of chickens. But why would they keep their chickens so far away from the barnyard?" I felt stupid for screaming and acting like a lunatic. On my hands and knees, I patted the ground, searching for my cell phone. Once I located it, I swiped on the phone, relieved to find it wasn't any worse for the wear. I stood and shined the flashlight inside the building. Metal cages lined each side of the long building with a colorful rooster in residence in each cage.

Tristan crept up behind me, now the danger of a boogie monster had passed. His flashlight beam joined mine as it glanced off cage after cage of roosters. "Jay's not growing pot," he said. "He's raising fighting roosters."

My mouth gaped open. "Fighting roosters? That's a thing? Like little miniature boxers?" I asked, confused by the terminology.

Tristan shook his head. "No, more like *Hunger Games* fight to the death, mean as they come, roosters. Two go into the arena, but only one comes out."

"Seriously?" I slapped a trembling hand over my open mouth. "What a terrible sport. Why isn't Nancy picketing Jay instead of the pig races?"

"Because I'm sure she's not aware of this little operation of his." Tristan stared at me, but all I could see in the dark building were the whites of his eyes. "Cockfighting is a felony, and there's got to be at least a hundred birds in here. Jay's keeping this side business of his hidden from prying eyes for a reason."

"Except for our prying eyes. And possibly Brandon's." With a hand covering my nose and mouth against the smell, I focused on what I thought I knew. "So instead of Brandon blackmailing Jay about pot, it was most likely about these fighting roosters."

"If your blackmailing theory holds water," Tristan reminded me. "We have no idea if that's what was actually going on. I still think he probably asked to be paid in cash since he'd lost his bank cards."

"Then why would Jay tell him it was the last time? He'd obviously given him cash before."

"It could've been a million things, all of them completely innocent. Maybe Jay bought something from Brandon. Maybe Brandon borrowed money from Jay. There's also a huge possibility the money he put into his pocket had nothing at all to do with their argument. Brandon could've been pulling something else out of his pocket and had to take the money out to get to it." Tristan shrugged. "Contrary to what you believe, there's nothing nefarious about carrying a wad of money in your pocket."

I sighed. "You have a point. My imagination is probably running away with itself."

"Yep, except these roosters aren't a figment of either one of our imaginations."

I took another long look around inside the building, then turned to Tristan. "Should we let them go?" As soon as the words were out of my mouth, I had visions of a hundred mean fighting roosters chasing me through the dark orchard. Aunt Ellen's flock of chickens included one lone rooster, and that son-of-a-gun had chased me more times than I cared to admit. Already traumatized by my altercation with the goose, I shook my head. "Never mind. It's quite possibly the worst idea I've ever had."

Tristan snickered. "Yeah, I think a better plan would be to inform Chief Barnhart about what we found and let law enforcement deal with it."

"Sure, but we're definitely going to have some explaining to do about our little trespassing adventure."

Something rustled in the bushes near the side of the building, and the image of a shotgun pointed at us exploded into my head. I slammed the door shut. "Speaking of trespassing, we need to get out of here. Fast."

"Agreed. It's getting a little dark for my liking in this hollow. Darkness can hide a lot of evil."

I shivered. "Well, that's a terrifying thought."

At a gallop, Tristan and I retraced our steps up the hill and through the orchard. Sticking to the deepest shadows, we made a wide circle around the barn and house. We hunched over and slunk behind the old stone wall and had almost made it to the end of the driveway when headlights swept over our crouched heads.

The Rowe family SUV pulled into the driveway, windows rolled down; chatter and laughter about the fun they'd had at the fair could be heard. They were completely unaware Tristan and I crouched behind the stone fence. As soon as their taillights turned the bend in the driveway, we shot across the road like two bullets launched from a gun.

Chapter Twenty-Three

My sleep was erratic that night, punctuated with disturbing dreams involving attack geese the size of King Kong, roosters playing *Hunger Games*, and apples exploding like bombs while pigs raced around willy-nilly, and carnival music played a frantic, nightmarish soundtrack. When I woke, my heart was pounding like I'd taken a wild dash through the scariest house of horrors I could imagine. To top it off, the goose bite on my leg throbbed.

While I took deep, cleansing breaths to rid myself of the nightmare, I stared at the bedroom ceiling. Despite Tristan's voice of reason, I stood by my theory Brandon had found out about Jay raising fighting roosters and had been blackmailing him over it. Had Jay gotten tired of the shakedown and decided to get rid of the problem? With the threat of exposure looming over his head, Jay had a lot to lose. Not only would he lose his standing in the community and his job as fair manager, but quite possibly his family and farm. It was a strong motive for murder. My pulse raced, fluttering in the base of my throat. Since Tristan and I found out about the roosters, the two of us could be in mortal danger.

It was obvious I needed to talk to Chief Barnhart about our little adventure and take any knocks coming my way for trespassing on the Rowe farm. Would he buy my story about going in search of apples from the Rowes of Apples farmstand? I sighed. Not a chance. While Chief Barnhart put out a laid back, jolly persona, he was no bumbling country cop. The man was as sharp as a tack, and I had no doubt he'd see right through any tall tale I tried to sneak by him. I pinched the bridge of my nose. I'd call him right after my morning goat yoga session and come clean.

Dawn was lighting the sky as I showered, rubbed some antibiotic ointment on my wounds, and pulled on a clean set of yoga clothes. Water bottle and yoga mat in hand, I jumped into Old Rusty's driver's seat and pointed the truck toward the Lupine County Fairgrounds. I rolled across the beautiful, covered bridge, enjoying the clickety-clack of the truck's tires on the wooden planks and the sound of the river flowing under the bridge. Breathing in the clean country air, I focused my thoughts on planning the morning's session. By the time I pulled into the parking lot at the fairgrounds, my mind was calm and centered. It was time to tackle the day, no matter what came my way.

The police checkpoint was still set up at the gate. I scanned the officers' faces, but there was no sign of Chief Barnhart. *Thank goodness.* It was a relief not to have to face him quite yet.

An hour and a half later, the goats were fed and watered, stalls cleaned, and I had all nine goats in the round pen waiting for our students to arrive. Even Bugsy hadn't caused any grief this morning. It was shaping up to be a great day, despite the nagging worry about having to admit to trespassing. I pushed the thought away, plastered on a smile, and greeted my students as they arrived. The woman with her two young daughters in tow got there first. While she unrolled her mat, the girls bounced among the goats, giggling with sheer delight. I was pleased to see Nancy's face light up with a smile as she spotted the goats. Jes grinned and greeted me with one of her warm hugs. More familiar faces from the last few morning sessions filled the pen, with three new people joining us for the first time. If numbers continued to rise, the round pen wasn't going to be large enough to hold all of us.

The last to arrive was Althea, the woman who owned Isis Herbal Apothecary. As soon as I saw her, I broke out in a grin. "Althea, it's so nice to have you join us for yoga."

"How could I pass up this opportunity on such a beautiful morning?" She smiled back and raised her hands to the sun. "How are those troubling allergies? Any improvement?"

I took a deep breath of the fresh morning air. "Gone. Even the goat dander isn't bothering me. You're a miracle worker. I didn't notice until someone else pointed out how I hadn't sneezed during the session yesterday morning."

A wise smile lit up Althea's face. "Oh yes. Isn't that just the way it is? We immediately notice when something's wrong with our bodies, but we fail to notice when the problem is no longer troubling us."

Because of the newbies in the group, I started with an explanation of goat yoga in case they'd never experienced it before. I was finishing my spiel when Emily scooted through the gate. Delighted to see her, I shot her a smile. Seeing Emily reminded me I hadn't given another second of thought to hiring her buck to have his way with my does. I made a mental note to talk to Uncle Will about it this afternoon. After I turned myself in to Chief Barnhart, of course. Hopefully, we wouldn't have to have the conversation about breeding goats through the bars of my jail cell.

We were halfway through the session and in the downward dog pose when I swiveled my head to see how everyone was doing. My heart jumped into my throat when I caught sight of Jay standing outside the yoga pen, arms crossed and a scowl on his face. His eyes locked on mine and held for a moment before he uncrossed his lanky arms and strode away. The hair on the back of my neck stood on end. Was I imagining the evil eye Jay gave me because of my own guilty feelings? Did he know I'd found his shed full of fighting roosters? What if Tristan and I weren't as stealthy as we thought we'd been? Did we inadvertently get picked up on cameras as we snuck around the Rowe farm?

With yoga still in session, there was nothing I could do yet except take a deep breath and keep teaching. I directed the class to the child pose so I could lie on my face and think for a minute. As laughter rang out all around me from goats using the students' stretched-out backs to play king of the hill, my stomach was in knots. I vowed to never trespass again. Well, unless it was absolutely necessary, of course.

As soon as the session ended, I wrangled the goats back into the barn and took off in search of Chief Barnhart. This time, I was in luck. I spotted his western hat from two hundred yards away from the police checkpoint table. As I approached, the chief stepped out from under the shade awning and met me halfway.

"Good morning, Miss Haybeck." The chief's large frame towered over me. "Any more problems with that escape artist goat of yours?"

"Just one itty bitty little incident." I held my thumb and index finger close together to illustrate how insignificant it had been. "Nothing to worry about."

"Good to hear it. How's everything else going? Things good out at the farm?"

"Yep, yep. No worries there, either." Except Tristan's slimeball of a father and his guardianship petition, but that's not what I was here to talk about. "There is one thing I wanted to discuss with you, though, if you have time."

"I have a few free minutes. What is it?" He pushed his hat back and studied my face.

"Well..." I hemmed and hawed, trying to decide how to tattle on myself.

"Whatever you're worried about, Callie, just spit it out."

"It's about Brandon Ebersole's murder."

Chief Barnhart huffed. "I was afraid of that. Now, you seem like an intelligent young woman, so I'm sure you're not snooping around where you shouldn't be and getting yourself tangled up in my investigation." He crossed his arms tight against his chest, drew his eyebrows together, and stared me down.

"Um, uh..." I stammered again.

The chief's eyebrows shot up underneath the brim of his hat. "Callie? You're not, are you?"

"I'm just speculating. Mostly."

He continued to stare at me.

I swallowed hard, then started talking at rapid-fire speed with my hands flying through the air. "Well, maybe a little bit, but Pete asked me to help him look into things because you guys have him pegged as your primary suspect and there's no way Pete killed Brandon. He's way too nice of a man and why would he murder the guy anyway? There're loads of other people who had tons of motive to want Brandon dead and you probably don't even know about them and are focusing on Pete when you should be looking at

Jay and Sam and Michelle and even Nancy, not Pete, and were you aware the checks from Hasty Hogs all bou—"

"Hold it. Hold it," the chief interrupted my rambling. A muscle in his cheek twitched. "Stop right there. Who are you talking about? Nancy who? And why Jay?"

"So, you admit Pete's your number one suspect?"

"I wouldn't call him my number one suspect."

"But he is a suspect?"

"No comment." He eyed me. "I'll ask again. Nancy who?"

"Nancy Achilles. The lady who was picketing the pig races the other night."

Chief Barnhart scoffed. "Nancy is nowhere near a suspect. The woman is completely harmless."

Everyone kept saying the same thing, but was she really as harmless as they thought? I wasn't so sure. "Fine, but what about Jay? The afternoon before Brandon was killed, Jay called me to his office, and when I got there, the two of them were having an argument."

"The two of who? Brandon and Jay?"

"Yes." I nodded. "I have no idea what they were yelling at each other about, but Jay threatened to pull Brandon's fair contract, and Brandon said things wouldn't turn out well for Jay if he did."

The chief squinted at me and chewed on his lower lip. I finally had his attention. "Why haven't you told me about this sooner? What made you decide to bring it to my attention this morning?"

I glanced over my shoulder nervously, hoping Jay wasn't lurking nearby listening.

"Should we go sit in my rig to ensure we have some privacy?" Chief Barnhart asked, hitching up his pants.

"Yes, please."

Once we were settled, he asked me to start from the beginning and tell him exactly what Jay and Brandon had said to each other. I repeated my story and finished with Brandon stuffing the wad of money in the front pocket of his jeans.

Chief Barnhart jotted notes into a small notebook he'd retrieved from the center console of his police-issue brown Bronco. "Why were you there to begin with?"

"Bugsy escaped his pen the first afternoon we were here and chased Jay around the fairgrounds." I repeated the story for the chief, who was hooting with laughter by the time I finished.

"I'm sorry I missed it. That sure would've been a sight to see." The chief wiped tears of mirth out of his eyes. "Alright, back to our task. Jay wanted to talk to you about your devil of a goat, but when you got there, he was arguing with Brandon. What did you do once Brandon stormed off?"

"I stood on the porch and waited a minute before I went inside."

"Why?"

"To give Jay a chance to cool off. He was already angry with me and Bugsy. I didn't want whatever was going on between him and Brandon to color the conversation he was planning on having with me."

"And how did he react when you went inside?"

I blew out a breath, remembering. "Fine, honestly. The meeting went far better than what I'd expected. I thought he was going to pull my fair contract and send me and the goats home, but he said we weren't even close to his biggest problem at the moment."

"I suppose you have a theory for me about what you think Jay and Brandon were yelling about?" The chief sighed. "Let me hear it."

"Remember the money I saw Brandon stuffing into his pocket? I think he was blackmailing Jay."

This time, the chief's sigh sounded tired. "Blackmailing Jay over what, pray tell?"

I fidgeted in my seat. "Okay, well, you see, Tristan and I..." Shoot. I'd meant to leave Tristan out of it. Maybe the chief wouldn't pick up on the mention of his name. "I took a little drive out by the Rowe's farm last night."

"By the Rowe's farm, or to the Rowe's farm?" Chief Barnhart was no dummy.

"Okay, to the farm. But what matters is how I think he's doing something illegal out there, and I think Brandon knew about it."

"Jay? Doing something illegal? Like what exactly?" His voice held a hearty note of skepticism.

"Well...so...." I gestured wildly with my hands, trying to get the words out. "Back behind the apple orchard, down the hill a ways, there's this long building that's pretty much hidden from view. Brush has pretty much taken over the side facing the orchard. You can't really see it unless you're looking for it and—"

"And, let me guess, you were trespassing on the Rowe's land and just happened to stumble upon it."

"Something like that." I blinked and swallowed hard. "Anyway, there were weird noises coming from inside the building, so I opened the door to see what was going on and happened to find the chickens."

"The chickens?" Chief Barnhart scowled at me. "I hate to be the one to break the news to you, but there's absolutely nothing illegal about having a coop full of chickens. Most folks around these parts do, including your Aunt Ellen, if I remember right."

I held up my hands, palms out. "You're not understanding. These aren't any old chickens."

"Oh yeah. What kind of chickens are they then?" It was clear the chief thought he was talking to the village idiot. "Enlighten me."

"Fighting chickens."

"Fighting chick-." He reared back and looked at me, eyebrows raised. "Are you telling me Jay has a coop full of fighting roosters on his farm? What makes you think they're fighting roosters and not a pen full of regular old birds."

I nodded with vigor. "Because they're all roosters, and they're all in individual cages. There's not a hen in sight."

"How many roosters, do you think?" His tone had turned serious.

I shrugged. "Close to a hundred, would be my guess. There are rows and rows of them."

Chief Barnhart let out a slow whistle. "I'll be a son of a gun." He tapped his pen against the notebook and stared out of the windshield. "Anything else you need to share with me?"

"I'm guessing you already know Brandon was having money troubles, right? The Hasty Hogs crew paychecks bounced and so did the check Brandon wrote to Uncle Will for their stay at the farm."

"He tried to pay Will with a check, too? I hadn't realized that."

I nodded. "Yeah. Brandon said he'd lost his wallet with his debit card in it. Uncle Will took the check instead, but when he tried to deposit it at the bank, they told him it wasn't any good. So now you have people with actual motives, unlike Pete."

"Sam and Jes Nowak were already on my radar, Miss Haybeck." The chief scrubbed a hand down his face. "Thank you for bringing Jay to my attention. Please keep what we've talked about this morning to yourself, and remember this is an active investigation. You seem to forget murderers and criminals are dangerous people. The repercussions if they find out you're on to them aren't something to be taken lightly. I don't want to have to explain to your great-aunt and uncle why you've gone and gotten yourself killed. Understood?"

"Understood."

The chief and I parted ways. As I took a step toward freedom and the sheep and goat barn, I breathed a huge sigh of relief. He hadn't even brought up trespassing charges.

"Oh, and Callie?"

I spun back around.

"You and your cousin Tristan had better watch yourselves. Not only are you going to find yourself with a goat-at-large ticket, but the both of you are going to be cooling your heels in the city jail for trespassing if you're not careful."

"Yes, sir." I turned back around and clenched my fists in victory. The chief warned me to be careful. He hadn't said a word about stopping my investigation. I'd take that as a win.

Chapter Twenty-Four

Chief Barnhart asked me to keep our conversation to myself, but he couldn't mean keeping it from Pete and Tristan, could he? Pete's the one who'd asked me to help clear his name, after all, and Tristan was helping me explore the other suspects. Nah. The Chief had to know I'd tell those two. I shot a text to Tristan, asking him to meet me at Sweet Pete's Snow Cones as fast as he could get there.

As soon as the three of us were gathered at a table in front of the stand, Tristan and I told Pete he'd been wrong about Jay's illegal activity.

"What do you mean I'm wrong?" Pete flashed a toothy grin. "I never said the guy was growing wacky tobaccy. You two jumped to that conclusion on your own. If you recall, I only said apples weren't the only thing Jay was cultivating on his farm."

I replayed the conversation over in my head, then smacked my forehead. "You're right. I'm the one who assumed you meant pot."

"And you know what they say about assuming. It makes—"

Together, Tristan and I finished the sentence for Pete. "An ass out of you and me."

Pete threw his hands in the air. "There you have it." He jumped up. "Who's up for a snow cone?"

"Me!" Tristan and I both answered, though what I really wanted was one of those delicious maple creemees, but I kept my trap shut. Beggars can't be choosers.

When Pete came back with a round of snow cones, he handed one to each of us and, remaining standing, raised his in a toast. "To Callie and Tristan."

"What for?"

"Clearing my name, of course."

I spooned root beer-flavored ice into my mouth. "Not so fast there, slick. Chief Barnhart is taking over the Jay part of the investigation, but it doesn't mean you're in the clear."

Pete's smile fell. "Why not?"

"Just because we think Brandon was blackmailing Jay over the roosters, doesn't mean Jay killed him. We have no proof of that." I shoveled in another scoop of ice. "Our investigation is far from over."

Pete sat down with a dejected plunk. "Alright. What's next, then?"

I eyed him. "Have you talked to your UFO buddy yet?"

"I've called half a dozen times and left messages, but he hasn't gotten back to me yet." Pete sighed.

"Maybe he was abducted by aliens," Tristan offered in a deadpan voice.

Pete's eyes widened. "Holy moly! You could be right. I hadn't even considered the possibility of an abduction. Maybe I better call the team."

Tristan shot me a bugged-eye look. "I was kidding," he attempted to reassure Pete.

"Well, it's no joke, man." Pete crossed his arms over his chest and leaned back. "Those things do happen, whether you believe in aliens or not."

To quickly change the subject, I filled them in on my conversation with Jes the day before and how she was adamant her husband would not have killed his friend over the bounced paychecks. "I'm not so sure. It only stands to reason she would defend her husband. Nobody wants to believe their spouse has a killer dark side."

"Agreed," Tristan chimed in. "What's the guy's name again?"

"Sam."

"Right. I think we need to take a closer look at Sam. Any idea how to go about it?"

I chewed on my bottom lip while I contemplated.

"The answer's right here in front of you." Pete swung out an arm to indicate the fairgrounds. "The fair's a big attraction. Why not invite them to enjoy the attractions with you this evening? Then you can feel Sam out for yourself, instead of getting the information second hand from his wife."

"Good idea. They probably don't have much else on their plate today, given Chief Barnhart asked the Hasty Hogs crew to stick around. I'll send Jes a text and ask her."

After agreeing on our next plan of action, we sat and chatted for a bit.

"Have you guys noticed the carny wearing the top hat and tails? The British fellow?" Pete asked. "The guy's a hoot."

"Oh, you mean Keith," I answered. "I've gotten to know him a little bit, and he seems like a super nice guy. By the way, he'd take offense at you referring to him as a carny. Keith likes to be called a showman."

"Well, la-tee-da." Pete bobbled his head.

Tristan snorted out a laugh. "Callie and Keith are great friends. She thinks he's the world's greatest scholar and only works for the carnival because he enjoys the travel and people he meets."

"Why is it so hard to believe someone would choose to travel with the carnival?" I lightly slapped my cousin's arm. "Knock off your attitude. You're so judgmental."

"No, he's mental."

I turned to Pete, ignoring Tristan's rude comment. "Did you know Keith's writing a book about his life with the carnival? It's going to be fascinating, and I can't wait to read it."

But Pete was frowning and not paying attention to me.

"What is it?" I asked. "What are you thinking?"

He pinched the skin between his eyebrows. "Hang on. I'm trying to remember something." After a minute, he snapped his fingers. "Got it!"

"Got what?"

"Listen to this. Remember the first afternoon of the fair when you got your snow cone but then had to take off to chase your goat?"

I nodded. "How could I forget? I ended up wearing blue snow cone syrup down the front of my shirt."

"You looked like a tie-dye session gone bad." Pete hooted with laughter.

"What about that afternoon? Did something else happen?" Tristan prodded, trying to keep the conversation on track.

"Well, so Brandon had been in line a couple people behind Callie, if I'm remembering right. I was taking his order when your buddy Keith walked up. I'd just handed Brandon his cone, and when he turned to leave, I remember he stopped and stared at the carny. Brandon said something like, 'Larry, is that you?'"

"To Keith? He asked Keith if he was someone named Larry?"

Pete nodded. "Yep, that's the scoop of my story. The color drained out of the carny's face like all the blood had been sucked out of him. He stammered around a second before he hightailed it out of here."

I frowned. "Did Keith answer Brandon's question?"

"Yeah, he said, 'Sorry, mate. You've got me confused with someone else,'" Pete replied in his best British Accent. "He took off like a shot. Guess he changed his mind about getting a snow cone."

"Weird. What did Brandon do?"

"Nothing. He just stared after the guy. I asked him if he knew the carny, but Brandon said he didn't. He thought he'd recognized him for a second but must've been wrong. I didn't give it another thought until now."

"Probably because there's nothing to think about. Sounds like a simple case of mistaken identity. I can't tell you how many times since I've moved to Bobwhite Hollow I've thought I've seen someone from Seattle only to realize it's not them. Sometimes I think it's wishful thinking more than anything, wanting to see someone from home."

"Maybe so, but I think we need to find out if he is who he says he is," Tristan said.

Pete agreed, so we decided to add Keith to our growing list of suspects. The strange interaction between him and Brandon was worth keeping in mind.

I shot Jes a text, asking if she and Sam would like to meet up with Tristan and me at the fair later.

She replied right away.

We would LOVE to!!!!!

The words were followed by three heart emojis in shades of purple, green, and yellow. The overabundance of exclamation marks made me chuckle.

Jes texted with the same level of excited energy she spoke with. I grinned and sent off a quick reply.

With our evening plans settled, Tristan ran off to spend the afternoon with Spencer, and I drove back to the farm for a day of chores.

I'd never gardened before coming to Bobwhite Hollow but had quickly learned digging in the dirt was a satisfying, and cheap, form of therapy. Out in the garden by myself, listening to the birds singing and feeling the breeze in my hair did wonders for bringing clarity to my chaotic mind.

The most prolific thing in the garden these days were the weeds. With a hoe, a hand trowel, a spade, and a wheelbarrow for company, I sank to my knees and started hacking away at the pesky intruders. Between Aunt Ellen and me, we'd done a decent job of keeping up on the weeding this summer, but it still amazed me how thistles and crabgrass could spring up overnight. It was nearing the end of the growing season, and even the creeping bittercress knew its days were numbered. They went to seed lickety-split, so it was imperative to dig them out before their offspring took a stronghold or we'd have a huge mess on our hands next spring. Or Aunt Ellen would, since I probably wouldn't be around to help her out.

As soon as the thought of leaving New Hampshire entered my mind, my brain seized on the thought, pushing all the other noise aside. Was teaching yoga on the beach still what I wanted to do, or was I clinging to an old dream that no longer fit my narrative? Honestly, I wasn't sure anymore. The idea of building a new life on a tropical island didn't hold the same appeal it had in the past. The relationships I'd formed with Tristan, Aunt Ellen, and Uncle Will meant the world to me, and I loved every minute I spent at Haybeck Farm with them. As soon as I'd arrived in Northern New Hampshire, I'd felt as if I'd come home to a place I'd never been before. The thought of it all coming to an end made my chest feel tight.

And what about my goats? How could I possibly run off and leave Bugsy behind? Maybe Uncle Will would want to keep him, but he was kind of a troublemaker. Even in the off chance I could talk Uncle Will into keeping Bugsy, I'd have to sell the rest of my herd. What would become of them?

CHAPTER TWENTY-FOUR

Tears welled in my eyes as I hacked at a stubborn patch of crabgrass.

I was wrapped up in my angsty thoughts when someone slapped a hat onto my head. Startled, I tipped over from the squatting position I'd been locked into for the last few minutes. Sprawling in the dirt, I looked up at Uncle Will towering over me. The bright sun outlined his head like a halo.

The sight of me spilled in the dirt and looking like a startled deer sent Uncle Will braying. "Sorry to give you a fright, Callie-Kat. I spied you out here and thought you might be in need of a sun hat."

"You were absolutely right. Thank you." I was grateful for the shade the floppy straw hat provided to my burning face and thankful for a chance to tap into my great-uncle's wisdom. "Do you have a minute?"

"Sure do. What's on your mind?"

Brushing dirt off my elbows, I pulled myself into a kneeling position and looked up at him. "The goats. I was talking with Emily from the Bobwhite Hollow Dairy Goat Association earlier, and she mentioned I should be thinking about breeding the mama goats. She said I could hire her buck to do the job, and we should do it soon so the kids would be ready for spring yoga. What do you think?"

Uncle Will pushed his hat back and scratched his head while he studied me. "Are you thinking about staying in Bobwhite Hollow?"

I focused on jerking another weed out of the ground. "Maybe." My staying around hadn't been part of the deal when Uncle Will and Aunt Ellen had agreed to let me run goat yoga from the farm for a season. What if I wasn't welcome to stay any longer?

"Maybe? This is the first I've heard you mention you might want to stick around."

I stood and brushed dirt off my derriere. "Well, I haven't settled on anything for sure, and if I do decide to stay, I'll find a place to rent in town, so I'll be out of your hair. Would I still be able to keep the goats here and teach yoga from the farm, though?" My face fell. "I guess I should've thought this through better before asking you."

Uncle Will chuckled. "Slow down. Of course, you can stay if you want to. Nobody else can make the decision for you. We'd love to have you, and there's no need to rent anything. Your place is right here with me and your Aunt Ellen."

"I haven't decided for sure yet, but thank you for being so…you." I threw my arms around him and squeezed his neck.

"Now, about those goats of yours. From my viewpoint, getting them bred is the only way to go. Like Emily told you, if you choose to stick around, you'll have the baby goats you need in the spring to continue your business. If you decide to sail on out of here, you'll get a better price when you sell the pregnant does. It's duck soup, in my opinion."

"Duck soup?"

"Yep. An easy decision. A no-brainer."

"That's a new one for me. I like it." I laughed. "Anyway, what you said lines up with everything Emily said, too. I appreciate your input more than I can say. Thank you."

Uncle Will patted me on the shoulder. "You're welcome. Sounds like you have a bit to chew on. Don't stay out here too long. Looks like you already sunburnt your nose. Those weeds aren't going anywhere." Walking away between a row of cucumber plants, Uncle Will left me with another tidbit. "While you're mulling over your options, try to remember the grass isn't always greener in the other pasture. Sometimes the other pasture is filled with weeds."

He was right, and from where I stood, the grass was pretty darn green and tasty. Duck soup. Before I got back to work, I placed a call to Emily and reserved her buck for the month of September.

Chapter Twenty-Five

Three hours later, freshened up from a shower and a change of clothes, Tristan and I drove separately to the fairgrounds. Since Sam and Jes were staying at Haybeck Farm, I extended an offer for the Nowaks to jump in Old Rusty with me. They'd mentioned they didn't want to stay out super late, and neither did I. Tristan had plans with Spencer later, and I had plans with my pillow.

Sam, Jes, and I met up with Tristan at my goat stalls, and the four of us spent the next hour chatting and wandering through the various animal barns. The evening's stage entertainment was a magic show we all thought sounded like fun, so we grabbed giant corndogs and climbed into the bleachers to enjoy the show.

"This is boring," Sam declared after half an hour of watching the magician fumble with a deck of cards. "How about a ride on the hammer instead?" He grinned at Jes and wiggled his eyebrows.

She shivered. "No way. You know I hate those scary rides."

"You and me both," I chimed in.

"Not me," Tristan said. "I'll go with you, Sam, since the girls are a couple of chickens."

"You're on," Sam answered, before he and Tristan ganged up on us by flapping their arms and clucking.

I smacked Tristan on the arm, but Jes simply ignored her husband.

She rolled her eyes and shrugged. "I've gotten used to his bad behavior after eight years of marriage."

Sam clucked louder.

"Tell you what. Let's all go together on the giant Ferris wheel first. It's my favorite ride." Jes clapped her hands in excitement. "Then you guys can go get your adrenaline fix on whatever scary rides you want without dragging Callie and me with you."

"Sounds like a great plan to me." I stood and slung my backpack across my shoulders.

Stars twinkled in the dark sky as the four of us took our place in the line at the giant wheel. The crowd wasn't nearly as dense as it had been the first few nights of the carnival, so we made it to the front of the line a lot faster than the previous times I'd ridden.

"Hey, Keith. How's it going tonight?" I greeted the showman. The story Pete had told Tristan and me earlier ran through my head. Was Keith who he said he was? Or some guy named Larry instead?

"Good evening, Callie," he greeted me with a nod to Tristan. "I'm glad to see you have a full carriage of friends tonight." Keith glanced between the four of us, his gaze stopping on Sam. He read the logo on Sam's T-shirt aloud, then made a clucking sound with his tongue. "Hasty Hogs Racing Pigs Crew. What happened to that poor man the other night is tragic indeed. What a terrible freak accident. Are you honestly a part of the crew?"

Sam hooked a thumb at Jes. "Both my wife and I are. Or were. Hasty Hogs won't be making a comeback."

"Oh. Michelle isn't going to keep the pig racing business going?" Brandon had only died a few days ago. It seemed like the decision to disband the business had been made awfully fast.

Sam shook his head. "No, she doesn't have any interest in running the business by herself."

"I'm sorry to hear the pig races won't continue," Keith chimed in. "And I'm sorry for your loss, mate. Were you and the owner close?"

"There was a time we were as close as brothers." Sam stared at his shoes, but I caught the gleam of a tear before he dropped his head.

"I know exactly what you mean," Keith said, his own eyes glistening. "It's hard to lose a mate, no matter what causes the split."

Empathy was another point in favor of the British carnival worker. Even

Tristan would have to agree.

Sam's comment about there being a time he and Brandon had been as close as brothers gave me pause. A time, but not anymore? I guess money issues could ruin a friendship as fast as they could ruin anything else. Still, I'd like some more information. I noodled around various ways to ask Sam more without coming off as callous and nosy. Keith opened the gondola doors as the journey for the current riders came to an end. It was our turn to load up for our trip to the top of the world, and I still hadn't come up with anything subtle enough.

"Enjoy the ride." Keith waved us off.

Our group was silent as the showman loaded the other gondolas with riders. Once we were perched on the top of the wheel with a spectacular view, Sam piped up. "Sorry about my mood. It's been a rough week."

"You're fine. Seriously, no worries at all. I can't even imagine how hard all of this must be on both of you." I took Jes in with my glance. "If you need to talk about anything, Tristan and I are happy to listen." I glanced at Tristan, who nodded his agreement.

Sam and Jes stared out separate sides of our gondola for a moment before Jes broke the silence. "Like Sam said, it's been an incredibly rough week. We're both kind of wrecked. We never thought our last fair with Hasty Hogs would also be the last time we saw Brandon alive. It's been so crazy, and then the problem with the paychecks bounc—"

"Jes!" Sam admonished her. "You don't need to be spouting off our business."

"Seriously? Callie already knows." Jes stared at her husband. "How could she not, with you yelling about it the other morning? The whole world heard you."

Sam's mouth gaped open, and red flooded his cheeks. "Sorry. I didn't realize anyone heard me. I was upset and not thinking clearly."

Jes tapped him lightly on the leg with the palm of her hand. "You have a loud voice. I keep telling you it totally carries."

Sam tore his gaze away from the scenery. "So, yeah, like Jes said, it's been rough. And with Brandon's death, we'll never see the money he owed us."

155

He looked at Jes and a tear stole down his face. "I can't tell you how sorry I am, babe. I never meant to put us in this position. I have no idea what we're going to do."

Jes stared at her husband. "What are you talking about? The money issues aren't your fault. Brandon's the one who put us in this position, not you." Jes reached for Sam's hand. "We're fine, anyway. Sure, it would've been nice to have our paychecks for the last two months, but we've still got the money from selling your half of Hasty Hogs socked away. It's not like we're destitute."

Anguish poured out of Sam's eyes as he shook his head. "That's what I'm trying to tell you, Jes. We don't have the money anymore."

"We don't? Sure we do. There's plenty of money in our savings account for a down payment, and with your new job, we'll be set. It's not a big deal."

"Jes, I'm trying to tell you we don't have it. The money's gone." Sam took both of her hands in his and turned to fully face her.

Tristan and I side-eyed each other without saying a word. It felt like we were imposing ourselves on an intensely private moment. I looked over the side of the gondola, but we were about one hundred and fifty feet in the air. There was no way to escape the awkward situation we were in.

Unblinking, Jes stared at her husband. "I don't understand."

"Brandon got himself in a pickle and I loaned him back most of the money from the sale. The rest we've had to use just to get by for the last several months. We don't have anything left."

Jes' eyes flared as big as saucers. "What do you mean? What kind of a pickle, and how do I not know about this? I can't believe you would hide something so important from me. We tell each other everything." She jerked her hands away from Sam's and cradled them around her face. "How could you have done this to us? To our family?"

"Brandon had a gambling problem. He was in deep with some nasty loan sharks. I lent him the money so they wouldn't hurt him. He promised he'd pay me back by the end of the summer, before we were ready to put a down payment on a house. I'd planned to tell you all about it after the money was safely back in the account."

Loan sharks? Are we in a mobster movie?

"I would've still been mad." Jes swiped at angry tears rolling down her cheeks.

Sam slammed a fist into the palm of his other hand. "If Brandon wasn't dead, I'd kill him myself." Rage played across Sam's face as our ride ground to a halt.

As soon as we were off the Ferris wheel and away from the crowd, Jes placed a tentative hand on my arm. "Callie? Would it be okay if you took us back to the farm? I'm sorry to cut your evening short, but I'm not in much of a festive mood anymore."

I nodded. "Of course. I understand completely." We said our goodbyes to Tristan and trudged wordlessly to the truck.

Tense and uncomfortable didn't even begin to describe the ride back to Haybeck Farm. Sam and Jes didn't utter a single word to each other for two-thirds of the drive. Thankfully, it was only five miles back to the farm. At about mile three, I couldn't hold my questions in any longer.

"Brandon had a gambling problem? What kind of gambling was he into?" I blurted into the silence.

Sam jerked the ballcap off his head and slapped it against his knees. "Slot machines, horses, poker, greyhounds, boxing, you name it. If he could lay money down on something with even a remote possibility of winning a few bucks, he did it."

"Do you think the loan sharks you mentioned are the people who killed him?"

Sam shook his head. "No, we paid them in full just a few days ago."

"And you're positive Brandon didn't already run up another tab with them?" Jes asked.

"He promised he wouldn't," Sam answered. "I believed him."

"I don't," Jes said.

Another scenario skidded into my head. "Did Brandon ever mention betting on cockfights to you?"

"Oh yeah. He went all the time."

Jes gasped. "But aren't they illegal?"

Sam scoffed. "Illegal doesn't stop gamblers. In fact, it makes it even more exciting for them. The whole lifestyle is an addiction. Brandon thrived on the idea of getting away with something."

"Did you ever go to any of the cockfights with him?" I asked.

Jes looked horrified while we waited for her husband's answer.

Sam shook his head. "Heck no. I don't want anything to do with that. Fighting roosters is barbaric. Not my cup of tea."

Jes sighed in relief. "Well, it's a dang good thing, too. It would've been the last straw."

"Did he talk to you about them, though?" I asked. "Did Brandon ever mention seeing anyone in particular at one of those fights?"

Sam tapped his ballcap against his leg as he thought. "Yeah, he did only a few days ago. Didn't tell me who it was, but I remember he was almost, I don't know, gleeful about whatever he'd found out. He said something about the information he had was going to keep him flush for a while."

"What do you think he meant?"

"Honestly, I'm at a loss. I guess I assumed he had insider information about which roosters to bet on." Sam shrugged. "Not sure how a person goes about determining which rooster is going to win. It's a fight to the death, and anything goes."

I drummed my fingers on the steering wheel. "Could Brandon have meant he knew someone who was involved with, say, raising the fighting roosters? Maybe it was going to be lucrative for him because whoever the person was would have to pay him to keep his mouth shut?"

Jes gaped at me. "Like blackmailing someone, you mean?"

I drummed my fingers on the steering wheel. "Possibly. I'm just tossing a theory out there."

"Damn." Sam whistled. "Blackmail hadn't occurred to me, but I wouldn't put it past Brandon. He was out of control."

Jes pivoted her shoulders to face her husband. "If you thought he was out of control, why in the world did you agree to lend him our money?" she demanded.

Sam pulled his neck deep into his shoulders and answered in a quiet voice.

"Because he was my buddy, and you don't give up on your buddies."

I pulled into the driveway at Haybeck Farm and cut the engine. Sam and Jes got out and headed for the guest cottage while I sat in the truck, alone in the dark. Our conversation had given me a lot to think about. With Sam's information bouncing around in my head, I was ninety percent convinced Brandon had stumbled upon Jay's involvement with illegal cockfighting and had been blackmailing him. I'd update Chief Barnhart with the information I'd learned in the morning.

As for the theory of Sam Nowak as a suspect in Brandon's death, I wasn't completely convinced. His comment about not giving up on your friends sounded genuine. And why would he kill Brandon and then have to admit to Jes he'd given the guy all of their money? From what I'd witnessed, I was pretty sure Sam would've done anything to keep that information from his wife. There was the comment he'd made about killing Brandon himself if he wasn't already dead, but people said stupid stuff all the time. On the other hand, it wasn't such a long shot to think Sam could've confronted Brandon about the money and snapped when Brandon still didn't pay him back. There were still too many unanswered questions. I couldn't cross Sam off my list of murder suspects quite yet, even though my gut was screaming Jay.

Chapter Twenty-Six

I t was only a quarter to ten when I slipped through the front door of the farmhouse. Aunt Ellen and Uncle Will had been lifelong farmers—up before dawn and hitting the hay early—so they normally went to bed around nine. I'd toed off my sandals and padded barefoot toward the kitchen when a soft rapping at the front door stopped me in my tracks. Did Jes leave something in the truck? I hurried to open the door before she had a chance to knock a second time.

Pulling open the door as quietly as possible, I was startled to find Michelle Ebersole standing on the front porch instead of Jes. The grieving widow's dark curly hair was pulled back in a ponytail, and purple shadows rimmed her dark eyes. Her skin had the sallow complexion of someone who'd been ill. Was her ragged appearance caused by grief, or from the guilt of having her husband killed? The image of her slipping the mysterious man a handful of cash at the fair the other night ran through my mind.

"Hi, Michelle. Is there something wrong at the cottage? What can I help you with?"

She glanced down at her feet and shook her head. "No, everything's fine with the cottage. It would be absolutely perfect if it wasn't for everything else." She sighed. "I realize it's late, and I'm sorry to bother you, but I noticed the lights still on and was hoping to be able to visit with you or your grandparents."

"Will and Ellen are my great-uncle and great-aunt," I corrected her. "Not that it matters." I stepped out onto the porch and pulled the door closed behind me. I wasn't about to invite a possible murderess into the farmhouse.

160

Gesturing to the twin white wicker rocking chairs, I offered her a seat. "They've gone to bed, so I hope I'll do as a substitute. Do you mind if we sit out here?"

"Not at all. It's a beautiful night." She moved toward the chairs. "And yes, you'll do fine."

A three-quarter moon lit up the night while wispy clouds drifted across the midnight blue sky. Crickets chirped out their nighttime songs with frogs providing the musical backup.

As soon as I sat down, I realized my hands were empty and my feet were bare. *Fudge.* I should've put my sandals back on and grabbed something to use as a weapon if need be. My only saving grace was knowing my great aunt and uncle slept with their bedroom window open. They'd hear me and come to my rescue if I yelled loud enough.

"Was there something I can help you with?" I asked.

"It's more of something I can help *you* with." Michelle launched into the reason for her evening visit. "When Sam and Jes came home, they probably thought I was asleep, but I've hardly slept since Brandon..." she gulped and tried again. "Since Brandon died. They were arguing, quietly, in their room, but not as quiet as they thought. I'm convinced Sam's deep voice could penetrate thick stone walls."

"I've noticed that phenomenon myself," I added.

"Anyway, I overheard them talking about Hasty Hogs and how they haven't been paid for either July or August." She glanced at me, tears threatening to spill out of her eyes.

I touched her arm. "Take your time."

Michelle swallowed hard. "Hasty Hogs was Brandon's business. He took care of all the financial details. I honestly thought it was doing fine. I had no idea there was a problem until tonight." She grimaced. "I mean, Brandon bought Sam's half of the business in June. How could things have gone wrong so fast?"

Understanding the question was hypothetical and she didn't expect an answer from me, I waited for her to continue. If Michelle was truly in the dark about Hasty Hog's money issues, was it possible she was in the dark about Brandon's gambling addiction? Or how he'd "borrowed" all of the Nowaks' savings?

Finally, Michelle spoke again. "My reason for knocking on your door tonight was about those bounced paychecks. While listening to Sam and Jes, it occurred to me Brandon had given your grandfa—I mean great-uncle—a check for our stay here at Haybeck Farm. If the Nowaks' paychecks weren't any good, then it stands to reason neither was the check Brandon wrote for the cottage. I mean to make it right with them as quickly as possible. You have all been so nice. Ellen even brings over breakfast every morning."

I smiled, thinking of my nurturing great-aunt. "Aunt Ellen's a wonderful cook and loves to feed people. It's her way of caring for the world. The woman has a heart of gold."

Michelle tentatively asked, "Do you know anything about the check Brandon gave your great-uncle? Was it bad?"

I looked into her eyes and nodded. "But you don't need to worry about it. Uncle Will and Aunt Ellen were going to reimburse the money anyway, after what happened to Brandon."

"There's no way we're going to sponge off of you guys." Michelle frowned. "Brandon's death had nothing to do with any of you or Haybeck Farm. Why would they not want payment? I don't understand."

"Because Uncle Will and Aunt Ellen are the nicest people in the world. They care about everyone and always want to do their part to make things easier for others."

"Well, I'm going to make it right anyway. I have money set aside for emergencies, and I'll get enough transferred tomorrow to pay everybody. My mom was right when she said women should always keep a stash of money secret from the men in their lives. She called it a get-away fund to use in case things went sideways."

"Interesting. And great advice."

Good thing Michelle's emergency funds had been a secret from her husband, or the money would have been long gone. Though it was entirely plausible Michelle's denial of knowing anything about the money issues was all an act. Would she have killed her husband if she found out he'd run the business into the ground? Maybe she'd finally snapped and paid the stranger I'd seen her with at the fair to knock her husband off. I pursed my lips. How do you find and hire a hitman, anyway? Dial 1-8-KILLMYHUSBAND? It's not like they advertised in the local newspaper. But the hitman theory didn't explain the hug I'd seen the two of them share later. An affair?

"Callie? Are you listening?" Michelle touched my arm and I startled.

"Oh, gosh. It's been a long day. Sorry. What were you saying?"

"I was wondering how I should pay the cottage rental. I don't carry the debit card for that account with me, but I can set up a direct transfer or go to the bank for cash. Which one do you think your aunt and uncle would prefer?"

I shook my head. "I'm sure Will and Ellen will appreciate your concern, but I can tell you without a shadow of doubt, they won't accept it. No, use the money toward what is owed to the Nowaks, please."

Michelle cupped her face in her hands and sobbed. Her slim shoulders shook as she wept. "I feel so horrible about all of this." Her voice was muffled behind her hands.

After a few minutes, she wiped the tears off her face and took a deep breath. "I'm so sorry. I didn't mean to come over here and cry on your shoulder."

"There's nothing to apologize for. You need to cry, and I'm glad to sit here with you so you can."

She seemed to truly be devastated. I wished there was more I could do, but sometimes the best thing a person could do was to keep their mouth shut and let the other person grieve.

"Thank you." Michelle hiccupped. "This is going to sound terrible, but if Brandon were still alive, I'd kill him myself."

There it was again, another person close to Brandon threatening his life. I made an agreeable murmuring sound.

"I'm sure the money went to fund Brandon's secret life." Michelle swiped angry tears from her cheeks.

Apparently, she was aware of his gambling habit. Feigning ignorance, I asked, "Secret life?"

Michelle nodded sadly. "Yeah, more and more often, Brandon was disappearing for days at a time. I'm sure he was having an affair. An expensive one, it seems."

Okay, so maybe she didn't know about his gambling. "And you had no idea where he was when he'd disappear? He didn't tell you anything?"

"Nothing that made sense, no. He'd always say he was going on business trips to nail down more racing venues." She threw her hands in the air. "Hasty Hogs is racing pigs. Our venues are fairs and other rural events. That's it, end of story. I never once saw any of his business trips come to fruition with racing venues other than the ones where we were already booked to perform. Sometimes Brandon would come home full of excitement with elaborate gifts for me, things I never wanted. Other times, he'd be almost despondent. Whispering into the phone and acting half-crazed until the next time he disappeared on one of his so-called business trips." She made air quotes around the words business trips as she said them. "Believe me, he was one hundred percent having an affair."

"Did you ever confront him about it?" I danced around the question I really wanted to ask. Michelle wouldn't have been the first wife to have a wayward husband killed.

"Sure, but Brandon always denied he was cheating on me. I'd had enough and was planning on leaving him as soon as we got home from this trip." A wry tilt of her head. "Thus my get-away fund."

"Do you think he had any inkling you were planning on leaving him?"

Michelle shook her head. "No, but if he'd been paying attention, he should've realized it. Things had been tense between us for a good long time."

My mouth ran ahead of my brain. "Are you sure it was an affair? I'd heard Brandon may have had a gambling problem." *Ugh. Idiot, why'd you have to blurt that out?*

Michelle abruptly stopped her rocking chair and stared at me. "A gambling problem? What? No." She shook her head, her ponytail swaying from side to side. After a few seconds, she turned and squinted into the dark. "Gambling? Was that what was going on? It would explain the missing money and even his long disappearances." Michelle swiveled her gaze back to me, her eyes wide. "Maybe Brandon wasn't having an affair at all! Oh my gosh. I've been such an idiot. How did you hear he was a gambler? Who told you?"

"Um…" I hated to throw Sam under the bus, but Michelle had brightened so much at the prospect that her husband hadn't been cheating on her. Still, it didn't feel like it was my place to spill the beans. "It's not my story to tell, but tomorrow I'll talk to the person I heard it from and ask them to get in touch with you. Sound good?"

"Yes. Yes, please." She set the chair rocking again, this time at a frantic pace.

"Okay, I promise to let you know how it goes." We stared out into the darkness for a moment before I broke the silence. "I need to ask you something."

Michelle stared at me as if anticipating where I was going with this. "Ask away."

I took a deep breath. "It's about the man I nearly knocked over the other night at the fair. The man you were with?"

"Yeah. What about him?"

"Well…um…I noticed you paid him for something. In cash."

Michelle stared at me for a minute, then laughed. "You think I paid someone to kill Brandon, don't you?"

"The thought had crossed my mind." My legs jiggled so hard they might as well have been dancing a polka.

"Evan's going to get the biggest kick out of that!" Michelle's tears had turned to belly laughs.

Her laughter was contagious and I found myself chuckling along with her. "I'm glad to provide the comedy for the evening. So…not a hitman, then?"

Michelle wiped her eyes. "No. My brother. He lives less than an hour away, so he drove over after he got off work the other night under the pretense of making sure I was all right. Turns out he was in a tight spot and needed money again."

I let out a sigh of relief. "I kind of feel like an idiot. And it sounds like your mama should've warned you to keep your emergency stash secret from your brother, as well." I made large circles with my hands. "ALL the men in your life."

"Boy, isn't that the truth?" She blew a raspberry with her lips.

"I'm truly sorry about this whole mess. I can't imagine how hard it must all be for you."

Michelle dissolved in a shower of tears again, and I belatedly wished I'd kept it light.

"He was my soul mate. At least I thought he was until recently," she sobbed.

"How did you and Brandon meet?"

"At college. We were both trying to better our lives by taking business classes at a community college in Fall River, Massachusetts. Before we met, Brandon worked as a prison guard back in Nebraska where he grew up. I'm not sure what happened; he never wanted to talk about it, but there was an incident, and he quit his job. He didn't want anything to do with law enforcement after that, so he was taking classes to learn as much as he could about the business end of things before he and Sam started their pig racing venture."

"Do you work somewhere else other than for Hasty Hogs?"

"I do. I'm the CFO of a university near Boston. The last few years I've saved my vacation time to use during the summer so I could help out with the Hasty Hogs during peak season. Luckily, Brandon's business wasn't our only source of income." Michelle sighed and stood. "I've taken up enough of your time tonight. I'll let you get to bed."

"Good night. Try to get some sleep yourself."

Michelle walked along the stone path to the guest cottage, while I sat alone in the dark with my thoughts for the second time that night.

Chapter Twenty-Seven

The usual early morning cheer filled the sheep and goat barn when I arrived at the fairgrounds the next morning, but with each step I took toward my goat stalls, people stopped what they were doing and turned to stare at me. The back of my head tingled as their eyes drilled into my skull. *What the heck is happening?* Did I have toilet paper stuck to my shoe? My shirt on inside out? I glanced down to make sure I had remembered my pants. Yep, all clothing firmly in place. It felt like the walk of shame, but for the life of me I couldn't think of anything I'd done recently to merit a public shaming. At least not yet, though the day was young. By the time I reached Bugsy's stall, the silence inside the barn was deafening. Even the animals were quiet.

As I glanced up at the Zen Goat banner hanging above my stalls, my stomach leapt into my throat and I gasped. A white, stuffed goat dangled by a rope from the banner. The rope was tied into a small noose around the toy's neck, and a long wooden stick stabbed clear through its little stuffed body. What appeared to be bright red blood dripped from around the skewer hole. The same thick red substance had been used to write STOP across the goat's side in bold lettering. I stared at the gruesome toy, then twirled around. The other sheep and goat owners were gathered silently behind me like a bunch of grim reapers.

I pointed to the swinging toy. "Who did this? Did anyone see who is responsible for this?"

Heads shook no, and a few people spoke up, trying to help me out.

"I didn't see a thing."

"It was there when I got here an hour ago."

"It must've happened in the middle of the night."

A teenage boy holding a curry comb added, "They're giving those stuffed goats away as prizes at the carnival. I won one for my girlfriend last night." He shyly glanced at the fresh-faced, long-haired young woman standing beside him. The girl blushed and giggled.

Levi strode into the barn and approached the group. "What's going on here? Something wrong with one of your goats, Callie?"

"Only that one," someone said, pointing upward to direct Levi's attention to the murdered stuffed animal.

With a few good lucks and I hope you figure it outs, the people who'd been crowded around my goat stalls disbursed. I whipped out my phone and snapped a handful of pictures of the threat.

Levi balanced on the third rung of Bugsy's stall and jerked the stuffed goat down. He jumped back to the ground and held it out to me. "What's this about? Stop what?"

"I'm not sure. I guess somebody thinks I'm getting too close to the truth."

Levi narrowed his eyes. "Truth of what?"

"The truth of who killed Brandon Ebersole."

He arched his eyebrows. "I didn't realize you were working with law enforcement these days."

I rolled my eyes. "Pete Kennison asked for my help, so I'm helping. They've pegged him as a suspect." I turned the toy over in my hands a few times, careful not to touch the blood. "You know what? Somebody killed this goat with a corndog stick." I recognized the pointed stick from the three giant corndogs I'd eaten at the fair so far. I handed the stuffed goat to Levi so he could take a closer look.

"Seriously?" Levi brought the toy up to his nose and sniffed. "And the blood is ketchup. I'm really sorry, Callie."

I glanced up. "About what?"

"I can't save this goat. He's dead as a doorknob." When I didn't laugh at his attempt to lighten the mood, he tried another tact. "Okay, I'm listening. Who do you think did this?"

I leaned back against the goat stall and crossed my arms, thinking about my suspect list. I'd seen every single one of them eating a giant corndog at some point over the last few days. Everyone except Nancy, who was a self-proclaimed vegan. "Anyone could've done this. Corndogs, ketchup, and stuffed goats are in abundance at Lupine County Fair." I sighed.

"Which is exactly why you need to tell Chief Barnhart about this threat right away."

"I will. Right after my goat yoga session, which I'm going to be late for if I don't get a move on."

Levi eyeballed me. "Don't you think you should cancel the session and talk to the chief immediately?"

I jerked the murdered goat toy out of his hands. "No, there's no reason to cancel. I'll be fine. Goat yoga is right out in the open, with twenty to thirty participants watching my back. I promise I won't be in any danger."

"Sure, you won't. Just like Brandon wasn't in any danger with a crowd of several hundred people watching."

I shuddered. He made a valid point. "Good thing I'm not planning to use a starter gun." I entered the little goat's stall and took two by their collars.

Levi followed me into the stall and grabbed two other goats. "Fine. If you're going to be stubborn, I'll help you get the goats to the round pen and hang out until it's over and you find the time to call the chief."

"Your concern is completely unnecessary, but whatever you want to do is fine by me." I shrugged, acting nonchalant about Levi's apprehension about my well-being while inside, butterflies danced in my belly. "Since you'll be there anyway, you should join us. A little yoga might help you loosen up a bit." I headed outside with my goats in tow, not willing to let Levi see how grateful I was to have him watching my back.

As with each morning of the fair so far, the morning's group was a bit bigger than the day before. All of the regular faces were there, minus Nancy. It was the only session she'd missed since I'd talked her into putting down her protest sign and joining in the first morning. I managed to squeeze everyone and their mats in the round pen and got the session started. When we finished and all my students had filed out of the pen, I left the goats right where they were and dialed Chief Barnhart's number while Levi hovered by my side.

"Callie. Good morning. This is getting to be a habit," the chief said as he answered my call.

"Two days does not a habit make," I informed him.

He chuckled. "To what do I owe this pleasure?"

"Tell him about the warning," Levi instructed.

I whispered through clenched teeth, "I'm trying!"

"Speak up," Chief Barnhart said. "I didn't catch what you said."

"It was nothing." I glared at Levi. "This morning, I discovered a murdered stuffed goat at my stalls here at the fair."

"What?" the chief bellowed into the phone. "One of your goats was murdered?"

I flinched and held the phone away from my ear. "No, not one of *my* goats," I assured him.

"One of whose, then?"

"Nobody's goat. It was a stuffed toy from the carnival."

Silence on the other end of the line. After a beat, the chief's voice came across eerily calm. "Oh, my gravy. Miss Haybeck, did you honestly call me to report someone has murdered a stuffed animal?" His voice rose in both pitch and cadence. "Have you lost your ever-loving mind?"

"But it was a stuffed goat, hanging by a noose from my Zen Goat banner with a corndog stick shoved through its heart and the word "Stop" spelled out on its side with ketchup. Someone was trying to send me some kind of sick warning."

Silence again. Chief Barnhart cleared his throat. "Well, why didn't you say so right up front? Are you at the fairgrounds still?" Without waiting for a reply, he continued, "Stay there. I'll be right over."

Levi helped me clean the goats' stalls while we waited for the chief. My hands were clammy with nerves. I wasn't sure if the jitters had more to do with wondering if Levi was checking out my butt as I bent over to rake the stalls, or concern over who left me the grisly warning. As far as I knew, neither Sam nor Michelle had left the farm after Michelle and I had visited on the porch last night. Nancy was a vegan, which left Jay as the wild card on my list. Well, and Pete. But Pete wouldn't have asked me to help clear his name and then warn me to stop looking, would he? Surely not.

When Chief Barnhart arrived, Levi excused himself. "Sorry to run. I've got a full day of appointments at the clinic. You going to be okay, Callie?"

I frowned. "Well, yeah. I was fine before."

Levi held up his hands in surrender. "Right. Sorry I asked."

"Thank you for all of your help this morning," I called after his retreating back. A little too late, as was my forte when it came to Levi.

I steered Chief Barnhart through finding the murdered toy earlier. He asked more questions, took notes, then stuffed the toy goat into a plastic evidence bag. "Anything else you need to tell me?"

"Just that I found out last night about Brandon having a gambling problem." I told the chief what Sam had said about Brandon's gambling habits and how he'd seen something at a cockfight that was going to provide him with cold, hard cash. "It proves my theory right. It had to have been Jay who Brandon ran into, and Sam said Brandon mentioned the inside information he had about someone, or something, was going to be lucrative for him. It makes sense Brandon was blackmailing Jay, just like I suspected."

Chief Barnhart raised a palm. "Whoa there. While your theory holds merit, it's all speculation at this point. I want you to keep as far away from Jay as possible." He shook a beefy finger at me.

"How am I supposed to stay away from Jay?" I protested. "He's the fair manager and I'm part of the fair line-up since I'm teaching goat yoga here."

"Okay, and how many times so far have you had to deal specifically with Jay since the fair opened?"

I rolled my eyes. "Once."

"I rest my case. There are only two days of the fair left. Like I said, try to avoid him as much as you can, and if you can't for whatever reason, act normal. Do you think you can handle that?"

"Yes, of course I can."

"I'm counting on you. The last thing we need is for Jay to get wind that something's off."

"Are you going to search his farm?"

"Things take time, Miss Haybeck. Leave this to me." He held up the bag with the murdered stuffed animal inside. "In the meantime, watch your back."

Chapter Twenty-Eight

My phone pinged with a text message from Tristan.

MEET ME AT PETE'S IN 10? AND IT'S YOUR TURN!

I replied with the thumbs-up symbol because I knew it would irritate him. If I couldn't annoy my best friend-slash-cousin every chance I got, then what was life even all about? Poking each other's buttons was our love language.

Stuffing my phone into my backpack, I headed for Pete's snow cone stand. Pete and his teenage employees, Mazzy and Noah, were already buzzing around, getting ready for the day. I waved and settled in at the picnic table to wait for Tristan to arrive, then dug out my phone and thumbed over to the word game app to study my tiles so he'd stop yelling at me to take my turn. A weird sense of excitement filled my chest over the warning I'd received earlier in the morning, and my thoughts were too scattered to think straight. Usually, I'd pick out a fairly high-scoring word easily, but not this time. I rearranged my tiles, added the word alias to the board, and hit enter. Six points. Oh well. I'd make up for the low score later.

Tristan scooted in next to me and placed a drink carrier holding three steaming coffees on the table. He pulled it away when I greedily reached for a cup. "Not sure you deserve this after the stupid thumbs-up you sent me."

No surprise Tristan wouldn't let his pet peeve slide without making a comment. I grinned, knowing I'd gotten a rise out of him, but I genuinely wanted, needed, a jolt of caffeine. "I'm sorry for the stupid emoji. It's been a super rough morning already and you're a lifesaver. Please give me the coffee. You're my most favorite cousin ever." I wasn't above whining and wheedling for a little caffeine.

"And handsome. Don't forget how handsome I am."

"And handsome." I rolled my eyes.

Tristan grinned and slid a coffee my way before he handed the third cup to Pete as the snow cone stand owner joined the two of us. "Refreshments are my treat today," Tristan said.

"Thanks, kid. Any progress?" Pete asked, taking a sip from his coffee.

I opened the gallery on my phone and showed them the pictures I'd taken of the dead stuffed animal.

Tristan spit out a few choice words.

"I'd call that progress, all right. You've got somebody running scared," Pete added.

"Right? Exactly what I thought. It might not look like it at first glance, but the murdered toy is a good thing." I grinned.

Pete frowned in my direction. "I suppose, if you thrive on danger."

I shrugged. "Maybe I do. I've never thought of it that way before, but I feel way more excited than I do scared. Like we're on the right track, and something's about to break loose."

"Adrenaline junkie." Tristan winked at me. "Seems odd, though, for someone who won't ride anything except the Ferris wheel."

I shrugged, then told them how I'd deduced it had to have been Jay who'd killed the toy goat and the reasons I'd come to that conclusion.

Pete was quick to shoot holes in my logic. "You're leaving Nancy off the possible toy murderers because you think she's vegan?"

I blinked at him. "Well, yeah. She told me herself. There's no way Nancy would eat a corndog."

Pete laughed. "She's a sly one and wants everybody to believe she's a strict vegan, but obviously you've never noticed Nancy sitting in her car at Meadowbrook Park on Tuesday afternoons."

"Um, you're right. I haven't. Why? What does the park have to do with anything?"

"She seems to think she's incognito when she wears dark glasses and a big floppy hat pulled down over her face, but everybody in the village is familiar with Nancy's car."

"Okay, and why is sitting at the park in her car nefarious? What's she doing?"

"Scarfing down hot dogs from Mustard Stains."

My jaw dropped. "What? No way! Nancy eats meat?"

"Is a pig's bum pork?" Pete laughed, and his eyes twinkled, clearly getting a kick out of my disbelief. "She's only a vegan in her make-believe world. Find out for yourself. You can set your watch by her. Every Tuesday at two forty-five in the afternoon, right before they close, Nancy dons her disguise and orders three hot dogs from the drive-up, then drives to the park to enjoy her snack. She's been doing the same thing for years. The whole town knows what she's doing, but we all pretend we don't see a thing."

The image of Nancy sneaking around eating hot dogs tickled my funny bone, and I laughed until I cried. Once I got myself under control, I wiped my eyes. "So, Nancy goes back on the list of possible toy killers. It had to be either her or Jay."

Tristan eyed me. "Are you sure it could only be one of those two?"

"Well, yeah. I took Sam and Jes back to the farm myself, and Michelle was there. We sat out on the porch and talked for quite a while. Why? Do you have something else to share with us?"

"Sam and Jes must've left again after you went to sleep. You apparently didn't hear their truck leave."

"Why do you think they came back in?"

"Because Spencer and I stayed at the carnival until they shut down at midnight. Sam was there right before closing time."

I stared at my cousin. "You saw Sam around midnight? Are you sure it was him?"

Tristan nodded. "Yeah, of course I am. We spent a few hours with Sam and Jes earlier. It's not like I wouldn't recognize him a couple of hours later. He was even still wearing the Hasty Hogs Crew T-shirt he'd had on earlier."

"What was he doing? Jes wasn't with him?"

"Yeah, she was." Tristan drummed his fingers on the table while he thought. "Sam was hanging out by the giant Ferris wheel."

"Did you talk to him at all?" Why did it feel like I was pulling teeth to get this information out of Tristan? Sheesh.

"Yep. He was waiting for Jes so they could ride the wheel one more time. She was off getting a bag of cotton candy before everything shut down."

Strange. Jes had been adamant about wanting to go back to the farm, and the two of them barely acknowledged each other on the ride home. Well, good for them. They must've gotten over their mad. Funny, Jes didn't mention they'd gone back to the carnival at goat yoga this morning. Maybe she felt guilty for cutting my evening short, but she shouldn't have. A solid night's sleep had been exactly what the doctor ordered.

I scratched my chin. "Interesting. Anyway, Chief Barnhart wants us all to stay away from Jay as much as possible, so my plan today is to see if I can get Nancy to answer a few questions. She's been coming to goat yoga most mornings, but I haven't talked to her about Brandon's murder at all. And with the revelation she's a possible corndog eater, I think it's time to find out what she knows. Plus, Nancy wasn't at yoga this morning. I'll use her absence as an excuse to check up on her."

"Sounds like a good idea." Pete nodded. "And before you ask, I finally got a hold of my UFO buddy. John's out of town, but he said he'd go in to talk to the police and provide my alibi as soon as he made it home today."

"Excellent news. So, it sounds like he hadn't been abducted?" Tristan asked.

"Nope, just down in Connecticut for his wife's family reunion. He said being abducted by aliens would've been a whole lot more fun." Pete laughed.

"Hopefully, with your friend's statement, the police will clear your name," I said.

Pete nodded. "I gave Chief Barnhart a heads-up John would be by to talk with him today. The chief said he'd let me know if I'm off the hook as soon as they have a chance to verify John's story." His cell phone rang, and he flipped it face up from where it'd been sitting on the table. "Speak of the devil." Pete stood and bounded a few feet away. "Yelloo?"

I looked at Tristan. "What're you up to today?"

He shrugged. "Not sure. I could go with you to talk to Nancy, I guess."

"Nah. She seems pretty shy and reserved. I think she'll do better one on one."

Tristan frowned. "I guess I'm at loose ends, then."

"You don't have any plans with Spencer today?" I asked.

"Nope." Tristan shook his head and shrugged. "He's headed back to D. C. today."

"Bummer. Are you going to keep in touch? Try to make the long-distance thing work?"

Tristan wrinkled his nose. "It was a fun couple of days, but no. We're just too different." He slapped his palms against the table. "It was just a short summer romance at the fair. We both had them this year, right?"

He wiggled his eyebrows at me, and I laughed. Tristan was right. The fun evening with Levi was probably nothing more than a too-short blip in time. So why did I want to break out singing "Summer Nights" from the *Grease* soundtrack?

Pete ended his call and bounced on his heels on the way back to join us. He grinned and threw his hands in the air. "Celebration time! Chief Barnhart gave me a clean report. He talked to my buddy and was able to verify our whereabouts the afternoon and evening Brandon was killed."

Tristan and I both clapped. "Yay! That's great news," I said.

Pete's smile of relief could've powered a thousand light bulbs. "It sure is. You can drop your investigation now, Callie. I really appreciate you trying to help me out, but thank goodness it's over."

I shook my head. "No, it's not all over. I mean, I'm glad you're no longer considered a suspect, but the murderer hasn't been caught, and I'm in too deep to back out. I'm going to see this through to the bitter end."

Tristan sighed and ran a hand through his thick curls. "How did I know you were going to insist on finishing this thing out?"

Pete sat down and leaned toward me. "Callie, remember the murdered goat this morning."

"It was a toy. A stuffed goat."

He stared into my eyes and shook his head dramatically. "Not the point. It was a warning for you to stop. You need to heed the warning. Next time, it could be you."

"Nope. I'm way too close to figuring it out. Besides, I can take care of myself." I threw a fake karate chop his way.

Pete and Tristan glanced at each other with a frown. As if practiced, they both sighed and shook their heads with exasperation.

"She's like a dog with a bone," Tristan said.

Chapter Twenty-Nine

Nancy worked as an insurance agent in an office on Main Street in downtown Bobwhite Hollow. I didn't call ahead, choosing to pop in unannounced instead. The insurance company was housed in a well-kept red brick building with large plate-glass windows on either side of the glass door. Concrete urns full of pink and blue pansies flanked the entrance.

Inside, a blue pleather couch harking back to the 1970s and two stiff upholstered chairs anchored a beige area rug and worked as the office waiting area.

"Welcome to North State Insurance Group. Did you have an appointment today?" A dark-haired woman seated behind a tall, half-moon wraparound desk greeted me as soon as I stepped through the door. The silver name plate on her desk read, "Lindsey Canfield."

"Thank you, but no, I don't have an appointment. I was hoping to speak to Nancy Achilles. Would that be possible?"

"Well, let's find out. Who should I tell her is here?"

"Callie Haybeck."

Lindsey pushed a button on the phone and told Nancy I was waiting, then hung up the receiver. When she stood to direct me to the offices behind her, it was abundantly clear she would be welcoming a new baby before too long. "Nancy's office is the second door on the right. Go on back." Lindsey smiled, then gingerly sat back in her chair, letting out a small huff as if the task had been strenuous.

"Thank you. I'm sorry to have disturbed you and made you get up."

Lindsey laughed. "No worries. It's not you, it's him." She pointed at her belly. "I'm so ready to be done."

"I imagine you are!"

Leaving the woman to her work, I found Nancy's office with ease. I rapped quietly on the doorframe and poked my head into her office. The distinct odor of cats that accompanied Nancy wherever she went filled the air. I sneezed and glanced around the room for a cat. Not a single fluffball in sight, but with the scent, it stood to reason Nancy was a walking ball of cat dander. I sniffled and attempted to breathe through my mouth.

"Come on in, Callie. My, this is sure a treat. Have a seat. What can I do for you today? Are you needing some business insurance?" Nancy tucked a strand of dull hair behind her ear and clutched her hands together on top of her desk.

Did I detect a hint of nerves? Had Nancy killed the toy goat and was afraid I was on to her? I slid into one of the low-backed client chairs in front of her desk and set my backpack at my feet. "I'm all set with insurance for now, thank you." I sneezed a second time, wishing I'd thought to take another dose of my allergy oils.

"Well, keep me in mind should your needs change." Nancy held a box of tissues out to me. "If you're not here for insurance, to what do I owe this pleasure?"

I gratefully took a tissue and blew my nose. "Thank you, and you'll be the first person I call when I need more coverage," I assured her. "We missed you at goat yoga this morning. I was downtown, so thought I'd stop in and make sure nothing was wrong." I slipped my hand under my thigh and crossed my fingers against the lie.

Nancy blushed and rocked forward in her chair. "How sweet of you. Everything's fine. I somehow slept right through my alarm this morning, so wasn't able to make it to yoga. Believe me, I was mad at myself about it."

Her face was ruddy and makeup-free, her thin hair threatening to fly away at any hint of electricity in the air. She wore a gray scoop neck cotton shirt topped with a cardigan the color of bologna. A splat of red jelly had dried on her shirt. It certainly appeared as if she'd rolled out of bed and dressed in a hurry.

Or had Nancy been at the fairgrounds in the wee hours of the morning murdering a toy goat as a warning to me? Could the spot of dried jelly on her shirt actually be ketchup? A late night, or early morning, adventure could cause a person to oversleep once they finally fell into bed.

"You're still teaching tomorrow, though, aren't you? On the last morning of the fair?" Nancy asked.

"For sure. The goats and I will be ready to go bright and early."

"Oh, good. I'll make sure to be there. I certainly don't want to miss the last session." Nancy shot me a shy, tight-lipped smile.

"Don't forget you can come out to the farm for my Zen Goat sessions, as well. I'll still be teaching them through the entire month of September. Hopefully even into October, if weather permits."

Nancy frowned. "But those sessions aren't free like they are at the fair."

I tilted my head. "No, I'm afraid they aren't."

"How much does each session cost?"

"Twenty-five dollars." My fee was middle of the road, as goat yoga sessions went. I'd seen them anywhere from fifteen to fifty dollars a session when I searched online.

"Hmm." Nancy frowned. "I'll need to see if I can work a few sessions into my budget. Do you have punch cards that offer a free class after so many paid sessions? You know what I'm talking about? Like the cards you get at the coffee shops?"

I snapped my fingers. "No, I don't have any, but I love the idea. I'll tell you what, I'm going to make a few up and you get to be my first punch card user. You get two free sessions for giving me such a great suggestion." Why hadn't I thought of punch cards earlier in the season? Every small business seemed to incentivize valued customers in a similar fashion these days.

Her eyes lit up behind her glasses. "Yes, please. I'll take you up on the offer!"

My stomach rumbled, and I glanced at the clock on the wall. It was only ten-forty-five, but my belly didn't care about the time. "I know it's early, but I'm starving. Can you get away for lunch? My treat." We hadn't gotten around to the actual reason for my visit. I hoped to be able to get Nancy to open up over a good meal.

"Let me check my appointments real quick." Nancy turned to her computer, getting close to the screen and squinting to see her calendar. "Looks like I'm free until one." She beamed at me. "Where would you like to go?"

"How does Bunny Hill Bistro sound?" The bistro had a variety of vegan options on the menu, so I was confident Nancy could get a great lunch there and walk away with her illusion of being a vegan intact.

"Absolutely perfect. The bistro is my go-to lunch spot if I don't bring lunch from home." Nancy opened the bottom drawer of her desk and pulled out a large, black leather purse. Standing, she dug around in her bag and pulled out a pink metal spray can. She shook the can before liberally spritzing herself with a cloying rose perfume. "Ready?" she asked.

Fantastic. *Now my lunch date smells like cats and overpowering fake roses.* My eyes watered as I stepped out of Nancy's office and waited for her to lead the way. She stopped by the receptionist's desk first. "Lindsey, I'm going to lunch with my friend, Callie." Nancy smiled widely and indicated me with a wave of her hand as if I was royalty and she was proud to be in my company. "Would you like me to bring anything back for you?"

"No, I'm good. Thank you anyway, though. With the amount of lunch Nick packed for me today, you'd think he was feeding a party of six. I'm not complaining, however." Lindsey plopped a miniature chocolate muffin into her mouth. "You just go enjoy yourself with your friend."

I got the impression Nancy didn't get invited to lunch often. My smile faded as a lump of guilt for my reason to invite her rose into my chest. As Nancy pushed open the front door, my eyes glommed onto the purse slung over her shoulder. Leather? Wait a minute. Vegans don't own leather, do they? It appeared I'd discovered another chink in her vegan armor.

When we stepped outside, I took a second to scan the shops across the narrow street—Bookmarks, a farmhouse cottage converted to a bookstore, was flanked by Mountain Daisy, a flower shop, on one side, and Cranky Bear Coffee, my go-to coffee stop, on the other. Locals and tourists alike moseyed in and out of the shops, with nobody seeming to be in a big hurry. In the sparkling sunshine, my charming new town could've been the setting for a Hallmark movie. Until moving here, I'd thought the small-town life on the screen was all make-believe. I grinned. *Nope. I basically live in Stars Hollow now.*

On our way to the bistro, the window display at Timberline Outfitters drew my attention. The store's logo was painted on the window with a tagline underneath-For All Your Hunting Needs. A pyramid of bright red Wiley Explosives canisters took up center stage in the window display. Canisters exactly like the one Pete had found in the snow cone stand.

Nancy chattered away about how much she was loving participating in goat yoga, but the second I noticed the display, I'd stopped listening. As we passed the hunting store, my head swiveled while my gaze remained glued on the explosives. *Yikes!* I hadn't realized the powder was so easy to obtain. Anyone could have simply waltzed into Timberline Outfitters, bought a can, and stuffed Brandon's starter gun with the volatile substance.

"And that Bugsy of yours. What a hoot he is! I just want to squeeze his little ears."

"What?" I shook my head and tried to tune back in.

Thankfully, we'd reached Bunny Hill Bistro and I had a minute to pull myself back together while the hostess showed Nancy and me to our table. One of the perks of indulging in an early lunch was that the place wasn't mobbed yet. Only one other table was occupied—an elderly couple finishing a late breakfast. The bistro was airy and bright, with Tiffany blue walls and plenty of windows to let the light in. The honey-gold hardwood floors gleamed, anchoring the room with warmth and charm.

A smattering of tables dotted the space, while a long, polished wooden table for larger parties took up the east side of the bistro. Our small round table was covered with a blue-and-white checkered tablecloth and tucked in the corner next to the front window. A large Fiddle-Leaf Fig plant stood between our table and the next one over, giving the spot an air of privacy.

Nancy and I both studied the menu for a few minutes. Nancy squinted and held the menu an inch from her face. She finally pulled a magnifying glass out of her purse.

"Ah, better," she exclaimed. "I can actually see the menu now."

I hadn't realized how bad her eyesight truly was.

"Do you see anything that sounds good?" I asked, then squirmed in my chair, wishing I'd phrased my question a little differently.

Nancy didn't seem to notice my faux pas. She smiled and cleared her throat. "Oh, yes. The only problem I'm having is deciding which delicious item to choose."

I laughed. "I'm having the same issue myself."

Nancy finally decided on the Thai noodle salad with tofu chicken. After debating with myself over a cheeseburger piled high with all the fixings and a side of fries, I decided to follow Nancy's lead and ordered the same noodle salad she did. After placing our orders, Nancy and I made small talk. She was funnier than I'd expected, and when she regaled me with a tale about the afternoon two of her cats worked together to bring a live pigeon into her house through a kitty door, I laughed until tears rolled down my face. My earlier assessment about the woman being as dull as plain oatmeal was miles from the truth.

We were having such a fun chat, it seemed like only two minutes had passed by the time our orders were delivered. The chilled noodles, fresh veggies, greens, and fake chicken were topped with a delicious peanut sauce.

"Mm. This is so good. It was an excellent choice. I have to admit, I'm pleasantly surprised by how tasty the meatless chicken is." I wiped a bit of peanut sauce off my chin with a cloth napkin.

Nancy chuckled. "It's the peanut sauce. I'm telling you, it can make anything taste good."

I licked my lips. She was probably right. "Can I ask you a question, Nancy?"

The woman glanced up from her salad and drew her eyebrows together in a straight line. "Sure, I suppose so," she replied tentatively.

"Well, it's just…the night the Hasty Hogs Racing Pigs owner was killed, my family and I were in the grandstands."

Nancy sighed and set her fork on the side of her plate. "And you saw me there protesting the pig races and wondered if I killed Brandon. Am I right?

I should've guessed you had an ulterior motive for inviting me to lunch besides your desire to spend time with frumpy old Nancy."

"No, no, that's not true." I've never been a good liar, so I decided to come clean before I dug myself into a hole. "Alright, yes, I was hoping to get your opinion on what you think happened the other night, but I'm honestly having a great time getting to know you better. I'm glad we decided to have lunch together. You're great company."

A little flattery was all it took, but I meant what I'd said. Nancy blushed and picked her fork back up. "Thank you, Callie. I'm enjoying this time with you as well." She took a bite of her salad. "What questions do you have for me?"

"Did you kill Brandon?" I winked to show her I was kidding. Kind of.

Nancy blinked and continued to chew her lunch. "Oh, yeah. A couple of times," she deadpanned.

I laughed at Nancy quoting an iconic line from *Practical Magic*. "Touché." I forked another bite of noodle salad into my mouth. "But seriously, did you see anything the night of the pig races? I noticed you entered the arena and then were escorted out, so I realize you weren't in the vicinity very long, but maybe you remember something that might help."

While we were eating, Nancy had placed her cell phone on the table next to her glass of tea. When her phone rang, red circles emerged on Nancy's cheeks like someone had turned on an internal furnace. She quickly swiped the call to voice mail, but not before I caught a glimpse of the caller's name as it flashed on the screen. Timberline Outfitters. I choked on a piece of lettuce as the sight of those Wiley Explosives canisters flashed in my mind. What possible reason could a vegan like Nancy have to do business with the local hunting store? What if the police had approached the owner to find out who had bought a can of explosives lately, and they were calling Nancy to give her a heads up? My gaze laser-focused on the red stain on her shirt. When I finally glanced up, Nancy was staring at me as intently as I was staring at her.

"You want to know if I saw anything suspicious?" She cleared her throat before picking up her glass of iced tea and taking a long drink. "The police already asked me all of this, you realize, but I didn't tell them everything."

My eyes went wide. "You didn't?"

She shook her head and leaned forward, whispering. "No, but I'm not sleeping well anymore because of my secret. It's why I overslept this morning and missed yoga. It's time to come clean and clear my conscience."

Was Nancy about to confess to murder? "Should we go to the police station after we finish lunch?" I asked. "And do this there?"

Another vehement shake of her head. She pushed her plate back and folded her hands on the top of the table. "Gosh, no. I want to tell you what I saw, not anyone else."

I reached across the table and laid my hand over the top of hers. "You realize, depending on what you tell me, I may have to take the information to Chief Barnhart, right?"

Nancy tightened her lips and nodded. "Yeah, but I'd rather someone else tell him than me."

"Gotcha." I sat back. "Okay. I'm listening."

"During the pig races, I was only there a short time, as you observed."

I nodded. "Go on."

"But before the races started, a couple of hours prior, in fact...," she paused and rocked nervously in her chair, her eyes shining with unshed tears. "And I'm not proud of what I'm about to tell you."

I kept quiet and let her continue.

"I was sneaking around the Hasty Hogs trailer and equipment. There. I've said it." Nancy leaned forward and rubbed the back of her neck.

My gaze narrowed on my lunch companion. "Why, though? What were you doing back there?"

"I was looking for something to handcuff myself to in order to put a stop to the pig races. I had settled on using the starting gate for my protest. They wouldn't be able to open the gates with a woman handcuffed to them."

"But you didn't go through with it? Why not?" Nancy hadn't been handcuffed to anything that night, but I wanted to hear what she had to say. Maybe she'd changed her plans and had decided to tamper with the gun instead.

"No. I was about to clip the handcuffs on when I figured out my timing was all wrong. There were still nearly two hours to go before the races were scheduled to start, and that was far too long. What if I needed to use the restroom or get a drink? I decided to wait until only half an hour before race time, but that timing turned out to not be ideal either. By then, there were already too many people arriving."

"Sure. Everyone wanted to get there early enough to grab the good seats." I took a sip of my iced tea. "When you were nosing around, was everything already set up for the races?"

She nodded. "As far as I could tell. The gates were all in place, the podium and big speakers were set out, and the pigs were in the pen waiting for the races to start. I was too late." Nancy pushed her empty plate aside and pulled a tube of ChapStick out of her purse.

I recognized the yellow label right away. It was my favorite brand. A local woman made it out of beeswax from her own hives. Nancy's veganism was cracking wide open right before my eyes. A true vegan doesn't use products made with any type of animal byproducts, including leather and beeswax. Not being vegan myself, I wasn't judging, but with Nancy so vocal about her 'beliefs,' the leather purse and beeswax ChapStick took me aback. It shouldn't have, I suppose, after Pete's hot dog revelation. I pulled my attention back to the murder. If Nancy had been sneaking around the Hasty Hogs equipment, she would've had the opportunity to sabotage the starter gun. With her advocacy for animals, it stood to reason Nancy wouldn't take a human life either, but the hot dogs, leather, and beeswax told a different story.

I had another question. "Since you didn't actually handcuff yourself to anything, you didn't do anything wrong. I honestly don't see any reason why you should need to tell your story to the police. It's not like you witnessed anything. Unless I'm missing something?"

She swiveled her head to look around the room, making sure no one was listening. Satisfied, Nancy leaned across the table, talking so low I had a hard time hearing her over the clatter of the lunchtime bistro. "I haven't told you everything yet."

I leaned in to match her posture. "What else happened?"

Nancy looked stealthily around again before answering. "You see, I wasn't the only one sneaking around the Hasty Hogs equipment that evening. I'm afraid I might have seen the killer, and they might have seen me. What if they think I can identify them and come after me next?" She shuddered.

I gasped and dropped my fork with a clatter. "Someone else was sneaking around? Could you tell who it was?" Now we were getting somewhere.

She shook her head. "No, I don't have any idea. As you may have noticed, my eyesight is terrible, even with my glasses on. I heard gravel crunching, you know, like someone walking around? As soon as I heard it, I hid behind one of the big speakers. I snuck a look a couple of times, but, like I said, I couldn't really make out too much."

"Is there anything at all you can tell me about the person? Was it a man or a woman?"

"I'm pretty sure it was a man, but can't say so with complete certainty. Whoever it was wore a shirt and dark pants. Black, I think, or maybe dark blue."

"Okay," I dragged the word out. "We have a human wearing clothes."

"Well, when you say it like that, I suppose none of this is very helpful."

Ya think? This time I kept my sarcasm to myself and smiled. "No, this is good. Is there anything else you can remember?"

"The person was there a good fifteen minutes. It seemed like I was squatted behind the podium forever, and my legs were screaming from being tucked into the same position so long."

"Did you see what they were doing?"

"Not really. I kept my head down for the most part, but I did hear noises. Rattling and banging about. Whoever it was went inside the pig trailer, then came back out and snooped through every bit of equipment the racing crew had scattered around. There was a squeaking noise. It reminded me of the sound a file cabinet drawer makes when you open and close it. Afterwards, there was like a slight pounding sound. Not loud at all."

I sucked in a sharp breath. "A quiet pounding? Like maybe the person was tamping something into the barrel of a gun?"

Nancy's eyes widened, and she sat back. "Maybe. I hadn't put two and two together, but it sure could've been. When the person finally left, I got out of there as fast as I could. I didn't stick around to find out what they'd been doing or take the chance they'd double back and discover me."

"Understandable. Was there anything else strange about the afternoon?"

"Earlier, after I'd decided to wait to handcuff myself to the starting gate, I was getting into my car to go home for a quick nap when I overheard the fellow who worked for Hasty Hogs screaming into his phone."

Sam. "Could you make out what he was saying?"

Nancy blew a raspberry. "Anyone within a country mile could've heard him. He was raging about not getting paid, which I'll admit would make anyone blow their top. The guy was kicking rocks in the parking lot and having a full-blown temper tantrum. I tried to rush past him but heard him yelling at whoever was on the other end of the line about how he should've knocked their block off when he'd had the chance. Brandon Ebersole was murdered later the same evening." Nancy leaned back with a wry smile. "Coincidence? You decide."

Chapter Thirty

After Nancy went back to work, my head swirled with everything she'd told me. Who was the mystery person she'd seen sneaking around the Hasty Hogs setup? And what had they been doing snooping through all the equipment? Or was Nancy throwing up a smoke screen to send me down the wrong path? I cast my mind back to the night of the pig races. Michelle had been behind the podium, announcing each race and getting the crowd amped up. Brandon and Sam had been working the pigs—hustling them into the starting chutes before each race and then back into the bigger pen afterward. The last race was the only one they had attempted to start with the gun. Where had Brandon kept the gun before the final race? I chewed on my lower lip while I tried to remember.

Wait a minute. An image snapped into my head of Michelle handing him the gun. Did I have her pegged all wrong? Maybe she did kill her husband. She had admitted to me she thought Brandon was involved in a clandestine affair. An affair in itself was definitely motive enough. It wasn't until after Brandon was killed that Michelle found out, from me, he'd had a gambling addiction as opposed to being involved in an affair. Could it have been Michelle who Nancy had seen sneaking around the equipment? As the wife of the owner, she wouldn't have had a reason to sneak, unless she'd been sabotaging the starter gun when she thought no one else was around.

On the other hand, Sam had as much access to the gun as Michelle did. With Nancy's bad eyesight, she could only tell me a human being had rummaged around in the Hasty Hogs equipment, but not if the person had been a man or a woman.

For that matter, as the fair manager, it would've been easy for Jay to casually stroll over and mess with the racing team's equipment. If he'd been caught, he could've claimed he was making sure everything was good to go for the pig races later in the evening. The more I thought about it, the more I convinced myself it had been Jay who had been sneaking around the same time as Nancy. Those fighting roosters Tristan and I discovered on Jay's farm threw a whole new light on his personality. Someone capable of such gross cruelty to animals would be capable of anything. But was I projecting and wanting Jay to be the murderer since I had such a nasty distaste for him in my mouth since finding out about the roosters?

I sighed. I was beginning to like Nancy and didn't want it to be her. Sam seemed easygoing until you messed with him or his family, and then he was a loose cannon. Jes was a sweetheart, and I hated to think of her life imploding if Sam turned out to be a killer and went to prison.

My gut told me Michelle was in the clear. She seemed nice, and I think she was truly grieving, but there was nothing to clear her name with complete certainty. Or accuse her, if I was being honest.

At least Pete had been taken off the suspect list. One down. I sighed, no closer to narrowing the suspects down than I'd been on day one. In fact, I was more inclined to move Nancy up the list of suspects than I had been before we ate lunch together.

I shook my head. *Nope. It's totally Jay.* He'd been wearing brand new dark blue jeans that day, which Nancy could easily have mistaken for black. There was the argument he had with Brandon and the wad of cash I'd witnessed Brandon shoving into his pocket seconds later. With Brandon's gambling habits, history with loan sharks, and the comment to Sam about having information on someone that would keep him in cash for a while, I was certain he'd been blackmailing Jay. And Jay had killed him over it.

Old Rusty was parked on Main Street, so I picked up my pace, climbed into the truck, and sped back to the Lupine County Fairgrounds. I needed to talk over all the jumble in my head with someone and hoped Pete would have a few free minutes. The long line snaking away from the snow cone stand stopped me in my tracks. Crickey. I wasn't about to stand in line for the next half hour. Might as well go check on the goats and make sure all was well in the barn.

A family of five stood in front of my goat stalls. The dad carried a baby strapped to his chest in a front pack. He smiled indulgently while the mom and two preschoolers oohed and aahed over the little goats, who were eating up the attention by clowning around and begging for their ears to be scratched.

"Those goats are loving the attention you're giving them," I said to the kids. "Would you like to feed them some carrots?"

The little boy jumped up and down, clapping excitedly. "Can we?" His eyes sparkled, as did his little sister's, who peeked at me with a shy smile from behind her mom's leg.

I dug the bag of baby carrots out of my cooler and showed the kids how to feed the goats. The most aggressive goats stood on their hind legs with their front hoofs on the top rail and bleated at us until the boy gave them their carrots. I held one out to the little girl. "Would you like to try?" When she nodded and reached for the carrot, I knelt down with her and helped her give the treat to a little white goat who was quietly waiting for her turn. The baby in the carrier waved his arms and let out a contagious belly laugh at the antics of the goats. Before long, we were all laughing right along with the little tyke.

I stood and rested my elbow on the top of the stall while the kids finished giving the goats the carrots. Bugsy made sure I knew he was also in dire need of a carrot or two with a sharp tug on my braid. The baby chortled again. I dug a couple more carrots out of the bag and fed them to my favorite, and naughtiest, goat.

Once the family moved along to see the other animals in the barn, I freshened up the goat's water, then headed back out. The line in front of Pete's stretched to Timbuktu now. I wasn't getting a snow cone anytime soon, so I flopped onto my favorite bench in the shade with a dramatic sigh. Flinging my backpack to the ground, I opened the word game app on my phone. Tristan had played a thirty-point word, and with my lousy six-pointer earlier, I needed to up my game. The pressure was on. I was fully focused on the tiles on the board when someone slipped onto the bench beside me.

"Hello, pet." Keith's smooth British accent caressed my ears. "What's so intriguing inside that phone of yours?"

I grimaced and showed him the word game. "Tristan and I've been playing all summer. He won't let it go until he beats me." I grinned. "And I'm not about to let that happen. How about you? What're you up to today?" I closed the app, grateful for the short reprieve.

"Oh, not a lot. Just taking in this glorious day. I was hoping to get an ice cream, but the line is ridiculous." He jerked a thumb over his shoulder at the ever-growing line in front of Sweet Pete's.

"I know what you mean." I sighed and sat back against the bench, crossing my legs at the ankles. "So, our little fair is almost over for the year."

Keith nodded. "Only tonight and a partial day tomorrow to get through; then we'll be moving on." He made a gesture as if he was done with this place.

I eyed him. "You sound like you're ready to get out of here."

"My apologies." Keith placed a hand over his heart. "I didn't mean for it to sound disrespectful in any way. Your village is charming, and I've greatly enjoyed my time here in Bobwhite Hollow. But I've shared with you how I derive great pleasure from experiencing new places and new people. It's the draw of this job for me, never staying in one place too long. I love the excitement of the road. I'm a true rolling stone."

"There's nothing wrong with looking forward to the journey ahead. I can understand the appeal." An image of a Puerto Rican sunset flashed through my mind. "Life on the road is what's going to make your book so fascinating. How's it coming, by the way?"

Keith smiled. "I'm glad you asked. Actually, we didn't run into each other by chance. I was hoping to find you here."

"Oh, okay. Is there something I can help you with?"

"Recognizing you're an avid reader, like myself, I thought it would be nice to get your opinion on the opening pages of my book before the troop pulls out of town. Would you be willing to read my first chapter and give me your honest thoughts?"

"Absolutely. I'd be honored." Excitement flared in my chest. "How would you like to get the pages to me? A Word document would be great. You already have my email address."

Keith laid a gentle, tattooed hand on my arm. "You misunderstand me. I don't have a Word document to send to you."

I frowned and cocked my head. "You don't? What program do you use then?"

He shook his head. "No program. I'm writing my book the old-fashioned way, with the use of a typewriter."

My eyebrows shot to my hairline. "A typewriter?"

"Yes, of course. I would've used a quill and inkwell if it wasn't so time-consuming." He chuckled. "And if my handwriting wasn't so atrocious."

"They still sell quills and inkwells?"

"Certainly. They come in all kinds of fancy cases with various colored feathers and ink. Calligraphy is an art form. A dying one, but an art form nonetheless."

"I'm not questioning the art. I just picture a fancy calligraphy pen, not a feather. So interesting." With Keith's vintage showman persona, it wasn't a far stretch to picture him scratching out his book with a feather pen. "Are you going to bring me the pages to read, then?"

Keith pressed his lips together and frowned. "Forgive me for being forward, but I was hoping you would agree to come to my caravan to read." At my hesitation, he held up a hand, palm out. "Nothing forward, I promise. The only issue is, with only one copy of my pages, I'm loathe to let them out of my sight. It's not that I don't trust you per se, but anything could happen. A brisk wind might come out of nowhere and whisk the pages out of your hand while you're reading, for instance. You understand where I'm coming from, don't you? I'd hate to have to reinvent the wheel because of some terrible misfortune befalling my precious pages."

I nodded. "Of course. I'm not a writer, but it makes perfect sense. Should we go now? I have a little bit of time."

Keith looked at his watch. "We have exactly an hour before the midway opens. It should give us plenty of time."

I stood and grabbed my backpack. "Lead on, mighty scribe."

Chapter Thirty-One

Even though the carnival wasn't yet open for the afternoon, classic rock music pumped out of the speakers, and the smell of fried food wafted from the food trailers as the workers prepared for the afternoon and evening to come. We wove our way between game booths and rides where carnival workers were restocking stuffed animals and inspecting the rides for safety. Keith greeted various co-workers as we made our way through the midway. I noticed a lot of smiles, nods, and a few handshakes and hugs thrown his way.

"You seem to have a lot of respect from your co-workers," I remarked.

Gripping another man by the hand and patting him on the back, Keith answered, "Aw, love, these people aren't my coworkers. They're my family." He winked. "When you've been together as long as most of us have, you either grow to love or hate each other."

I glanced around as we walked. "Most of the carnival workers are long-term employees? I guess I've always thought of it as more of a seasonal job. Sure, a few long-haulers like yourself, but I assumed the majority of jobs were only temporary."

"You have it backwards. The majority are lifers. Sure, most of us start out thinking it's only for one season, but the midway draws you back time and again. One day, you wake up and realize you've been with the midway for fifteen years, seen the country, and can't picture yourself in any other kind of life. Take Riff over there, for example," Keith waved to a worker oiling the hinges on the gate to a carousel. "Riff is third generation."

"Third generation?" I gaped, quickly doing the math. "You mean like his

196

grandparents, parents, and now him, have all worked for the carnival?"

"Indeed, I do." Keith waved at another man polishing the ginormous apples on the Spin-the-Apple kiddie ride. "As is his brother Ron over there."

"You've got to be kidding me?"

"Not in the slightest."

I chewed on his comments for a minute. "Have you really been with the carnival for fifteen years?"

"As I've mentioned before, I prefer the term midway," Keith reminded me with a hint of a scowl. "Yes, fifteen years or thereabout."

"Wow. Impressive."

We came to the edge of the midway grounds. Keith pointed to a collection of travel trailers and tents pitched in a shady campground a football field's throw from the midway. As we neared the camp, the smell of breakfast permeated the air. Bacon frying and coffee brewing.

"Breakfast? It's one in the afternoon," I said.

Keith shrugged. "It's our lifestyle. We work until at least midnight, then need time to unwind. Midway workers are up regularly until the wee hours of the morning. Our days start around noon."

I nodded. "Sure, as a former waitress in a seafood restaurant on Seattle's waterfront, I understand those late nights. It was impossible to go home and go right to bed most nights because I was so wound up from work."

"Right, so you get what I'm saying."

"Completely."

"Here we are." Keith had led me through the campgrounds and to a small white, vintage travel trailer on the farthest edge of the grounds away from the midway. His nondescript trailer was backed into a secluded spot underneath a large oak tree. A small white pickup was parked in front of the camper.

"Does everyone have their own trailers?"

"Caravan," he corrected me. "And no, some of us do, and some don't. I make a terrible roommate, so started out with a tent, then purchased my own caravan as soon as money allowed."

I nodded. "I completely see the appeal in having your own space. I think I would do the same in your shoes."

Keith opened the door and gestured for me to enter with a theatrical sweep of his arm. Stepping out of the bright sunlight of a New Hampshire August day into the dimness of Keith's caravan, I felt like I'd entered into a 1920s writer's den. Cool air from a humming air-conditioner cooled my skin, and the masculine scents of leather and bergamot tickled my nose. While light from outside filtered through the shaded windows, the cabinets, walls, and ceiling were all covered in dark but gleaming wood paneling. A bottle of top-shelf, aged bourbon sat on the small kitchen counter next to a cut crystal highball glass. The standard travel trailer table had been removed, and a wooden desk had taken its place. Brackets and screws on the bottom of the desk legs secured the desk to the floor. A black vintage Royal typewriter took the place of honor on top of the desk, with a container of various pens and pencils placed next to it. An unlit candle sat to the left of the typewriter. The label on the candle read 'Hemingway's Den.' Aha. The source of the leather and bergamot scent. Three hardback books rested in a stack on the edge of the desk. I ran my finger down the spines—*A Tramp Abroad* by Mark Twain, *In Pursuit of Spring* by Edward Thomas, and *The Road to Little Dribbling* by Bill Bryson.

"Your inspiration?" I asked.

The smile on Keith's face told me I was spot on. "Here. Sit. Sit." He indicated the small chair situated in front of the typewriter. While I arranged myself in the chair, Keith lifted a brown leather briefcase from the floor. When his phone pinged, he pulled it out of his pocket, glanced at it, then set it on the corner of the desk. Leafing through a sheaf of papers inside the briefcase, Keith pulled a stack about half an inch thick from the top of the pile and laid them on the desk in front of me with a flourish. He spread his tattooed hands wide to cover the top sheet. "I want you to be perfectly honest but not too brutal. I know it's all piles of rubbish, and I have no right to call myself a writer, but I've poured my heart and soul into these pages, and you're the first person I've ever let read them. Please be gentle, and don't crush me like the cockroach I am." He paused and narrowed his eyes. "I'm not sure I should let you read them at all. You're not going to steal my story and try to publish it yourself, are you?"

Wow, what? I stared at him, my mind a blank slate as to how to respond to his ludicrous question. I never expected him to have such a fragile ego. Keith stared back, keeping his hands firmly in place over the pages he'd brought me here to read. Wasn't he the one who invited me to read his precious pages in the first place? Steal his story by reading a few pages? Was this guy off his rocker? For the first time since Keith had invited me to his caravan, I was starting to feel a bit nervous about accepting his invitation.

After what seemed like an eternity, I broke eye contact. "Listen, why don't I just go, okay? I really should be getting back to check on my goats anyway."

"No, no. Please stay. I'm sorry. I honestly do want your feedback, but there's a terrible push and pull inside me. It feels absolutely bonkers to show my baby to someone." The angsty writer sighed and removed his hands from the stack, revealing handwritten pages. "Don't listen to me. Please read them."

"Okay," I agreed. "I promise to be gentle. It's not like I'm an editor or anything, though, just a reader who knows what I like." *His baby? Yikes.*

"Brilliant. This is exactly why I wanted your opinion. Your job is to verify my opinion of my work. You're going to love it. Not to toot my own horn, but I'm certain I have written a masterpiece."

Alrighty then. I turned my gaze to the top page, feeling Keith's eyes boring into the back of my head. *Welcome to the Midway.* I squirmed in my seat. The title could definitely use some work to add some jazz to make the book pop, but I certainly wasn't going to mention I thought he should rename his baby. I hoped the title wasn't a harbinger of things to come. I reluctantly flipped the page.

'My life as a midway nomad began the day I became an orphan.'

Okay. Better. The first sentence drew me in, making me want to read more, though I'd be a lot more comfortable without the laser stare of the writer scorching my brain as I read. I'd flipped to the second page when Keith's phone rang, startling us both. I glanced up as the screen lit up with a name—Mum. *How cute is that? So British. I'm going to start calling my mom Mum.*

Keith scrambled to grab the phone off the desk. "Hello, Mum."

He was standing right beside me when he answered, and I heard a woman's voice coming over the line. It was clear Keith's mum was upset over something. "Have you seen the news about Larry?" the woman screeched.

I glanced up from the page I was reading, the name Larry ringing a bell in the corner of my brain.

Keith immediately slammed his hand over the phone and looked at me. "I'll take this outside so you can read in peace."

As soon as he stepped out of the trailer, I couldn't hear either Keith or his mum's voices over the rumbling of the air conditioning. I pushed aside the niggling bell in my mind and turned my focus back to the words in front of me, already intrigued by Keith's writing style and vivid descriptions of midway life. A couple of misspelled words grabbed my attention. *Does he want me to point them out?* If I was the writer, I think I'd want someone to tell me if I'd spelled something wrong. One thing I was certain of was Keith wouldn't want me to write directly on his pages. I needed a blank piece of paper, but a quick glance told me there wasn't one on the desk. Keith had closed his briefcase and stowed it back in the corner, so I opened the desk drawer in search of something to write on. Everything in the drawer was neat and tidy, like Keith's entire caravan. I spied a small pad of paper in the back corner of the drawer and reached in for it. When I pulled the notepad out, an envelope came with it. I was about to put the envelope back when the return address caught my eye. Kate Palumbo, Ogallala, Nebraska.

Nebraska. Larry. A chill ran up my spine as things began to click into place. I replayed the one sentence I'd overheard Keith's mum say. *Wait a minute.* I flipped back to the first page. Yep, there it was in black and white. If Keith was an orphan, who was Mum?

On reflection, the woman's voice had sounded distinctly Midwest American with no hint of a British accent. Had she asked if he'd seen the news about Larry, or had she actually called Keith by the name Larry?

With a startled jerk, I remembered how Tristan, Pete, and I had agreed to tentatively add Keith to our suspect list. I'd been so focused on the other suspects, the conversation had completely slipped my mind until the name Larry came up again. The day Brandon was murdered, Pete said the two men had been at the snow cone stand at the same time, and Brandon seemed to think Keith was someone named Larry. I was sure Michelle told me Brandon grew up in Nebraska. She mentioned he'd been a guard at a prison in the Midwest before they met. Was it possible Keith was living under an alias, and Larry was his real name? What if he'd been a prisoner and Brandon recognized him? Keith may have killed him to keep his secret safe. I remembered Keith telling me how important names were, how they could make or break a person. Suddenly, those comments weighed heavy as they seared into my brain. From what I'd learned about Brandon, he wasn't above distortion to line his pockets and feed his gambling habit. Maybe he'd rolled his dice one too many times. I'd been positive Jay was the killer. Could I have been drastically wrong?

Chapter Thirty-Two

When the caravan door creaked open and sunlight flooded into the small space, I was still sitting at the desk with the letter in my trembling hands. As quickly as I could, I shoved the envelope back into the drawer and shoved it shut.

Keith pulled the door closed behind himself with a quiet click and squinted at me. I tried to act normal despite the cold sweat raising goose bumps on my skin. In one step, he stood beside me, looking down at the envelope hanging partially out of the closed drawer. Dang it.

He tugged the envelope out of the desk. "Blimey, Callie. Were you going through my things?"

My gaze skated away from the incriminating envelope. "N...o...o," I stammered, tapping an ink pen against the notepad. *Redirect, Callie, redirect.* "It must've gotten caught in the drawer while I was looking for a piece of paper to write notes on. You do want me to point out any misspellings I find, right?" My voice shook.

Keith's gaze shot to the pages of his manuscript. "Misspellings? I have misspellings? Not possible. I'm an excellent speller. I'm sure you are quite mistaken, young lady. I don't see you writing a book, and until you have a go at being a writer yourself, you are in no place to criticize my work."

Sheesh. The writer's ego was something to contend with, but at least it had taken Keith's attention off the letter he gripped in his fist. I took a deep, calming breath, releasing it along with the stab of fear. "You are absolutely right. I'm not an author or editor, so I don't have any business giving you feedback. And I'm really sorry, but I only just remembered I'm supposed to be helping my aunt with canning vegetables from her garden this afternoon. It's going to take us several hours, and I can't let her do it alone." I flipped the two pages I'd made it through back to the top of the pile and laid my hand gently on his masterpiece. "I didn't get super far, but what I did have time to read was great. I have no doubt your book will be a bestseller." Without making eye contact, I stood and reached for my backpack.

Something sharp poked into my ribcage. "Not so fast, love. Go ahead and sit back down."

Keith pressed a silver letter opener against my side. My legs quaked like aspen trees in the wind as I eased myself back into the chair. "What are you doing, Keith? You don't have to threaten me. I'll finish reading the chapter if you want me to. No problem." I stared into his blue eyes, hoping he'd show mercy and let me go.

"Ah, love, we both know this isn't about reading my pages anymore." A pained expression crossed his face. "I do apologize. You're lovely, and I'm gutted to have to hurt you. If you'd only let it drop after I warned you off, we wouldn't be in this predicament, but no, you had to keep picking at the wound."

"Warned me off? Are you saying you are the one who killed the toy goat and hung it in my goat stall?"

Keith threw his arms wide, playing the showman until the end. "Among other crimes, yes. If you'd just let it go, I would've been out of here with the midway tomorrow, and nobody would be any the wiser."

"Why did you invite me here if you were worried about me discovering your secrets?"

"Like I said, to read my first chapter, of course. However, I didn't count on you being dodgy and snooping through my things."

Trying to appear confused at his accusations, I shrugged and attempted to keep the tremble out of my voice. "A letter fell out of the drawer. So what? It's not like I read it. Honestly, Keith, I have no idea what you're so worked up about. Please let me leave. No harm, no foul. Neither one of us will mention this little incident to anyone ever again. In fact, I've already forgotten it."

Keith shook his head. His eyelids drooped, and the corners of his mouth turned down. "Can't let you go, love. The look on your face when you heard me mum call me Larry spoke volumes. You're a smart lass, and I'm sure you've put two and two together by now."

Aha. So I hadn't misunderstood. But now I needed to hear him say it. For him to tell me who he really was. "Wait a minute. I'm confused. You're Larry, not Keith?"

"Larry no longer exists. He's who I was another lifetime ago. Remember our conversation about how a change of name can rewrite a person's entire existence? That's exactly how it worked for me. I've been Keith George for fifteen years. I don't even remember the other guy any longer."

"And you're not from England?"

He looked down his nose at me. "Listen to what I'm telling you. Keith is a Londoner by heart. Larry, however, was born and raised in nowhere Nebraska."

"As was Brandon Ebersole."

"I'm not surprised you put the clues together. You're a bright little bird. Which is why it pains me to have to do this to you." Keith, or was it Larry, jammed the letter opener a hair farther into my ribcage as a reminder to me that he was in charge.

In the small space, he was able to keep the threat imminent while reaching around to jerk open a kitchen drawer next to the stove. I had about a gazillion more questions but decided it might be a good time to keep my mouth shut. Keeping his eyes on me, Keith rummaged around inside the drawer with his free hand, finally coming up with a roll of silver duct tape. Yikes. I was in deep trouble. Panic rose in my chest as I wrenched away from the sharp letter opener and stood. Before I could make a move for the door, my captor shoved me back into the chair and held me in place with a bruising knee to my belly. Using his teeth, he loosened the end of the tape, then tossed the letter opener onto the desk and swiftly wrapped the sticky tape around both me and the chair at chest level. I hissed with pain as Keith grabbed my wrists and bound them tightly together. I screamed, kicked, and flailed the best I could as he bent down and secured my ankles to the legs of the chair.

Keith remained calm, totally unfazed by my antics.

"Screaming won't do you any good, love. The midway has started for the day, and there's not a soul left in camp." He ripped off another piece of tape from the roll and slapped it over my mouth, then cracked his knuckles to show me he meant business. "As much as I've enjoyed your company, I've got to rush off. You've already made me late, and we wouldn't want anyone coming to look for me, would we?"

Yes, we absolutely would.

He pulled the shades on all the windows, then snapped on a light over the stovetop. When he finished putting the caravan in order, Keith leaned down and peered into my eyes. "Try not to make too much of a fuss. No one would hear you anyway, tucked back here at the edge of the campground like we are." A hint of flat Midwestern vowels snuck into his language.

My eyes felt like they were going to explode out of their sockets, and my heart thrummed a crazy rhythm against my restraints. I'd managed to get myself into a huge pickle this time.

"Oh, love, do stop looking at me with those terrified eyes. You'll hurt my feelings. By this time tomorrow, we'll have put this entire situation behind us. Don't worry, I'll find somewhere safe, far from here, to throw you out on my way to a new life. My biggest regret is leaving Keith behind. It's really too bad. I was quite fond of the old chap." Keith straightened, pulled his showman's jacket off a hook beside the door, and shrugged it on. With a flick of his wrist, he placed his top hat on his head, then opened the door and stepped outside. Suddenly, he turned back to me. "I'll bring you something to eat later. How about a corndog? I know you're awfully fond of them." He pulled the door closed and was gone.

I gagged at the thought. If I ever saw a corndog again, it would be too soon.

Chapter Thirty-Three

As soon as the caravan door clicked shut behind Keith—or Larry or whoever he was—I wiggled and squirmed the best I could, trying to find any give in the duct tape holding me to the chair. I grunted with the effort, but the tape held fast. I'd seen a video once showing how a person could free their hands from duct tape by raising their arms as high over their head as they could, then bringing them down fast while attempting to pull their wrists apart. Unfortunately for me, Keith was smart enough to strap my upper arms to the back of the chair, so I couldn't use that method. All I managed to do was bounce the chair from side to side and make myself hot and sweaty in the process.

My breath was coming quick and shallow behind the tape on my mouth. I couldn't take in enough oxygen to fill my lungs. My chest was tight. Were my toes going numb? *I'm going to die in this blasted caravan.* Tears rolled down my cheeks. *I'm never going to see Mom and Dad again. And Bree. I love you guys so much. I'm sorry for being such a pain in the....*

Muted voices filtered through my terrified brain. Was someone close enough to hear me? I tried to yell for help, but the duct tape prevented any volume. In an attempt to make noise, I tried to slam the chair into the desk but only managed to bruise my knee. Whoever had been talking had wandered off, and all was silent outside the caravan again.

I stopped struggling and sat still for a minute, meditating to get control over my panicked thoughts. Getting hysterical wasn't going to help me to get myself out of this mess.

From inside my backpack, my phone chirped with a message. My backpack lounged against the bench seat across from the stove where I'd dropped it when Keith and I first entered the caravan. Strapped to the chair with my hands and feet bound, I had no way of reaching it. Even if I could hop the chair around the desk and over to the bench, how in the world could I possibly get the phone out and call for help?

After catching my breath and cooling down a bit, I decided the best plan of attack was to work on getting my shoulders free. Rocking back and forth and twisting my body as much as I could, the tension of the tape around my chest and arms started to feel slightly looser. With no idea how much time was passing, I worked away, going from barely able to move to feeling a slight give in the tape. Optimistic, I doubled down on my efforts. I kept up a constant pep talk in my head. *Everything's going to be fine. You've got this, Callie. Keep going.* I rocked harder, amazed at how the slightest movement was loosening up the tape. Muffled sounds from the carnival provided the background music as I worked to free myself from the restraints. The sunlight behind the closed window shades became muted and soft. Dusk. *Come on. Faster. Let's go.* I had to get out of there before Keith returned with the corn dog. An image of myself skewered in the chest with a corndog stick was all the motivation I needed.

By the time the duct tape loosened and stretched enough to fall to the crook of my arms like a loose belt, my phone had chirped with an incoming text at least a good twenty times, and the *Jeopardy* theme song, my ringtone for Tristan, had played no less than five times. With any luck, he'd noticed I was missing and was looking for me. I could only hope, but most likely the texts were only nagging me to take my turn on our word game.

Working the tape had made me hot and sweaty, despite the air conditioning keeping the caravan cool. In the process of freeing my arms, the tape around my wrists had loosened considerably from the movement and moisture from my skin. I'd managed to create enough movement for my arms that I could try the method from the video I'd seen. I lifted my bound hands to face level, then brought them down fast, pulling my wrists apart in the same movement, just like they'd demonstrated in the video. The tape split with a satisfying rip. I tore the gag off my mouth and yelped with pain as the sticky binding tore away a layer of skin and hair along with it.

Something slammed against the side of the caravan and stopped my heart. I was too late. Keith was back already. Another slam against the caravan and my heart jump-started itself. *You still got time, Callie. He's not in here yet.*

With my hands free, I scrambled to unwind the loose tape hanging off my shoulders and bent to free my feet from the legs of the chair. In record time, I was loose. I snatched the letter opener off the desktop where Keith had thrown it, grabbed my backpack, and with the sharp little blade gripped in my fist like a weapon, I wrenched open the caravan door. *It's not a caravan. It's a common camp trailer, you idiot.* I directed my mean thoughts at Nebraska-born Larry.

A large white creature flashed through the dim evening light and slammed against the side of the trailer.

"Bugsy! What are you doing, buddy?"

At the top of his lungs, he bleated his reply. To my ears attuned to goat lingo, it sounded like he said, "Rescuing you."

I rushed out of the trailer and wrapped my arms around my favorite goat's neck. "I've never been so happy to see you, my sweet furry friend."

Bugsy smiled and bleated again.

"I couldn't agree more. Let's get out of here."

Sprinting through the carnival worker's campground, Bugsy hot on my heels, I searched for the quickest route to get back to safety. Choosing to stay as far away from the midway—*carnival*—as possible, Bugsy and I made a wide arc, racing across an open field and circling around to the front of the livestock barns. When we flew around the corner, the area was in chaos. Goats ran wild all around us, kicking up their heels and bleating happily. I stopped to catch my breath, pressing a hand to the stitch in my side. *Hold on. Those are my goats. Why are they all out?*

I turned to Bugsy. "I expect this behavior from you, but did you have to teach them how to escape?"

He blinked innocently.

I reached out and grabbed the collar of one of the goats as she tried to fly by me. Tristan chased after another but changed course when he caught sight of me.

"Where've you been? I've texted and called a million times."

"Sorry. I was tied up."

Tristan glared at me. "Well, all your goats are out."

"Thank you, Captain Obvious." With my free hand, I unzipped the front pocket of my backpack and pulled out my phone. With my thumb, I dialed a number, then pressed the phone to my ear.

"What are you doing? We need to get these goats rounded up."

I held up a finger. When my call was answered, I began to talk. "Chief Barnhart, this is Callie Haybeck. I know who killed Brandon. He abducted me, but I've escaped and am safe now."

After the Chief yelled he'd meet me at my goat stalls in five minutes, I hung up the phone. Tristan's eyes were as large as flying saucers as he stood staring at me, his mouth wide open.

"What? I told you I'd been tied up," I said.

He gaped. "It never occurred to me you meant literally. Are you okay?"

"I'm good. Try to get the other goats. I'll be right back to help."

Once I had Bugsy and the one rogue goat I'd managed to snag tucked away, I sat on top of the cooler where I kept the goat's treats. With the rush of adrenaline from my kidnapping over, my body shook and my head spun like I'd just gotten off the Graviton.

Emily was feeding her goats, but when she saw me, she rushed over. "Callie, there you are." She looked into my stalls and made a sound in her throat. "Shoot. You've only managed to wrangle one of them back. I texted you after a guy let your goats out, but never heard back. I guess you were already out chasing them. Do you want help getting the rest of them in? I'd be more than happy to help, and I'm sure other people would, too."

"Thank you, but I think my cousin and I can get them in with a little grain. They're entirely food-motivated," I answered before my brain registered what she'd said. "Wait a minute, though. Did you say someone let them out?"

"Yep. At first, I thought he was just another person admiring the animals. Next thing I knew, the guy was fast walking out of the barn with all your goats running along beside him. I yelled, but he didn't turn around. By the time I got outside, the goats were scattered all over the place."

"When was this? What did the guy look like?"

She shrugged. "Fifteen, twenty minutes ago. It was the carnie who dresses like the ringmaster of a circus. Do you know who I'm talking about? He usually runs the giant Ferris wheel."

My eyes went wide. "Keith. Larry. Whoever he is." I'd gotten out of his camp trailer in the nick of time. By letting the goats loose, he was trying to create a diversion.

Chief Barnhart rushed up, two deputies on his heels.

"There's no time to explain, but Keith George from the carnival is the murderer. Keith isn't his real name, though. It's Larry. Larry Palumbo, I think, and I'm pretty sure he's trying to make a break for it right this second." I explained where Keith's camp trailer was parked, what it looked like and spouted off the model and make of the pickup he'd be pulling the trailer with.

The chief glanced at his deputies. "Go get him," he ordered. He pulled a two-way radio from the holster on his hip and called for more backup. With a pointed finger, the chief addressed me, "Stay right here, Miss Haybeck. I'll be back." He turned and ran out of the barn.

With seven goats running loose, I couldn't follow the chief's orders to the letter. Instead, I grabbed two feed bowls and filled them with the oat and molasses mixture my goats were so fond of. Once outside, I handed one bowl to Tristan. "Come on. Let's get them back in their stalls."

"Should we split up?" Tristan asked.

With the worry Keith-Larry might still be lurking around the fairgrounds, I shook my head. "Stay with me. Please," I pleaded.

He wrapped me in a quick hug. "You got it, cuz. I'll always have your back."

Once we spotted the rogue goats, a few shakes of grain caused them to come running. They followed on our heels, clamoring to get back in their stalls so they could indulge in the sweet treat. The way they acted, you'd think I never fed them. By the time the chief came back forty minutes later, I was sitting in the exact spot where'd he left me. My legs had finally stopped shaking.

Chief Barnhart settled himself on a bale of hay, stretched his long legs out in front of himself, and crossed them at the ankles. He removed his hat, placed it on the hay, and ran a hand through his thinning brown hair before he addressed me. "You were a lucky young lady tonight, Callie." The chief cleared his throat, clearly trying to pull his emotions together.

"Were you able to find Keith-Larry? Did you arrest him?"

He nodded. "We did. Your tips proved invaluable. My deputies were able to stop his vehicle as he was pulling out of the campground. I'm happy to report your abductor was apprehended without incident."

"He was trying to create chaos by releasing my goats so he could get away. And take me with him."

"Correct. I'm glad he wasn't successful." The chief turned his attention to Tristan. "Were you aware Callie was missing?"

Tristan grimaced and wobbled his head. "No, I just had a feeling like something wasn't quite right. I'd texted her a handful of times but hadn't gotten any response. It's not like Callie at all. She usually answers right away unless she's in a yoga session."

I elbowed my cousin. "You were trying to harass me about taking my turn, weren't you?"

"Maybe." His cheeks flared pink.

"You're turn with what?" the chief asked.

"A word game the two of us play online. It's similar to Scrabble."

"Ah, okay." Chief Barnhart looked at Tristan again. "You thought it was unusual for Callie not to answer you. Did you go in search of her?"

"Yes and no. I'd been out at the farm with my grandparents and knew Callie usually checks on her goats around five, so since she still wasn't answering, I came in to see if she was here." A pause. "She wasn't, so I went to ask Pete if he'd seen her, but he hadn't either. When I got back to the barn, all the goats had been let out."

Chief Barnhart asked a few more questions, taking notes as we answered. I told him everything I'd learned about Keith-Larry, and the conclusion I'd come to about how he knew Brandon, and why he decided he had to kill him.

"Did the man share this story with you? Did he admit to killing Brandon Ebersole?"

"Yes," I started, then stopped and shook my head. "Well, no, actually, now that I think about it. He didn't outright admit to anything, but didn't deny it either. I had a lot of questions, but he put the tape over my mouth before I got the chance to ask them all."

"Smart man," Tristan replied.

I smacked him.

Finally, the chief rose, his knees crackling as he stood. "Well, I've got to get back to the station and interview the suspect." He stretched. "I have a feeling it's going to be a long night."

Chapter Thirty-Four

"Ow." Every muscle in my body screamed as I stretched. "Why do I feel like I've been run over and spit at?" As soon as my eyes squeaked open, the entire ordeal came flooding back. Turns out wrestling your way out of duct tape restraints uses a whole different set of muscles than either yoga or even farm chores do.

The skin around my mouth was raw and on fire from where the tape peeled a layer off when I'd ripped it off my face. *Welp, if I had a moustache growing, I don't have to worry about it for a while now.* Throwing off the comforter, I went in search of face cream to soothe my distressed skin. My aching muscles clamored for a long soak in the bathtub, but there wasn't time. I settled for a quick shower instead.

Downstairs a few minutes later, I poured a cup of coffee from the pot Aunt Ellen already had brewing. Even at this early hour, she bustled around, filling the kitchen with homey smells—sizzling bacon, heavenly pancakes, and sweet maple syrup. I added a splash of vanilla creamer to my coffee and cradled the mug between my hands, breathing in the comforting scents.

"Sit and relax a minute, ladybug." Aunt Ellen scraped back a kitchen chair for me. "You had quite a fright yesterday."

I shook my head. "Thanks, Auntie, but I've got to get my chores done and get to the fairgrounds for the last goat yoga session."

My aunt flashed me her trademark no-nonsense frown. "I've already fed the chickens this morning, and Uncle Will's out checking on the sheep and goats. Now do as I say." She pointed at the chair with her chin. "Sit."

I sat. Aunt Ellen slid a plate in front of me piled high with a stack of hot, golden pancakes and a side of bacon. "With all you've been through, you need to eat to regain your strength. I bet you haven't eaten anything but greasy fair food for the last week."

"I had a salad yesterday," I protested through a mouthful of delicious pancake. I wasn't sure bacon, pancakes, and maple syrup were a much healthier choice than a corndog, but, wisely, I held my tongue.

Aunt Ellen poured herself a cup of coffee and sat at the table next to me. She stirred a teaspoon full of sugar into the dark coffee and sat back. "Tell me what happened."

After rehashing my wild day with my aunt, I took my empty plate to the sink and rinsed it. I didn't generally practice yoga on a full stomach, but the homemade meal was worth the flagging energy I'd most likely feel during the session. I leaned in and gave my aunt a tight squeeze. "Thank you for taking care of me." I placed a loud kiss on her weathered cheek.

Aunt Ellen blinked back a tear. "It's my pleasure, ladybug. My pleasure." She patted my arm and slipped out of my embrace. "You better get going. You don't want to keep your students waiting."

Yes, ma'am.

Old Rusty rumbled to life as soon as I turned the key in the ignition. I threw the truck into gear as the farmhouse door banged shut. Tristan flew down the sidewalk and jumped into the passenger seat before I could take off. He looked like the picture of summer, dressed in a navy blue tank and a pair of white shorts.

"Haven't seen you up this early all week."

Tristan shrugged. "Thought the least I could do is join you for yoga this morning."

"Mmhmm. You just don't want to miss out on any gossip we might end up being privy to."

He grinned. "You've got me pegged, girlfriend."

Back at the fairgrounds, I was grateful for Tristan's help with the morning chores and getting the young goats into the round pen in time for the yoga session. All the regular faces showed up once again, with about a dozen more people who we couldn't fit inside the round pen. Everyone in a fifty-mile radius had heard about my narrow escape from Keith-Larry's trailer and his subsequent arrest. Jes had even convinced Michelle to join us this morning. I was proud of all the regulars who agreed to swap out and let a newcomer take their place in the pen so they could experience the actual goat yoga. The session ended up being fantastic, despite my full belly and aching muscles.

Afterward, I passed out more business cards than I'd managed to give away all summer so far. With only one or two months left before The Zen Goat was no more, I was thrilled to see so many locals interested in attending sessions at the farm. And who knew? With Emily's buck scheduled to service my does, my options were wide open. Bobwhite Hollow felt more and more like home every day, and the idea of the beach in Puerto Rico seemed like a distant pipe dream, especially since my conversation with Uncle Will about the possibility of me sticking around. More often than not lately, I found myself picturing my future right here.

Nancy approached me to inform me I'd be seeing her at the farm, and she invited me to a do-over lunch. I'd already talked to Althea about what to do about my strong histamine reaction to Nancy and her cloud of cat dander. She'd suggested next time, I make sure I took an extra dose of my allergy oils just a few minutes before being in that close of contact with Nancy, so I felt like I had that little problem covered.

"Yes, let's do lunch soon. I have one question for you, though," I said.

"Shoot."

"Yesterday I couldn't help but notice the call you received was from Timberline Outfitters. I'm pretty sure the killer bought the explosives from them. Do you mind telling me why they were calling you?"

She cocked her head and squinted as if confused about why I was asking. "Nothing nefarious there, I assure you. They purchase their business insurance through me."

Of course, they did. I grimaced. "And I promise not to interrogate you at our next lunch."

Nancy sniggered. "Oh, that was half the fun. It might sound strange, but I was flattered you thought I had enough gumption to be a murderer." With a sly smile and a wink, Nancy turned and strolled away.

215

Alrighty then.

Jes had chosen to practice yoga outside the pen this morning, giving up her coveted spot to Michelle, who still sat on the ground cuddling a goat. With most of the other students gone, Jes entered the round pen and wrapped me in one of her giant hugs. "Callie, this has been amazing. Goat yoga is my new favorite thing."

"You're so welcome." I hugged her back, then glanced at Michelle. "I hope you enjoyed the session, Michelle."

Sadness spilled out of her eyes, but she nodded and gave the goat one last embrace before standing and wiping grass off her leggings.

Sam was waiting for the two women, so we said our goodbyes while Tristan finished rolling up yoga mats and stowing them in a tub. As the Hasty Hogs crew was walking away, a deep voice called out to them. I spun around to find Chief Barnhart approaching. He beckoned for the crew to rejoin us at the yoga pen.

"Good morning," he greeted us once we were assembled. "I'm glad to catch you all here. It'll save me a trip out to Haybeck Farm." He cleared his throat. "First of all, I wanted to thank you for your patience and cooperation and for agreeing to stay around Bobwhite Hollow during this horrible time." Chief Barnhart removed his hat and bowed slightly to Michelle. "You can rest easy knowing we've charged someone with your husband's murder."

Michelle nodded while tears ran down her face. Jes placed a comforting arm over her friend's shoulder.

"Did Keith admit to killing Brandon, then?" I asked.

The chief frowned and shook his head. "Not until we uncovered the truth of his identity. With your help, of course."

"Was I right? His real name is Larry Palumbo?"

The chief nodded. "Spot on. And his fingerprints proved it. You were also correct in figuring out Larry knew Brandon from Nebraska. They spent time in prison together."

"This Larry was incarcerated at the same facility where my Brandon worked as a guard?" Michelle asked.

The chief wobbled his head and clicked his tongue. "Not quite. The two men were childhood best friends. It seems they robbed a convenience store at gunpoint when they were little more than teenagers. They were both sentenced to serve a stint in prison and were sent to Sand Hills Correctional Center outside of Omaha."

Michelle frowned and shook her head emphatically. "Brandon wasn't an inmate. He worked as a guard. You've got your wires crossed somewhere."

Chief Barnhart slowly shook his head. "I'm sorry if that's what he led you to believe, but it's far from the facts. No, Brandon served his time. As a prisoner. Five years. Larry, however, did not."

Michelle gasped and threw her hands over her mouth.

"He didn't?" I stared at the chief. "How did he get out of it? Did he throw Brandon under the bus?"

"No, Larry did serve some time, just not his full sentence."

"He was let out on good behavior?" Jes guessed.

The chief paused. It was clear he was enjoying telling this story to his captive audience. "Not quite. You see, for the first two years, Larry was a model prisoner. Now, what you need to understand is Sand Hills isn't a high-security facility, and the best-behaved inmates are put on work details. Larry Palumbo was one of those lucky few, but one day he simply up and walked away from the work crew."

It was my turn to gasp. "And nobody noticed him leaving? They didn't catch him?"

The chief shrugged. "Apparently, his absence wasn't noticed until the end of the workday. By then, he'd been gone for hours. An APB was put out, but Larry was long gone."

"What about Brandon?" Michelle asked in little more than a whisper.

"Like I mentioned, Brandon served his full sentence."

Michelle put a shaking hand over her mouth. "How long ago was this?"

"It's been fifteen years since Larry walked away from the work crew. Brandon spent another two years in the facility." The chief hitched his thumbs into his belt loops and rocked back on his heels. "It was a chance encounter that had them face to face again. Imagine Larry's astonishment when he went to buy a snow cone on a hot day and ran into the one person who could knock his world off its axis."

"Which is why Keith, I mean Larry…killed Brandon. He was scared he'd have to go back to prison." A stab of compassion for Larry welled up in my heart. It must be horrible to think about going back to a prison cell. I pushed the emotion down. This was no longer about a robbery. The guy killed another man. His former best friend. As much as I'd liked the showman named Keith, his persona had been nothing but smoke and mirrors. "And after he filled the starter gun with explosives, he must've disposed of the container in Sweet Pete's stand in an attempt to throw suspicion off his own trail."

"Not quite," Chief Barnhart said. "Larry was frantic to stay out of prison. He says he remembered being able to see the garbage can from the order window at Sweet Pete's stand. He thought since they were so busy, they'd be taking the trash out often so it seemed like a good place to get rid of the empty canister, thinking nobody would have a reason to dig through the snow cone stand's trash."

"Oh! He wasn't trying to set up Pete at all," I said. "He must've missed the garbage can when he tossed the canister in and didn't realize it."

"Right, not the smartest move. Of course, the whole thing may have been avoided if Brandon hadn't attempted to blackmail an escaped convict in the first place. It wasn't the best idea I've ever heard."

Michelle gasped again. The poor woman was receiving one blow after another this morning. "You think Brandon tried to blackmail this Larry character? My husband would never have done something so vile."

The chief looked at Michelle with pity in his eyes. "I'm sorry, Mrs. Ebersole. He would, and he did. Larry wasn't his only target."

"What do you mean? Brandon was blackmailing someone else besides Larry?"

Almost as if it had been choreographed, two deputies escorted Jay Rowe past our gathered group. We all swiveled to watch them go. Each deputy had a hand on one of Jay's elbows. Gone was the competent fair manager, replaced by an unhappy and red-faced criminal. Jay's hands were handcuffed behind his back, his shoulders hunched, and his head down as he marched by us, not making eye contact with anyone. While I felt terrible for his family, I hoped Jay was ashamed of himself and would find a way to make amends for his despicable crimes once he served his time.

When they got to the parking lot, one of the officers placed his hand on top of Jay's head and guided him into the back seat of a police cruiser. Our group remained silent until the car pulled away from the fairgrounds.

Chief Barnhart waved a hand at the retreating police car. "Brandon was blackmailing our Lupine County Fair manager as well."

Michelle gaped at the chief. "Jay? What could Brandon possibly have had to hold over Jay? We're only up in this part of the state once a year." Her voice shook. "I didn't know my husband at all, did I?" Jes squeezed Michelle's shoulders.

"A few days ago, we received an anonymous tip," Chief Barnhart winked at me. "After a rapid investigation, it was uncovered that Jay was raising fighting roosters on his apple farm. As it turns out, he was well known in the cockfighting circles, providing the meanest, nastiest roosters in the northeast."

"Holy cow. What a terrible thing, but what does Jay's fighting roosters have to do with Brandon?" Michelle asked.

Before the chief could answer, Sam spoke up. "Brandon told me he'd gotten information at a cockfight that was going to keep him in money for a long time. He found out about Jay's side business, didn't he, and was shaking him down?"

Chief Barnhart nodded. "Yep, exactly right. Jay has admitted to everything. He's looking at jail time and a hefty fine."

Tristan let out a low whistle. "Looks like Lupine County is going to need a new fair manager."

Chapter Thirty-Five

"Rambo will be a lot more excited about being with the ladies than the nanny goats will be at first. They'll warm up to him eventually." Emily chuckled as the two of us crossed our arms on top of the fence rails while Rambo raced around the field. His top lip curled up in excitement as he caught the unique scent of the females.

"I hope so," I added.

All six of my does had backed away in a synchronized group. Fanny, the largest and bravest of the nannies, stood neck and shoulders in front of the other girls and stomped a front hoof in warning when Rambo got too close. With her ears perked and the one horn on her head from a botched dehorning when she was young, Fanny resembled a magical avenging unicorn.

"Don't worry. It won't be long before the ladies will be feeling just as randy as Rambo and take him up on his offer. Then you'll have new babies bouncing all over this field come spring."

The thought of stiff-legged bouncy baby goats sent a zap of pleasure through me. "I'm going to be a goat grandma."

We made arrangements for Emily to return in a month and take Rambo back to her farm. I'd settle up her invoice for the buck's stud fees when she came to get him, and then we'd keep our fingers crossed for the first sign of pregnant goats.

"Oh, hey." Emily had one jean-clad leg in the cab of her pickup. "You're going to have a ton of goat milk in a few months. The dairy association will be holding workshops on making goat cheese, yogurt, and a ton of other stuff. Even soap. You should seriously consider joining the association and attending a few of those workshops. It's only fifty bucks a year and well worth the cost." She climbed in her truck and drove away, throwing a smile and one last wave my way.

I stared at the dust flying up from her tires and blinked slowly. A ton of milk? It hadn't crossed my mind I was going to have to learn how to milk the goats.

Uncle Will stepped out of the barn and strode to my side. "I see Rambo's getting acquainted with the ladies." He chuckled and looked at me. "You're white as a ghost. What's going on?"

"Emily informed me I'm going to have bunches of extra goat milk and have to take classes to learn what to do with it. Won't the nursing kids use it all? I'm going to have to milk six goats? What in the world have I gotten myself into?"

Uncle Will's blue eyes twinkled with amusement, and he lay a weathered hand on my shoulder. "Now, settle down, young one. You can handle this." He pointed to the nannies. "All of them won't produce more milk than their offspring will need. Take Fanny there, for instance. She's not a dairy goat. She comes from meat goat stock and most likely won't have an overabundance. Same goes for Clara and Blossom, so you can cut the number of does you'll have to milk down by half. Besides, it'll give you something to do in those late winter months."

Aunt Ellen had wandered over and heard the tail end of Uncle Will's remarks. She rubbed her hands together. "Are you talking about goat milk? I've always wanted to try my hand at making goat milk soap. This'll be fun!"

I blew out a breath. If my eighty-two-year-old aunt was excited about this new venture, I decided I could muster up a little enthusiasm of my own. "You're right. It will. Oooh, lotion and ChapStick would be fun, too!"

Uncle Will ruffled my hair. "There's that Haybeck spirit."

I still wasn't overjoyed with the thought of milking a bunch of goats every day, but with a little prodding, I could warm to the idea. Who ever thought a city girl from Seattle like me would be turning into a farmer at such a rapid pace? It'd been less than four months since I'd boarded the plane at Sea-Tac with plans to be back in the Pacific Northwest two weeks later. I glanced around at the picturesque farm with the two-story white farmhouse and big red barn and sighed with pleasure. I didn't regret my decision to stay for even a minute. New Hampshire was becoming more and more like home every day.

Uncle Will's cell phone jangled from the front pocket of his overalls. He pulled it out, tilted his head back, and raised his eyebrows, trying to read the screen. He poked a thick finger at the lit-up green ringing phone icon a couple of times before finding success. "Morning, Roger. I hope you have some good news for me."

Aunt Ellen pursed her lips together while she listened intently to her husband's end of the conversation.

"Mmhm. I see," he grunted into the phone. "Well, we'll just keep after it then. Thanks for the update."

"Well?" Aunt Ellen licked her lips. "What did the attorney have to say? Tell me!" She grasped Uncle Will's arm.

"Not a lot he can tell us yet. He spoke to Jim..."

Better him than me. I imagined taking Bugsy to Jim's fancy office and letting the goat unleash his fury on him. He deserved any amount of wrath Bugsy could hand out.

"And that stubborn son of ours refuses to drop the petition. Roger still stands by his initial response that the petition won't hold up in court. It'll be several months before it makes it to the dockets, so with any luck, we'll be able to get the little weasel to change his mind in the meantime."

Aunt Ellen slammed her fist into the palm of her hand. "I've never been so angry at my own child. Since he refuses to come home and discuss this, I have half a mind to fly to Chicago and give him a good dressing down."

Uncle Will set a hand on her shoulder, calming down the second woman in his family in a matter of minutes. "We're going to work through this, Ellen. I promise. He won't get away with it."

"Dang right he won't, but my son even trying to pull this nonsense has me in a tizzy."

"How about we all take a rest on the porch with a slice of the delicious lemon tart cooling in the fridge? That should fix us all up good and proper."

The mention of making all our problems feel smaller with her cooking was the balm Aunt Ellen needed to rub on her mad. She whirled around and beat both me and Uncle Will to the house.

A slice of pie and cup of coffee later, I stood and gathered up our dirty dessert plates. "I'm going to wash these dishes real quick, then return a few phone calls from people who want to book yoga sessions."

Uncle Will patted my hand as I reached for his plate. "You just remember, this thing with Jim isn't your fault."

Tears sprang to my eyes, and I nodded. "Gotcha." We were all well aware that if I wasn't living at the farm, this never would have happened, but I appreciated Uncle Will trying to take the guilt off my shoulders.

With my hands in the soapy dishwater, I replayed the mayhem of the past week. Tristan had left for Boston yesterday morning, right after the last goat yoga session at the fair. He needed to get back to cutting and styling hair at the salon, and what was left of the Hasty Hogs crew pulled out right behind him.

That same evening, Levi had stopped by my stalls at the fair to see how I was doing. His timing couldn't have been better since the clock had just struck seven, which was the time exhibitors were allowed to take their animals home.

I clipped lead ropes to two goats and handed them over to Levi, then attached another to Bugsy's collar and one more of the yoga goats. A makeshift ramp I'd constructed out of two-by-fours and thick plywood worked to load the goats into the back of Old Rusty. If I ever needed to transport the goats again, I was going to have to invest in something sturdier. Maybe even an actual livestock trailer. For now, I didn't mind looking like the *Beverly Hillbillies*.

We got all of the goats and supplies loaded in quick order. Levi leaned against the side of Old Rusty and fiddled a piece of hay between his fingers. *What is he waiting for?* While I appreciated his help, I was dead tired and ready to go home.

"Okay, well, thanks a lot for your help," I squeaked out in an awkward, high-pitched voice.

Levi looked up from the hay he was worrying to death. "Glad to help. Um, by the way, I was wondering if you'd want to catch a movie," he shrugged, "you know, maybe have dinner sometime?"

My heart stuttered and flames leapt into my belly. *Am I melting?* I fluttered my hands in front of my face to ward off the sudden heat. *Is Levi asking me on a date?*

"Um...yeah, I guess I could." *You guess? Idiot.*

"Thanks for the enthusiasm. Makes a guy feel good." Levi grinned. "It's a date, then."

He *was* asking me out on a date.

Levi leaned in and gave me a quick peck on the cheek before wandering off toward the cattle barn. Would it be uncouth to yell after him—When? Where? Probably.

Now, I pulled the stopper in the farmhouse sink and rinsed the remaining soap suds down the drain. It was only last night Levi had asked me out, so I wasn't terribly concerned about not hearing from him yet. Even so, I racked my brain for a reason to stop by his vet clinic that wouldn't seem completely fabricated.

I snapped my fingers. "It wouldn't hurt to find out the good doctor's protocol for caring for pregnant nanny goats." Pleased with my plan, I dried my hands and hung the dishtowel on the oven handle as my cell phone jangled.

"Hi, Bree. What's up?"

"Have I ever got some news for you." Bree's voice sounded both gossipy and uncertain at the same time.

I pulled out a chair and sat down at the kitchen table. "Hit me with it."

"First off, and as your big sister, it's the only time I'm going to say this, so listen closely. You were right."

I rolled my eyes. "Okay. About what?"

"Grandma was the one who filed for divorce all those years ago. Not Grandpa Orville. I was able to dig up the records from the archives here in King County."

"Oh no." This wasn't a scenario where I wanted to be right. The news had the potential to change the entire truth of our family story. "How are we going to tell Dad?"

"There's more." Bree hesitated. "Remember how I said one of my friends from college works at the courthouse? Well, Jennifer did me a huge favor. She really hooked me up. I didn't just get names and dates, but I was also able to get my hands on all of the records. The entire file with all the juicy details. Are you sitting down?"

I nodded before realizing Bree couldn't see me. "Yep. Tell me everything."

"Grandpa contested the divorce. He wanted to stay married and was willing to move to Washington. He even came to Seattle to go to court. I read the transcriptions. Grandma claimed desertion; he said no, he'd been shipped out to fight in Vietnam, and she's the one who left without a forwarding address while he was gone."

"No way," I whispered, breathless, even though I had begun to suspect as much.

"Yes, way. And he fought for partial custody," Bree said.

"But I'm going to guess the judge didn't grant it."

"Nope. It was the 1960s and custody almost always went to the mother back then. However, Grandpa did petition the court for visitation rights. They were granted, and he was supposed to be able to visit Dad for one week, twice a year, though he couldn't keep him overnight without Grandma's permission."

"In Seattle? Or like partial custody, and Dad and Grandma would have to go to New Hampshire?"

"No, visitation only, and Grandpa would need to come to Seattle. And he did. Several times. But further records show Grandma was never at home, or at least didn't answer the door, when it was Grandpa's time to see Dad. Not even once."

"You've got to be kidding me. I can't believe Grandma would do something so rotten."

"Yep, and all his letters were returned to him with 'refused' scrawled across them. There're pictures of a few in the file. He tried to take her back to court, but wasn't successful in getting the case reopened. Eventually, he probably did give up. It must've been heartbreaking."

I couldn't wrap my mind around what my sister was telling me.

"Callie," Bree's voice sounded urgent. "Grandpa Orville did not abandon Dad. Grandma lied to all of us."

Acknowledgements

A big thank you to my family for putting up with my incessant blathering about the make-believe worlds that live in my head. Thank you for helping me solve plot problems, keeping your eyerolls to a minimum, and actually being excited to read the books when they're done. You guys are the best!

To my Inky Fingers critique crew. You know who you are. You guys provide priceless support and encouragement. You keep me on the balance beam when I want to tip over the edge. Your critiques are on point and your feedback is invaluable!

Thank you big to Larry Kurtz, for way more than one reason. Not only was Mr. Kurtz one of my high school English teachers, he's been a huge support in this journey, even driving several hours to come to my book signing. Larry also provided a name for one of the sheep being shown at the Lupine County Fair in this book—Ichabod Schnoozer!

To my whole herd of writing and reading besties. The very best surprise about this whole writing thing has been you. Not in my wildest imagination could I have dreamt up the support, connections, and friendships that I have found in the mystery community. You are my people.

About the Author

AUTHOR WEBSITE:
Cozy Mystery Writer | Paula Charles Cozy Mystery Author

SOCIAL MEDIA HANDLES: Rainy Day Mysteries on both FB and IG
FB: Facebook
IG: Paula Charles / Janna Rollins (@rainy_day_mysteries) • Instagram photos and videos

Also by Janna Rollins

An Escape Goat

Hometown Hardware Mysteries, written as Paula Charles
  Hammers and Homicide
  Axe Me No Questions (Jan. 2025)

www.ingramcontent.com/pod-product-compliance
Lightning Source LLC
Chambersburg PA
CBHW020624110726
47899CB00002B/644